SUCCORANCE

Teens discover that great power does not come with wisdom

VICTOR KIRKSEY-BROWN

SUCCORANCE

Teens discover that great power does not come with wisdom

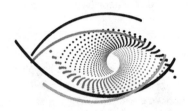

VICTOR KIRKSEY-BROWN

Little Big Bay LLC

LITTLE PLACE ~ BIG IDEAS ~ ON THE BAY

littlebigbay.com

SUCCORANCE

Author: Victor Kirksey-Brown
Designer: Roslyn Nelson
Publisher: Little Big Bay LLC

ISBN: 978-0-9968071-5-9
Library of Congress Control Number: 2017957377
To contact the author:
Instagram@thelovephoenix
vdkb125@aol.com

Little Big Bay LLC
littlebigbay.com

ACKNOWLEDGMENTS

I can't thank everyone by name because I'd have to thank everyone in my life. I've taken inspiration from songs, movies, books, people in my life, those I've bumped into on the street or sat across from in a class, but never spoken to. All of that shaped me and made this book happen.

I thank my mom, Candace Kirksey. If she hadn't strongly encouraged me to write creative ideas down when I was a child, I don't think this book ever would have been made. My memory of her teaching me to do this is so vivid. It was like a plea, like something she wished she had done, something she didn't want her only child to make the mistake of not doing. Anytime I had an idea and thought, "I'll remember it later," I'd see my mom telling me to write my ideas down and I would remember the urgency in her voice. The few times I didn't listen and waited until later, I'd usually forget. Or I would lose the strength of the idea. So I take note of all my creative ideas. *Thanks, Mom.*

The idea for *Succorance* wasn't even totally mine. It spawned from something a friend said; something that stuck with me and inspired me. Months later, with the encouragement of another friend to start writing for NaNoWriMo, (National Novel Writing Month) I expounded on the idea and it grew over five years into *Succorance*.

I want to thank my dad, Leonard Brown. He shaped a lot of the character of Rachel and a lot of my own. He loved me with his whole being and showed me as much as he could in the 12 years we had together. He encouraged my artistic endeavors and pushed me to do not just what I was good at, but to try my hand at different aspects of my interests. I've always loved writing, but never imagined writing a book. Without his advice to look past my self-imposed limits, I would not have completed this book and would not be the person I am today. There are many things I wish I could ask him and tell him. I've been able to ask and say a few of those things with *Succorance. Thanks, Dad.*

Thanks to those who read early drafts and gave me feedback. Without you, many elements of the story and of Jessica, Rachel, and Bright would not be what they are now. I was too stubborn to make some changes at first but in time took suggestions to heart and they helped make this story develop to what I wanted it to be. You wanted my voice to be heard, and you wanted me to grow as a writer. Because of your encouragement to stay true to myself, I was able to create a book that I'm happy with and that meets my inner goals instead of ego goals. Thanks to all of you, I accomplished something I am extremely proud of and a book that has helped heal me in many ways. I hope it inspires connection both to oneself and to others.

I want to thank every person who has shown me love, every person who has asked me about my book, who has given me advice or written something with me. I want to thank everyone who has cried or laughed with me, danced with me, expected better of me, or pushed me to believe in myself. I want to thank every artist who has moved me: musicians, directors, writers, actors, talk show hosts, and critics. Thanks to those who have shown me affectionate care and social support; who have shown me that we're all connected, and though this world can be painful, none of that is endured alone. Thank you to everyone who has helped prove to me that my path is one of love.

Oh! And I definitely have to thank Xena: Warrior Princess. Your journey of healing and self discovery has helped me in more ways than you'll ever know.
– Victor Kirksey-Brown

TABLE OF CONTENTS

PROLOGUE

My name is Rachel. Rachel Crowley. I never really liked my last name. Always sounded creepy to me. But I do like the initials RC, like the remote control cars. I always found them a bit difficult to control.

It's about 11 a.m. on a Sunday afternoon and I'm over at my best friend—Jessica Walker's—house. Jess and I have been friends for a long time, since birth really. Well, her birth ... and her brother's. They're twins. I don't remember because I was only five months old, but they—our parents—tell us that Jess came out first and then Bright was soon to follow. I guess you could say I've been showing Jess the ropes ever since.

Like now, we're playing Xena: Warrior Princess. I'm playing the role of Xena. Jess, of course, is Gabrielle. Jess's dad, Edward—Mr. Walker to me—helped us find some spare toy parts to make a sword. A mini Minnesota Twins baseball bat with the blade of a red plastic sword held on top of it with a combination of duct and electrical tape. I don't know if it would be fitting for fighting ancient gods, warlords, and kings, but it definitely works for horsing around in their organized mess of a living room.

"Watch it!" Jess's mom, Marion, doesn't like us playing in the house, but she and Mr. Walker are about to leave and they don't like us playing outside if they're not here. They've got errands to run or something. Mrs. Walker is a guidance counselor at a nearby community college and Mr. Walker works at his sister's bakery Tuesday through Saturday. Sunday is the only day they both have off, so it kind of sucks they have to spend it running errands.

Jess is using a broomstick for Gabrielle's staff and nearly took Mrs. Walker's head off. "Why don't you two take a break while your father and I gather our things to go? Ed, come on!"

Jess and I shrug and she takes a seat on the couch while I go upstairs to use the bathroom. Mr. Walker is standing outside Bright's room giving him a lecture on being responsible for us all while he and Mrs. Walker are out.

"It's not like this is the first time we've been left home alone, Dad."

"Yeah but—"

"Call if anything goes wrong—call 911 first if it's an emergency, don't answer the door, don't leave the house, keep an eye on Jess and Rachel. I got it, Dad."

"And it's not like you have to boss them around or anything, just make sure nothing gets out of hand."

Bright looks up from the book he's reading—*Neverwhere* I think it's called—and he catches me eavesdropping. "Like they'd ever let me boss them around." He smiles and returns his attention back to his book. Mr. Walker, catching on that someone's behind him, turns around and greets me and I continue on my way to the bathroom.

I don't really get why Bright is put in charge. I'm 13. I'm the oldest. And I think 12- and 13-year-olds are capable of spending a few hours alone without requiring supervision anyway. As I'm washing my hands, I look in the mirror and can't help but notice—like I always do—the huge indent in my forehead where I ran into a coffee table as a baby. Others say it's not even noticeable, but I know they're just trying to be nice.

I hear Mr. Walker start lecturing Bright once more before Mrs. Walker yells for him again and he finally gives it a rest. He must have forgotten his keys or something because I hear him fumbling around in the master bedroom and Mrs. Walker scream a few more times before he runs through the hallway and down the stairs.

A few moments later, I hear the front door closing and locking as I'm exiting the bathroom.

"Have fun reading your book, little brother. We'll be downstairs having some real fun if you need us," I say as I pass Bright's room. I rush down the stairs before he has a chance to respond. Jess and Bright are family to me. I think of them as my siblings and this is my home away from home. After my mom died, Mrs. Walker—being my mom's best friend—made it clear I was welcome here whenever I wanted, and I took advantage of that whenever I could.

Jess and I are much more friends than Bright and I. I mean, I love him, but most of the time he'd rather have his nose deep in a book than play with us. When I get back downstairs, Jess and I pick up our weapons and start back up from where we left off.

"Can I be Xena this time? I like being a Warrior Princess too you, know."

I want to say no, but I know that'll hurt her feelings. I know Jess likes being the warrior badass and not the sidekick, but I'm just better in that role than she is. I want to be the good guy, but I want to fight as the good guy. Jess is more concerned with protecting than battling, so when she's leading the adventure, it can be a bit boring.

"Why don't you be Callisto in Xena's body, and I'm trying to get your soul back to the right place?" I suggest.

"But then I don't really get to play Xena, or even be a good guy. And we'd have to fight each other, wouldn't we?"

"Yeah, but aren't you tired of pretend fighting things? It'll be funner this way." After thinking about it for a moment, I can tell she's not sold, so I tell her that we'll do it for a little bit and if it's not fun we'll go back to fighting imaginary foes and she can be Xena for real.

She accepts this offer and we jump into our roles, as well as onto furniture, emanating battle cries, knocking over stacks of papers and magazines, generally causing a ruckus. Bright yells at us once or twice to calm down, but he's too lost in his own world up there to come down here and make us stop. After we've been at it for what seems like forever, I can tell we're both feeling an end to this storyline. I let Jess get a few good hits on me so that it seems I'm down for the count, which of course we both know I'm not, and then I go for the comeback knock out. Only I get a little overzealous and deck Jess right in the face with my broomstick.

Immediately realizing my mistake, I rush over to Jess, who's now kneeling on the floor in pain. Tears are rushing down her face, and when she turns toward me, I can see a huge red mark on her cheek that'll surely turn into a nice-sized bruise. "I'm so sorry," I try to tell her, but she doesn't want to hear it.

"You did that on purpose." She says, covering her face again, embarrassed by her tears.

"No I didn't! It was an accident!"

"Whatever. Just leave me alone."

"Jess, it was an accident!" I grab her arm, trying to get her to look at me, to forgive me. But that makes things worse, and she swings the bat sword at me with great vengeance and furious anger, striking me in the neck. The fierce growl she emits scares me and the last thing I remember before blacking out is thinking that maybe she's more warrior than I give her credit for. That and the agonizing look of betrayal in her eyes.

And then I woke up.

I thought it was a dream until I felt the stiffness in my neck. As my vision clears, I can see two figures above me—Jess and Bright—kneeling beside me. I'm spread out on their living room floor. My butt and shoulders are sore from lying still on their patterned rug for too long. I don't totally look at them for a while, but I stare at their ceiling fan, watching it go round and round, my mind going blank, until one of them asks me something.

"What?" I ask, surprised to find that my throat is hoarse.

"Are you okay?" Bright asks. I look over and his eyes are red and his brown cheeks are stained with tears. Jess looks the same, but she isn't looking at me directly.

"Wh—What happened?" I push my elbows into the rug to lift myself up.

Neither of them respond, and now neither are looking me in the eye.

"What's going on?" I'm starting to get upset. I attempt to sound authoritative, but I just sound like a sick old lady. Something about my performance must have worked, though, because Jess bursts into tears and starts repeatedly apologizing, but she doesn't make much sense. All I can get from it is that she got upset and I think knocked me out. I ask Bright to confirm this for me and he nods.

Jess continues to blabber and I take her hand. "It's okay," I tell her. I look into her eyes and I see intense pain. It's as if she's afraid to be near me, afraid to touch me, afraid to even look at me. "I'm fine, right?" I ask rhetorically, but Jess just continues to stare. We all sit in silence, the whirl and rattle of the ceiling fan above us becoming more prominent. "I'm fine," I finally decide. I bring myself to my feet, but then the room starts to spin, my head pounds, and my eyes water. I try to brace myself against the wall to my right, but soon realize the wall is not as near as I perceived it to be. Luckily Bright and Jess are able catch me.

They make sure I can stand on my own and I thank them. I tell them I have to use the bathroom and insist on doing so alone. I use the wall to brace myself up the stairs. I move slowly, dragging my hand, noticing as the roughly smooth white plaster transitions into the old, peeled, blue and silver wallpaper on the second floor.

When I reach the bathroom I shut the door and make my way to the mirror. My almond skin seems smoother than I remember, there are no breakouts, and my straight black hair is definitely silkier. I lift my bangs to feel my forehead, thinking I might have a fever or something. Something else is off though. I slide my hand up to my scalp and I examine my forehead. There's no indent. It's always been there, in between my hairline and my left eyebrow, and it's gone. Thinking it may be the lighting, I flip the other light switch, but there's still no scar. I back up and sit down on the toilet. I think I may be losing my mind.

I stare at the bathroom counter, but I don't really take it in. I'm racing through my memory of what was happening right before I blacked out. I remember laughing and screaming. And I remember Jess being in tears. The last fluid memory I have is of Mrs. and Mr. Walker leaving. I remember the excitement of knowing there was no parental supervision, that I was free to let go and be myself.

What happened?

Suddenly, my surroundings come back to me. I notice the faucet is slowly dripping, that it's way too bright in this bathroom, and I question how long I've been in here. I worry that they'll think I was pooping and then immediately feel silly for worrying about something like that at a time like this—a time where my friends are definitely hiding something from me. Something changed, something I don't know if I care to question. Whatever happened is over now. I'm fine. I'm up and walking. I'm sure there's nothing to be worried about. What could they possibly be hiding that's *that* bad?

RACHEL

"Seriously?" I ask. "Just teleport us back now, there's nobody here! Nobody's going to see." Jess opens her mouth to speak, but I cut her off. "Like, you feel this wind right? You see what it's done to my hair? You do understand that at any moment my head could be blown right off my shoulders."

Bright laughs and that triggers me to do the same. It's a cold and windy Friday in Minnesota. No, actually, windy doesn't cut it. It's like if Superman, Supergirl, Powergirl, Zod, and any other Kryptonian I may be forgetting were blowing at you with that icy breath blow thing they can do—superbreath?—all at once and then The Flash was twirling his arms at you providing an additional gust of wind, and then there was like a super tornado happening too. But like times ten.

"Do you guys have superbreath?" I ask.

"What, like Superman?" Jess asks.

"Or Supergirl!" I retort.

"No," Jess answers. "And we're walking to the park and using the bathrooms there to teleport like we always do."

"All it takes is once for someone to see us using our powers and get it on video or something, and then our lives are over." Bright says.

"Don't be so dramatic," I tell him.

"Well you try having your parents hold you responsible for everything your sister and her best friend do," Bright shoots back, defensively.

"Big Brother's always watching," Jess says matter-of-factly.

"You know I hate when you call me that. I don't want this put on me anymore than you want me always tagging along at your side. And besides, we're twins and you came out first," Bright shouts.

I laugh until another strong gust of wind smashes me in the face, prompting me to turn my laughter into a loud groan. I tighten my hood up and drudge forward. My cries of agony go ignored.

"First of all, I was talking about Big Brother. Like, 'the man,' the government, our almighty oppressors holding us down. And second, I love having you around," Jess says looking to me for my opinion.

"Yeah, me too. And do you just think of me as 'your sister's friend' after all these years? I'm hurt." I feel my phone vibrate in my pocket and I take it out to check it.

"I can barely hear you through the wind and your hoodie, but no, that's not how I think of you okay? I love hanging out with you guys. Who else would I hang out with? But my point is, it's my ass if any of us does something stupid. You know the rules, Rachel. No superpowers in public. So no superstrength, no superspeed, no flying, and no teleporting where prying eyes can see," Bright says.

"I know. I know. I'm just complaining, okay? Fuck this wind!" I yell, but it amounts to nothing, the wind swallowing it whole.

"We're almost there, Rachel. You'll survive," Jess says.

"Will I though, Jess? Will I?" I cry dramatically.

Jess just rolls her eyes and we continue walking. I take my phone out, having got another message, and type a response.

"Who ya texting?" Jess asks.

"My dad. Who else?" I respond, a little too defensively.

"I dunno, damn," Jess huffs.

I was lying though. I'm texting a boy. A cute boy. I'm texting Jason Holi, captain of the bowling team. I know, that doesn't sound that impressive, but at Farson High, the bowling team is pretty much like the Dillon Panthers from Friday Night Lights. They're our pride and joy. The only team that matters. Or I should say the only team that consistently wins. And it's pretty cool because it's a co-ed team, so both boys and girls allowed.

Jason and I have been texting a lot in class and we exchanged numbers a few days ago. There's a big game against our rival school, River's Edge— I know, it sounds like a '50s greaser gang or something—tonight. Jason wants me to come to the game, but I told him I already had plans with Jess and Bright. Pretty much the same plans we have every weekend. Every day really. Go back to their place and either watch a movie or show, play a video game, all sit and read—basically anything that makes us forget we're shutting ourselves in. It sucks, but I mean, we don't really have any other options. Their parents pretty much make it impossible for them to make any other friends. If I wasn't already their best friend when they got powers, I probably wouldn't even be in the picture. That day four years ago when Jess knocked me out with a hollow plastic sword, discovering she had superstrength, changed everything for us.

They didn't tell me right away. I was brought into the loop of few days later. Jess and Bright, who discovered he had the same powers, tried to hide it from me and their parents. However, 12-year-olds aren't particularly good at keeping secrets, especially when those secrets involve superpowers. So their parents were quick to find out. And after their parents knew, Bright and Jess forced them to allow me to know. They said I could never tell my dad and that powers were not to be used in public, especially at school. Those were basically the only rules, except for that Mrs. And Mr. Walker worry an extreme amount and tell us that just about everything we want to do risks someone finding out about the powers and therefore we can't do it. But I guess I'd worry too if I had superpowered teens for kids.

Anyway, my plans with Jess and Bright, and the fact that I'm afraid to tell them that I've been texting a cute boy because I know they'll overreact, are the reasons I turned down Jason's invitation to tonight's game.

> You sure you can't convince them to come?

> Haha, yeah. I'm sorry, I'll try to come to the next one :)

Do you put periods after a smiley face? I never use emojis, but that seems right. I mean, it's the end of the sentence. Maybe it's too flirty though? Smiley faces are flirty right? That's what all the popular media tells me. I don't even know if I want to be flirting. I mean, I clearly don't even really know how. But like, this can't end well right? This is dumb! Why did I even agree to give him my number?

> I'm gonna hold you to that ;)

Oh shit, a winky face! That's definitely flirting! Right? And he didn't put a period after it. Though I think I'm still going to. Is this what flirting feels like though? Modern flirting through technology at least. I mean, it's ridiculous how excited I get when my phone vibrates and I know it's Jason. It feels so good to … feel good about myself. Like socially. I mean, I know I don't need a boy or anyone to validate me, but fuck, it's really nice to feel liked—in any sort of way.

I have Jess and Bright, and I love them, but being 17 and never making any other friends, not because I don't want to, but because I'm not allowed to, it sucks. And if it was like just a regular overprotective parent, or even just my own parent, I wouldn't stand for this. But it's not my parents. It's not my life that's completely altered if someone finds out about these powers. It's not my place to say anything. I just wish I could talk to Jess and Bright about all of this. Especially Jason. I have no clue what I'm doing here. I need my best friends. But all that would be is me gloating about things they can't really experience, and then probably make this thing—whatever it is—that I'm experiencing end.

"You happy now, Rachel? We're here!" Jess says.

"Yes Mom!" I say, playing along.

It's still kind of weird for me to even jokingly call someone mom. I feel weird because I feel like they're going to get weird about it, and then I think they pick up on that weirdness and that's what makes them feel weird about it. I dunno, I mean, I don't think any weirdness even happens at all at this point with Bright and Jess and the subject of my mom. It's all in my head, but it's still kind of weird … .

"See you two at home," Bright says as he walks into the men's restroom.

"We're going to stop at my place first!" I call out.

"We are?" Jess asks, giving me a side glance.

"I gotta feed Rebel," I defend.

We walk into the women's restroom and check to make sure no one else is around. Once we're sure the coast is clear, Jess grabs my hand and a second later we're in the little crook that's completely hidden between my garage and my neighbor's.

We have these little safe spots for when we teleport places. This spot is the one we use for teleporting to my house. Since my dad doesn't know about their powers, and their parents don't want them using powers outside of the house, we can't actually teleport into either of our homes.

Our houses and school are the only places we ever really teleport to regularly, but we have a few other secret spots scouted out for other locations we might want to jump to.

Jess and I clumsily squeeze our way out of the crook and make our way into my backyard. I stop to look at our garden, which is on its last leg for the year. My parents loved working on the garden together, and Dad kept it up after Mom died. I'm glad because this place wouldn't feel like home without it, and I have no patience for gardening.

I fumble with my keys, dropping them. And before I can actually get the back door open, my dad opens it from the inside.

"Hey girls! How was school?"

I'm a little startled. He's usually not home for at least an hour after I get home. "Fine," I say, brushing past him and setting my backpack down.

"It was a pretty good day," Jess answers. She always tries to be extra nice to my dad to make up for how short I can be with him.

"Not planning on staying around long?" Dad asks.

I'm already out of the back entryway, through the kitchen, and into our pantry we keep at the top of the stairs to our basement when he asks.

"Not really. Just came home to feed Rebel. Didn't know you were here, though," I say.

There's an awkward silence as I scoop some cat food out of the bag and pour it into Rebel's bowl. Rebel is already mounted up on the counter waiting expectantly. Most people don't like cats on their counters, but my dad and I never cared much. We used to eat at the kitchen counter a lot and we wanted her to feel like she was part of the family. I mostly eat in my room now, but Dad still shares the counter space with her.

We continue to stand around in silence, me petting Rebel as she eats, Dad reading an article in *The Atlantic*, and Jess standing awkwardly near the back entryway.

"You going back to your place then?" Dad asks Jess, breaking the silence.

"Yeah, just gonna hang out and watch a movie," Jess responds.

"Which one?"

"*Argo*, I think," Jess looks to me for agreement, but I pretend not to notice.

"That's a good one! Have you seen it?" Dad asks.

"Nope," I cut in. "None of us have. That's why we chose it."

"I assume the rest of this 'us' is Bright?" Dad asks.

"Yes," I groan. "Why are you asking questions you already know the answers to?"

"I didn't know, maybe you invited some other friends," He says.

"Yeah, because we have so many of those," I say, and another short silence follows.

"Well, I need to run to the store. You guys want me to drop you off on the way?" Dad asks. "Unless, maybe you drove Jessica?"

"No, I didn't. That would be great though," Jess says. I give her a dirty look, but don't protest any further.

"Okay, just let me know when you're ready," Dad says.

"We're ready," I shoot back.

Dad rolls his eyes, "Okay, just give me a second." He lingers on his article for a moment, then closes the magazine and gathers his things to go.

Jess and I both give Rebel a pet and then follow my dad out the front door to the car. I take the front seat. Partly because my dad always likes someone to sit in the front seat because he doesn't like feeling like a chauffeur, partly because I feel like Jess deserves to sit in the back by herself for agreeing to Dad's offer for a ride, and partly because then I get to choose the music.

I turn on the radio and "Cuckoo" by Lissie is on, so I let it play. It's a song from her first album, *Catching a Tiger*. That song always make me think of warm summer days sitting in a park, or driving around with no real direction. It just has a summertime feel and vibe. It warms you up and gives you that gentle excitement you feel when you know you've got a whole sunny June day to do absolutely nothing.

I first found out about Lissie right around the time Jess and Bright discovered their powers. It was a really fun time. I mean, looking back, I'm sure it was scary as hell for Mrs. And Mr. Walker, and probably rather unsettling for Bright and Jess too, but all I remember is excitement.

My two best friends had discovered they had superpowers. I mean, as a kid, *anything* seemed possible. We're all told that powers and things like this are something that you can only pretend and imagine, but here it was actually happening. I was *actually* seeing it with my own eyes.

I didn't even care that I didn't have powers. The fact that powers even existed in my world at all was enough to give me a newfound belief in it. My mom had been dead a couple of years when their powers emerged, and I had pretty much stopped believing in magic and hope. I mean, I wasn't constantly sad or emo or anything—well, maybe a bit emo—but I guess even at that young age I had become more of a realist. I enjoyed fantastical things and stories of grand adventures, but I didn't really have hope that I'd experience anything worthwhile in my own life.

Their powers made me believe again. Gave me my childhood innocence back for a while.

Before overprotective parents, witnessing the cruelty of the world, and realizing we're all pretty much stuck in the same shitty system brought me back down to a base state of "meh."

The ride is spent entirely in silence, aside from the music. When we get to Jess's house, we get out promptly.

"Bye," I say, giving an afterthought of a wave as I close the car door.

"Thanks a lot, David!" Jess says.

"No problem." He waves and then drives off.

"I hope you know you wasted valuable movie time," I say to Jess as we approach her front door.

"Whatever," she retorts.

As soon as we walk in the door, Bright is on us. "What took you so long?"

"Jess wanted to let my dad drive us home," I say, casting the blame on her.

"He offered! And what sense would it make in his eyes for us to turn him down? Why would he think we'd want to walk in this cyclone?" Jess defends.

"I don't care!" I say. "I know you think you're being nice to him –"

"Yeah, exactly!" Jess cuts me off.

"Well, you're not!" I yell back. "You're not. I don't like being such a bitch to my dad, but … I can't help it. It just comes out. It's like a switch goes off in my head as soon as I walk into a room with him. And I shut down, and I don't want to talk to him, and … it sucks. But you forcing a situation isn't going to help. I have to go to him on my own. When I want to. I have to want to fix this. And right now … I don't."

I haven't admitted that to anyone. I hate it, but it's true. I don't know why, but over the past few years my relationship with my dad has gotten stale. I've been withdrawn and I just don't know how to fix it. And so I stay withdrawn, I move further away. I've distanced myself from him. To protect him I guess? So that I can't hurt him anymore than I have. And I plan to figure it all out. But I can't right now. Or more so, I'm not ready right now.

We're all standing around, not sure of what to say or do. I start to take my boots and other outside gear off. Jess does the same, and after hanging up her jacket she walks over to me and hugs me. I wasn't expecting it, so it's more of a bear hug, my arms pinned at my side. She uses a little bit more of her strength than I think she means to, and I let out a small cry of pain.

"Sorry," she says, slowly letting go and backing away. "And for more than the hug, I mean."

"It's okay," I say. "You were just being you."

"What does that mean?" Jess says with a laugh.

"Nothing. Just that you're kind, and you're caring, and you want to help. You're always trying to help, and there's nothing wrong with that."

Jess smiles halfheartedly, "Except for when I do more harm than good."

"Well, then you just listen, like you're doing now. And realize that sometimes the best way to help is to not get directly involved, but to talk to and assist those who are," I say.

Jess smiles and we let that be the end of it.

"You guys wanna go sit down?" Bright says, motioning toward the living room.

"Yeah," I respond, and we all make our way there.

"So how are we watching this movie?' I ask. "You guys don't own it right?"

"No, but isn't it on Netflix?" Jess asks.

"No, I'm just going to torrent it," Bright says.

"Let's just buy it," Jess counters, "I'm sure it's good. It did win an Oscar."

"That doesn't mean anything." I say.

"I know, I just don't want to torrent it," Jess defends.

"Jessica, you illegally download music all the time!" Bright rebuts.

"Yeah, but who doesn't?" Jess retorts.

"Okay, so then why do you care about this? They've already made millions of dollars," Bright says.

"I just like having physical copies of movies. I like my collection," Jess answers.

"Consumerism has got you," Bright says.

"Oh whatever, Mr. Room-Full-Of-Comics-And-Books," Jess spits back.

Jess gives Bright a playful slap and takes a seat on the couch. I sit next to her, and Bright takes the chair to our right.

"They should just release all forms of art for free: movies, music, books, whatever. Do it because you love it, not for the money," I say.

"That's easier said than done. Sure if you're a big name who's already got tons of money, you can do that, but other people have to make a living. It sucks, but supporting the things you like with money is kind of the only way to keep them going," Jess responds.

"Yeah, and even the big names have studios and investors to please. If they want their stuff distributed, it has to turn a profit, and a substantial one," Bright chimes in.

"So everyone's stuck in the system," I say matter-of-factly. "So how are we going to watch this movie?"

"We'll just torrent it," Jess says.

JESSICA

Do you ever watch a movie that just completely moves you? Well, it doesn't have to be a movie, but have you just experienced something that just motivates you and inspires you? Like, on a whole other level. This is what just happened for me. I think *Argo* changed my life. And not like—I dunno. It didn't really show me anything about life I didn't know, but opened up something inside me. It showed me a truth I knew, but … now I know it deeper? I think that's what I mean.

And I have a love-hate relationship with this feeling. It feels as if your mind is clear, like you know exactly what needs to be done, and you know how you want to do it. You feel this surge of energy running through your body and your emotions and it's awesome, but this feeling is impossible to hold onto. And even if you could hold onto it, it would exhaust you. You can't run on that high forever, bursting with energy and emotion. There would be no way to make any rational decision. You're too sure of everything. You're not supposed to be that sure all the time. That's how you become a tyrant. That's how you lose yourself, because you think you know it all.

We're not supposed to know it all.

"So how did you like it?" Rachel asks.

"It was good, kind of slow, though," Bright responds.

"The end was pretty intense!" Rachel says.

"I'm sure it wasn't really that close of a call in real life, but yeah, that was crazy," Bright agrees.

I don't say anything. I don't know what to say. I hate being the only who loved a movie. Well, I didn't *love* it. But it sucks when you're completely taken with something but the rest of the group just thinks it's "alright." I always feel silly, like I must be mistaken. Like since I'm the only one who really enjoyed it, I'm just not smart enough to see the issues with it. It's not that I didn't see the flaws—there were definitely flaws. It just … made me want to do more. It inspired me to do more, to help more, and I love it when movies do that. I love feeling empowered. And maybe it's not the movie, maybe it's something more. Maybe it's just life. Maybe no matter what I was watching today, this is what I wanted to see from the world, and I would have taken the same feeling away regardless.

Do you ever think about that? Like, you know when you're in a bad mood and you watch something and you just completely tear it apart, but then you watch it later on a clearer head and you find value in it. It's hard to know when you actually really enjoy something—or really love it—and when you're just emotional and it allowed you the release you needed. Whatever that release was. Maybe it was sad and you needed to cry. Maybe it was inspiring and you needed hope. Maybe it was awful and upsetting and you needed to rage. And so in that moment, whatever it is is exactly what you need. So it's impactful and memorable and maybe you think you love it, or maybe you think you hate it. But really your emotions change all the time and I feel like you can't be sure on how you feel about anything without multiple interactions and repeated dislike or love.

Though even with that there are exceptions.

"So, Jess, what about you?" Rachel asks.

"I really liked it. I never felt bored. I thought it had a good pace and it had a nice blend of humor mixed into it. However, I didn't like that Ben Affleck cast himself in the lead role and not a man of Mexican descent like he was in real life," I say.

"Yeah, well, whitewashing is nothing new," Bright responds.

"Doesn't mean we should just ignore it," Rachel challenges.

"I'm just saying that if we're judging it as a movie, which is supposed to entertain and tell a compelling story, it did that well," Bright says.

"Yes, but we're being naive if we try to pretend that movies aren't more than just entertainment. Directors, writers, and actors have a responsibility to be entertaining and tell a compelling story in responsible ways. Like not basing the movie on real life and then making the main character, who in real life was a Mexican-American man, a white man," Rachel asserts.

"But why does everything have to be so serious? Just take it for what it is. We don't have to deeply analyze everything," Bright argues.

"Well, if we don't analyze and critique things, they won't change. I think it's very possible to critically discuss something without completely trashing it," I reply.

"And maybe sometimes it needs to be completely trashed. Sometimes things just aren't good, or missed the mark, or were very offensive while claiming to be satire," Rachel adds.

"I know. Sometimes I just wish that we could all just be innocent. That we could watch something, or read something, or hear something, and not look deeper. But I know that's flawed. We live in a system that massively discriminates against people of color, women, members of the LGBTQ community, and more. To pretend that doesn't have an effect on our media, our movies and music and books, is naive and irresponsible. I know. I just get tired of having to do that. I get tired of caring. As a black person, I know I'm treated like I'm less than my white counterparts, and of course not by everybody, but institutionally. I don't want to spend all my time thinking about that though. I just want to watch *Argo* and *just watch*," Bright says.

"That's the problem though. People just want to turn off their brains. They don't want to confront the injustices in our world. I mean, I get it, what can we do? Why worry about it when there's no way to change it?" Rachel says.

"But we can change it," I say, desperately.

"What do you mean?" Bright asks.

What do I mean? I'm not really sure. I just, I feel like we can. I feel like we, as a people, have the power to do a lot. We have the power to do it all. Look at all humans have done already. We can change things. Especially us.

"We have superpowers," is what I get out.

"And?" Bright asks, still not getting it.

"*And* we can make a difference with them!" I declare.

"You're being crazy, Jessica."

I hate when people say that. When they just dismiss you and call you crazy when they don't want to talk about something, or don't understand. "Go fuck yourself." I say to him. He laughs, but I'm not joking. "I'm serious, fuck you."

"What? Okay, you want me to throw on a cape and fly around pulling people out of burning buildings? *That's* crazy, Jessica! It's not going to change anything," Bright exclaims.

"I'm saying we can do more than that. We can stop wars, save lives, call out corruption. We can stand up for what's right and not be afraid," I demand.

"Jess, you're still human. You have awesome powers, but you can still die. You still have reasons to be afraid," Rachel jumps in.

That's true, but it's also not. I can't die, but Rachel doesn't know that. I guess I'm not totally sure either, but I've tried to, and it doesn't work. I didn't try to kill myself. Well, I did, but the goal wasn't to die, it was to see if I could. Bright and I had reason to believe that we could heal ourselves, and so we got curious. We started out hurting ourselves in small ways and seeing what happened, and when those wounds rapidly healed, we escalated to more dangerous tests. We always healed though. We were always fine. We kept this secret from our parents and from Rachel. We were afraid to tell them. We were afraid they wouldn't understand. So she's right, I do still have reasons to be afraid.

"I guess you're right, but I just want to be doing something. I want to be making a difference. I want to not feel like I do nothing," I say.

"Well, you can do something without being a superhero," Rachel responds.

I just wish I knew how. Putting on a cape and giving your life to something seems so easy. You become the job. Saving lives is what I'd do, and I'd *know* that.

And most of all, I'd be doing something. Life sucks because you have to make decisions. Because you know you have a choice, but all the powerful choices are the hardest to make. And you never know what's right. You never know what's best. Will you hate yourself a year from now because of what you decide to do today? Will someone else hate you? Is there even any actual *right* or *wrong*?

And then if you can decide on a right and wrong, you still have to decide on good vs. great or bad vs. worse. How much of a reaction or consequence does one thing deserve against another? Case by case is probably what's best, but then nothing seems fair. In a large society, if it doesn't seem fair, people aren't going to want it. And if you're someone making decisions, then they're not going to like you.

So yeah, I know that I can do something and make change without trying to be a "superhero," but they make things look so easy. Even when they're actually tough.

"Okay, so what do you guys wanna do now?" Bright asks.

Before Rachel or I get a chance to answer, we hear my mom yelling, "Groceries!"

"Guess that's my answer," Bright laughs.

I teleport down to the back door where mom is standing, trying to manage three large grocery bags. Bright and Rachel just take the stairs.

"Jessica!" My mom exclaims.

"What?" I say, knowing full well what.

"What if someone was with me?" Mom asks.

"Well then, I assume you'd have said something." I maintain. Frustration and tension starting to build inside me.

"Don't sass me." Mom gives me a stern look, but then turns her attention to the bags in her hands. "The rest is in the trunk. It should be unlocked." She tilts her head toward the car indicating we should go. I know she wants to argue more, but she also knows that I'm a teenager and that we complain a lot, so she has to pick her battles. I'm glad she decided to change the subject and drop it because I'm in an arguing mood. Especially after the movie.

Bright, Rachel, and I all grab bags from the car, finishing off the load, and bring them back into the kitchen. Mom has started sorting the groceries into the places they belong, "So what are you guys up to?" She asks.

I don't even try to stop myself. "Nothing. What could we possibly be up to? You and dad won't actually let us have lives."

Bright rolls his eyes and Rachel just averts hers and starts taking more stuff out of bags.

"I'm not doing this with you right now, Jessica," Mom sighs, already over it.

"Of course not," I reply.

Mom slams a box of Honey Nut down on the counter. "What's that supposed to mean?"

"It means you never want to talk about this! You always try to brush it aside, or pull the 'we're your parents, we make the rules' card," I explain.

"Because this is what happens!" Mom says, now completely devoting her attention to me. "I brush it aside because there is no point in talking about it. There is no conversation to be had. You don't get to have a normal life Jessica! You just don't. What happens if you try out for a basketball team and you're defending yourself from being stripped of the ball, and you throw an elbow, but instead of just causing a foul, you cave in someone's chest? What if the government gets wind of you and your brother? You think they'll just let you roam free? You think the world will accept you?"

"Wow, what a great talk mom. 'The world will never accept you, so don't bother having a life.'"

Mom's eyes soften and I can see I hit her hard with that one. I don't mean to hurt her, I just want to make her understand.

"Do you think I like telling you these things?" Mom asks. There's no anger or bitterness in her voice though. At least not any directed at me. "You're a young black woman. You're already not accepted by a lot of the world. You've already got enough stacked against you."

"I don't believe that. Or, I mean, I don't see it that way. Right now the only thing I feel like I have stacked against me is the clutch hold you and Dad keep on us. I can do anything Mom! I have so much power, but all you guys ever say is that the world is too dangerous for me. That's bullshit! What can the world do to me?"

Mom shakes her head and smiles. "You've just helped me prove my point." She picks up the box of Honey Nut and puts it away. Bright and Rachel, being used to me bickering with our parents, have pretty much finished putting away the groceries while we argued.

"I don't get it," I say.

"Because," Bright answers, "You just said it. What can the world do to you? Not much of anything. They're going to fear you. They're going to fear us. And the fact that we're young and black is just going to add more fuel to that fire."

"So you're on their side now?" I shout. "You're the one who was *just* saying that you're tired of always having to be thinking about life like this. That you want to forget about race, and gender, and politics, and just be."

"Yeah, but I also agreed with you that that's not really possible." Bright responds.

I want to scream. I want to yell my fucking head off. I'm so frustrated! I look to Rachel for backup, but she looks away. I know she has a dog in this fight. I know she wants a life, too. Maybe I'm overreacting. Maybe my emotions are too high. Maybe I'm not thinking straight. But I feel clearheaded. I feel like this is right. Like I'm right about this. This is so tiring! I just –

"I'm tired of arguing, Mom," I say. There's no more fight in my voice. I don't have any left right now. I just know that from now on I'm not arguing anymore. From now on I'm not asking.

BRIGHT

It's Monday morning and my alarm is blasting. Rage Against the Machine is telling me to "wake up." It's sort of a jarring way to start the day, but that's kind of the point right? To wake up and "stay woke." And as far as staying woke, that's the whole purpose of the song. To open your eyes. Not be a sheep. To question the world around you. So I stay woke in both senses of the word.

I turn off the alarm on my phone. It's 6:45 a.m.. I'm sitting up in bed, legs swung over the side, but haven't motivated myself to move beyond that. I massage my face and eyes and groan rather aggressively as an additional jolt to stand me up. Just as I get to my feet, there's a knock at the door. Mom will have left for work by now and Dad had some day off stuff to take care of at the bakery, so I know it's Jessica.

I contemplate not answering, but figure she heard my alarm and that I couldn't pretend to still be asleep, so I respond after a few seconds delay, "Yeah?"

"We have to talk." Jessica says.

I slowly walk over to open the door, still in my boxers. "Right now? I literally *just* woke up. Can I at least get dressed first?"

"Look, I …"

I wait for her to continue, but she just stares at the ground with her mouth open, not saying anything for close to a minute.

"You …" I encourage her to proceed.

"I'm just trying to find a way to say this without sounding crazy or freaking you out," Jessica expresses.

"Well, prefacing it with that will surely do the trick," I joke with her, running my hand through my hair further trying to rouse myself.

"I …" Jessica pauses again.

"Jessica, come on. We have to get ready," I groan.

"I think I want to run away. *We* should run away—me, you, and Rachel." Jessica says. There's a sense of pleading in her eyes.

"What the fuck are you talking about?" I ask. I don't mean to sound so harsh, but I'm tired and I don't know what else to say.

"I haven't been able to stop thinking about it. We *have* to use our powers for good." Jessica demands.

"Fucking *Argo*!" I mutter "How is *that* the movie that does this to you? Not *Hotel Rwanda*, or *The Corporation*, or something a little more meaningful?"

"I don't know, Bright! What does it matter? This is how I feel now, and I don't think it's going to change," Jessica responds, exhausted.

"But what if I don't feel it? What if Rachel doesn't feel it? Are we just supposed to drop everything? You're being …" I rethink before continuing, "It just doesn't seem logical."

"Look, I know it's a bit extreme. I just—I have to do something, and I need you guys with me," Jessica pleads.

This honestly sounds crazy to me, but I can tell she's serious. If I dismiss this, she might just run off on her own, and I don't want that. I don't want to push her away, I just—I don't know what to tell her. I don't understand this. Or I do, but not completely. I don't have this call to do good that she does. Sure, I want to be able to go out and make friends and have a real life too, but even if Mom and Dad weren't stopping us, wouldn't we be doing it to ourselves? Just doesn't make sense to be letting more people into our lives who we can't tell the truth to.

This is all stuff I've told Jessica before. She knows my opinion on all of this. She knows I'm in between our parents' rules and what she wants. But I also know her well, and I know this isn't going away, so I know we should talk this out, "I don't know what to say. I think we should call Rachel."

I think my response surprised her. She doesn't move or saying anything for a few seconds. "So like … now?" she asks.

"Yeah, unless there's some reason to wait?" I reply.

"No, I just … I guess I was expecting more of a fight? Or … something. I dunno, I mean, I figured I could convince you eventually, but … cool! I'll call Rachel!" Jessica runs into her room to grab her phone.

"Hey, I'm not saying that I'm down for running away, and I can assume Rachel won't be either. What I'm saying is we should talk about this—all together," I say, trying to bring her excitement down a little.

Jessica comes back out, phone call to Rachel already in progress, and she gives me a hug and a kiss on the cheek. "Thanks, big brother."

I give her a "fuck you" look for the big brother comment. I know she uses it as a joke towards how ridiculous, unfair, and kind of sexist it is that Mom and Dad hold me responsible for us all—especially when I'm technically the youngest—but it still annoys me and makes me uncomfortable.

"Sorry, sorry," Jess holds up her hands in surrender while holding the phone to her ear with her shoulder and head as support. "I'll try to stop, I promise."

Just as she finishes, I can hear Rachel's angry voice through the phone. "What the fuck do you want?"

"Calm down!" Jessica laughs.

"You know I'm not a morning person, Jess. What do you want?" Rachel asks, clearly annoyed.

Jessica proceeds to ask if she can head over there and then teleport Rachel back here so we can talk about something. Rachel says that'd be fine since her dad has already left for work, but informs her that she has to get dressed and will not be rushed.

"She said …" Jessica starts.

"I heard," I say.

Jessica nods and then immediately teleports to Rachel's.

After Jessica's been gone a minute, I take a deep breath and prepare myself for the conversation to come. Jessica is just so hopeful. She's so caring and inspired. And it's hard—really hard—to have to bring her back down to Earth. I wish I didn't have to. I wish she could do the things she wants to. I wish it was possible. But it's not. At least not in the way she wants it to be.

I head to my room to put on pants. Rachel has seen me in my boxers before, but we both like to keep those instances to a minimum. I make my way downstairs and think of something to eat. I think I'll have enough time for a quick breakfast before they get back. I usually go for eggs and sausage or bacon and some of whatever fruit we have in house—usually red grapes—and some water and juice. But since time is a factor, I opt for just some cereal and a bagel.

I grab a bowl from the cupboard, a spoon and a butter knife from the silverware drawer, Honey Nut Cheerios that Mom picked up the other day, and milk from the fridge. Then I take a bagel from the bag of bagels on the counter, slice it in two, and pop the two halves in the toaster. I don't know why specifically this time and not all the time, but I was just reminded of that joke—or riddle I guess?—"What do you toast in a toaster?" It's supposed to trick you into saying toast when the answer is bread. I remember falling for that the first time. Maybe more than once, really.

I pour a bowl of Honey Nut while I wait for the bagel and grab some water too. Orange juice was tempting, but I hate drinking orange juice with cereal because the way it tastes mixed with milk is weird.

After the bagel pops, I grab the strawberry cream cheese and spread an unhealthy amount on each piece. I don't feel guilty about using too much because it's just for me. Nobody else in my family likes strawberry cream cheese. I don't understand it, but I'm also not complaining.

I sit down to eat my meal—is it a meal? I pull out my phone to google the definition of a meal. What I find is, "the food served and eaten especially at one of the customary, regular occasions for taking food during the day, as breakfast lunch or supper." So … I guess this is a meal then? I just imagine actually prepared food for a meal. Like maybe not quite a feast, but in that general realm.

I open up YouTube to play some music. I don't use Spotify or anything because I like to own my music I guess, and I don't put music on my phone because of space, and then it takes up battery for that instead of for the normal functions of a phone—not that I actually call or text anyone. But I have an iPod for my music and I use YouTube on my phone sometimes when I just need a quick listen to something.

I pull up the song "Numbers" by Daughter. Their music is kind of sad. Kind of like a hopeful sad. Mostly hopeful because you know that there's someone feeling these things and sharing them and that it's okay to feel, I guess. And to sort of be confused and sad, but also a little self-loathing, but also empowered. I don't know—that's all of the things that Daughter makes me feel. I wouldn't say that I'm particularly sad or depressed or anything, but I guess sometimes I just feel … directionless. Kind of numb to things in a way. And I think that's why this song has been sticking with me lately. The song is about a numbness inside of you. And having this habit of taking an awful situation and making it worse. And I can relate to that so much. Whenever shitty things happen, I make them worse because I worry so much about how I appear. I stress that I'm babying someone too much by trying to be there, or that I'm seeming too distant when trying not to do that, or that sometimes I don't feel sadness as much as someone else, and so I freak out that I'm a sociopath or something and that I have no real feeling. And I guess that all sort of goes back to feeling numb at times. I basically take situations and make them about me, in my head, and have to remind myself that it's not about me. At least most of the time it's not, anyway.

I just really love the singer's voice. Especially in this song. Her inflection on "you better" and "me better" as she repeats it in the bridge is infectious. It sticks to you and wraps you in the outro so you're thinking about it all day. Ultimately this song resonates with me because I do feel numb. I feel like I can't unleash. I feel like I lost the want to unleash. Like I lost the will. And I can't tell if it's a good thing or a bad thing. Maybe I don't need to unleash. I don't feel upset or sad about it. I only feel bad when I think I should be feeling upset about it. Otherwise, I'm fine I guess. I don't know if I actually have a problem or what, but this song is just … comforting. It's chill and soothing and a bit eerie. It makes you feel like you don't know. It's in between. You don't feel good or bad. You just feel. All of Daughter's songs are pretty calm, and most if not all of them are melancholic. Another one of my favorites by them is "Youth." Rachel played it for us one day and it just instantly got me.

I'm about halfway through my meal when the song finishes and I hear Jessica and Rachel upstairs. They must have just teleported back.

"Bright!" Rachel yells from upstairs. She sounds pissed, so I assume Jessica already mentioned the whole running away thing. "Bright!" she calls again.

"Yeah, I'm coming!" I call back. I think about teleporting, but just opt to walk. I'm not feeling that lazy. I take a few more spoonfuls of cereal and then shove the last of my bagel in my mouth—with cereal and milk still in there—and then make my way upstairs.

"What the hell is she talking about, Bright? We're running away now?" Rachel asks.

I open my mouth to answer, but Jessica beats me to it, "I never said we were running away! It's not like I'm making you go through with it, I just wanted to talk with you guys about it."

"What's to talk about? I'm not running away. Why do we have to run away? For what?" Rachel asks.

"I just thought it'd be easier," Jessica says.

"Easier how?" I ask.

"Easier in the sense that we could make a difference," Jessica says. "We could be out there saving the world, doing cool shit, having grand adventures, and not have to worry about hiding ourselves. I mean, we're all sick of that, right? Hiding?"

I look to Rachel because I know that last touch was mostly meant for her. I know she wants to branch out more than Jessica and I. I know she wants to have a life. It sucks for all of us, but at least Jessica and I get powers. But it doesn't seem like Rachel is taking to this idea, which I'm okay with. I'm not sure I could talk both of them out of it, and I couldn't let them go alone. And not because, like, I think they need me, a man—or like, not a boy, not yet a man— to accompany them and watch out for them. But because what the fuck would

I do without them? *And* because I can't deny that a part of me would love to just travel around and do nothing. Jessica could save the world, and I'd just tag along for the ride.

"I can't run away, Jess," Rachel voices, bringing me back into the moment.

"You're telling me that doesn't sound like fun?" Jessica pleads. "You're telling me you don't wanna get out of this place?"

"You know I do," Rachel concedes.

"Then what?" Jessica asks. "Why not?"

Rachel takes a moment to form her words, "Because even though I treat my dad like shit, I love him. I could never just leave him like that. He already lost my mom. I'm just supposed to up and run away? He'd be broken. And though your parents keep us on a short leash, they love us. They'd be so hurt."

I don't know how I didn't even think about what it would be like for David if Rachel just ran away, if she was just gone suddenly—just like her mom. I really don't think he could handle that. I was only nine when Katherine died, but I remember how lost he was. I remember how he held on to Rachel and how she did him. They saved each other. But then, because of us, she chose to start distancing herself from him. She gave up her remaining parent to help us keep a secret for something we didn't even ask for and probably don't deserve. We definitely can't run away.

"Rachel is right," I cut in. "We can't run away. We can't do that to our parents. And also, where would we live? How would we survive? If you don't plan on having a job, how would we pay for anything? Steal it? And are we wearing costumes and masks, or just using our powers in public as ourselves? And Mom and Dad know about our powers. Do you think they'd just think it was a coincidence that we ran away and then all this shit started happening?" I ask.

"I don't know," Jessica whines, realizing she's losing this argument.

"And what would I do? I don't have powers, Jess. Do I just sit around while you two save the world? And how are you saving the world? Just stopping crimes, pulling people out of burning buildings? What are you going to do to change the world? What are powers going to do to really change anything? People are still going to do the same shit. The world is still going to run the same way.

The poor will get poorer, the rich richer. People will die. Bad shit will happen," Rachel adds.

"I know that, okay? I know! But what am I supposed to do? Just pretend that I don't have these powers? Pretend that it doesn't mean anything?" Jessica asks.

"It doesn't mean anything, Jessica," I say.

"How can this not mean anything?" Jessica demands.

"Because we're still just kids. We have powers, but we still have lives to lead. I don't think that we have to burden ourselves with the fate of the world just because we have powers," I reply.

Jessica doesn't say anything for a while. None of us do. We're all still standing in the hallway at the top of the stairs. Jessica doesn't quite look mad, but ... defeated. Defeated doesn't even cover it, really. It doesn't do it justice. The look on Jessica's face is realization. It's knowing something you don't want to know. And that look scares me. It scares me because I don't know if she's coming around to our way of thinking—seeing that running away isn't the answer, or if she's just realized that she can't sell us on this. That we're not going to help her.

I don't want that to be what she's come to. I don't want that to be what she feels. That we won't help her. That we're against her. I don't want her to see Rachel and me like she sees our parents. I don't want her to see us as the opposition. And I don't think that our parents are the opposition. I just think that after all this time of being shut in, it's hard for her not to see it that way. And if she sees Mom and Dad in that light, and now we're on that side, then we become the enemy too. And maybe not right away, because she won't want to let go of us so easily, but if we keep saying "no," what other outcome can there really be? And we can't go along with things we don't agree with. I know I won't, and I know Rachel won't either.

After some time, Jessica starts to speak again. Her voice is lower than before, less sure of herself, or maybe less sure of us. "I don't know what to do. I just feel lost. I know it's stupid to run away. I've watched enough dramas to know that running away doesn't really solve anything. For the most part, your problems will still be there. And I know it's silly to get so worked up over a movie, and *Argo* nonetheless, but it's not like this is coming out of nowhere. I care about the world. I care about making a difference, and I don't know how our powers will help us do that, but there's got to be something we can do. There's got to be something I can do," Jessica expresses, hopelessness in her voice.

"Well, have you thought about just getting involved with community programs, or looking into clubs at school? I know you're big on helping the environment. Maybe you can find something to do with that? I know that the Farson High Green has done a lot of cool things locally. You should talk to them," Rachel suggests.

"That name is so stupid. It sounds like they're selling weed or something." Jessica says.

"Well, don't go then, whatever," Rachel huffs, crossing her arms in annoyance.

Jessica goes quiet again. I'm guessing she was mostly joking, but Rachel's response probably peeved her a bit, and now they're just both being stubborn. "Well, I think Rachel's right," I say.

"Big surprise," Jessica cuts in.

"What's that supposed to mean?" I ask.

"Why can't either of you think *I'm* right?" Jessica bursts out. "Why can't you speak up and try to help me when it comes to getting Mom and Dad to give us some freedom, huh? Why can't *either* of you back me up? I know you want to. I know you want to fucking do something other than go to school and come home and bullshit. Why are both of you acting like I'm being unreasonable for wanting to run away? You're honestly telling me you don't want to? You're telling me you haven't thought about it?" Jessica pauses for a moment then starts again with even more force, "I can't be stuck like this for two more years! Eighteen is too far away—it's too late."

"Too late for what?" Rachel asks.

The question catches Jessica off guard, "I don't know. I'm … that just came out. But it does seem too late. That's two more years of being trapped. Two more years of hiding. Two more years of lying to myself that I'm content with the way things are. I am *not* content! I barely even feel capable of doing this for another week, yet alone two more years." Jessica's eyes are red with tears. I look to Rachel and I can see that she's on the verge of tears also.

"I have something I need to talk to you guys about," Rachel says.

"Can we sit down first?" I ask, motioning to our rooms.

"Yeah, let's go to my room," Jessica says.

Rachel doesn't look happy to hold onto what she has to say, even for just a second, but we move into Jessica's room and all take a seat. Rachel sits on the floor, I take Jessica's computer chair, and Jessica sits on her bed. We sit in silence for a second before I inquire as to what it was Rachel has to tell us.

"I've uh … I've been talking with Jason Holi. Flirting really—I think," Rachel says. "I mean, I don't really know what I'm doing, but I'm pretty sure we've been flirting. I mean, we're going out tomorrow, so it had to be flirting right?"

Both Jessica and I just stare, mouths agape. Neither of us were expecting that. Neither of us knows how to respond.

"What?" Jessica asks, her tone a mix of anger, surprise, joy, and maybe a hint of jealousy.

"Jason and I are going out tomorrow night. He's gonna pick me up and we're going on a date. I'm going on a date," Rachel says, seeming to mostly be talking to herself, also in disbelief. "I'm going on a date!"

"You are not going on a date," Jessica retorts.

"Why not?" Rachel asks.

"You know why not," Jessica responds, anger and annoyance winning out amongst the battle of her emotions. "I don't get to run away, but you get to go on a date with Jason Holi? One of the most popular people at our school."

"I wouldn't say that. He's *maybe* one of the most popular people in our grade," Rachel says. "And me going on date with Jason is in no way comparable with you wanting us all to run away."

"Well, that's not totally true," I interject. Rachel and Jessica both turn toward me, eyes full of fury, both of them ready to attack if I side against them.

Which of course I don't want to do for either of them. I'd love to just sit all of this out, but staying quiet about something doesn't really keep you out of it. "No, going on a date with Jason isn't on the same scale as us running away, but what it can lead to might be."

"What do you mean?" Rachel asks.

I take a moment to gather my thoughts, "I mean, *you know* there's a reason we don't get close to people. You're not just finding out about these rules. You haven't been in the dark all these years. There's a reason why we don't have any other friends. And yes, one of them is that our parents won't let us, but another is because we don't want to—"

"But I'm telling you right now that I *do* want to," Rachel cuts me off, staring at me indignantly.

Her not letting me finish my point riles me a bit and so I stare right back at her, eyes hard and clear, "I was trying to say that we don't want to because we know that it leads to lies and cover-ups. And we know that in the end it doesn't work out. We know that at some point we're going to have to let the relation-ship—or whatever it is—go." My returned indignance falters toward the end because I realize just how shitty the reality of what I said is. I realize just how shitty our lives are.

"We don't know if we don't try," Rachel says.

"We can have a pretty good idea, though," Jessica responds.

Rachel shoots a fiery glare at Jessica, but it cools and she drops her eyes to the floor. Nobody says anything for a while. Eventually Rachel lets out a loud sigh and spreads out across the floor, "I thought you were supposed to be the one inspiring us," she says to Jessica.

"Well, since you're not going on the date, maybe I can convince you to take my side in running away now?" Jessica asks, halfheartedly.

I roll my eyes and say "No" at the same time that Rachel says, "I'm still going on the date."

"What?" Jessica and I both say together.

"I'm still going on the date," Rachel repeats. "I like Jason a lot, and sure I can't tell him that you two have powers, but it's not like you're well-known heroes with secret identities to keep safe or something. I'm not going to have to lie to him very much, if at all."

"Rachel ..." I start not knowing how to finish.

"You're not thinking this through," Jessica says.

"Again, this is coming from the person trying to run away!" Rachel retorts.

"So because I had a bad idea, yours is okay?" Jessica shoots back.

"So you admit it's a dumb idea?" Rachel asks.

"I said it was bad, not dumb," Jessica says.

"Yeah, whatever," Rachel rolls her eyes.

"I really—" Rachel cuts me off again before I can finish.

"I really don't care, Bright. I'm going on the date. There's nothing you can say to make me not go. You're right Jess, I am tired of hiding myself and shying away from everyone. And I'm not going to do that to myself anymore. I want you two to be able to branch out too, and I promise to help you do that in a more productive way than running away if you want. But I'm going on that date tomorrow. Because I want to. Because I need to."

I sigh and palm my face, forcefully rubbing my brows, trying to think of a way to combat what she just said. After a few seconds of coming up blank, I give up, "Look, I don't think this is a good idea, but it doesn't seem like we're going to be able to stop you. And honestly, I just really don't want to talk about it anymore because it's going to go nowhere." Jessica and Rachel offer no arguments. "We should get ready for school. I've got a math test first period that I can't miss."

"I guess school would be a good distraction from overthinking," Jessica says after another few moments of silence.

"I doubt that," Rachel retorts, propping herself up on her elbows. "Is it cool if I still ride with you guys? Don't think I'd get there on time otherwise."

"Yeah," I say.

Rachel nods and then gets up and stretches before leaving Jessica's room. She gets her stuff from the hallway and heads downstairs. I look to Jessica and we exchange a look that says that neither of us knows where to go from here. Even if we did know, we probably wouldn't be in agreement.

I leave Jessica's room and head to mine. While I pick out my clothes, I decide to listen to some music. I scroll through and end up playing "The Way" by Fastball. I wish I knew what was right. I wish I had the same urge to help that Jessica does. I really love this song, but it makes me feel conflicted. There's something both hopeful and helpless about it. I feel like it doesn't just apply to our lives directly, but the human race in general. I agree with Jessica that the world needs help. I agree that we could probably make a difference with our powers. But what can we really change if we don't know what we're doing? What's the point if we don't have an endgame?

After we're all ready, we hop in the van our parents let us use and we head to school. I can tell this is going to be an angsty week.

JESSICA

Rachel was right. The school day doesn't really provide much distraction. Why would it? I guess I don't really want to run away anymore though. Or, I really don't know what I want. I *do* want to run away, but what Rachel and Bright said makes sense. I don't want to hurt David, and I don't really want to hurt my parents either. I just want them to realize that there's so much shit on my mind. I'm thinking about the world all the time. I'm thinking about my place in it—or how I really have no place in it at all. I'm not allowed to.

I face being labeled and put in a box because of my race, because of my gender, because of my age. It's hard enough trying to find some kind of footing in society because of that. And because of my powers—something that should be a gift—I'm held down even further. It's like I'm in one of those nesting doll things. You remove one barrier and it just reveals another.

I know my parents know how hard it is to feel like you're really being seen for you. As a black person, I'm always aware of how I seem to others. Do I come off as angry? Do I act too "white" when around other black people? It's really hard and really frustrating navigating high school just as me—without powers. I want to fit in. I want to make friends. I want to do shit normal teenagers do. But besides all the, I guess, normal concerns a black teenager might have,

I always fear that anyone I talk to knows I have a secret. They know I'm not being truthful. They know I'm not being myself. And then I fear that I'm being judged because I'm withheld. Like people think I think I'm too good for them, or that I'm afraid of them, or whatever they think.

I just don't get why my parents don't understand. They have to know what it's like. How is not letting me explore society going to help me? Keeping me from the world only fosters more insecurity in me about it, my place in it, and the people living in it. Sure it protects me, keeps me from being hurt, but it doesn't allow me any chance to build up my own defenses. It doesn't allow me to learn how to handle the hurt of the world. Because there will always be hurt, but a part of growing up is learning how to manage that hurt. Learning how to be yourself in a world that can be hurtful.

I can't learn how to be myself. I can't explore anything. I can't form any relationships outside of the ones I was born into basically. What's the point of even going to school? What's the point of being let out into the world at all if I can't *do* anything in it?

A loud cheer from my classmates brings me back to where I am—in World History, my last class of the day. I realize I'm breathing heavily and I'm gripping the edges of my desk tightly. Too tight. Any tighter and I'd snap them right off. I quickly let go and relax my stance. I look to my right and see Dylan Lafferty staring at me. I look away and forcefully keep myself from looking back in that direction, now feeling even more self-conscious than I normally do.

Mrs. Fitz has the projector remote in her hand and the screen pulled down over the whiteboard. So now I'm caught up to why everyone was cheering. Though it's not like this happened at the beginning of the class. There's only about 15 minutes left so I don't know why everyone is that excited.

Mrs. Fitz is showing us a news clip from *BBC World News* about another oil rig that had a spill, then there's a bit about what's happening in Syria, and all of a sudden I'm thinking I don't know anything. Like seriously, I don't know a lot about the world. I can barely tell you where every state in the U.S. is located. If you were to give me a map test of Europe, or Africa, or Asia, well, I'd fail—hard.

I've been told—mainly by my parents—that the best way to help the world is to get an education. To learn about the world and use my mind and my intelligence to make a difference, not my powers. And it makes sense. There's so much I need to learn and so much I should study. I'm terrible with history. I'm terrible with dates. There's just so much. There's so much fucking history to our world. Our home on Earth. How am I supposed to remember it all? How am I supposed to learn it all? I can't. So then the question becomes what's the most important? How is there anything that's the "most important"? It all matters. What if we decide points A, B, and C are what's important, and D, E, and F don't matter, and then miss out on the fact that when you look at A through F all together, a bigger picture is revealed?

I mean that happens all the time now. We have so many different experts on different things—the economy, climate change, social issues, the judicial system, whatever, and it's like none of them speak to each other. None of them consistently and openly communicate with experts in other fields to see that they all relate, and if they all just work together *so* many solutions could be found. But I suppose you can't blame them. Being an expert in a field requires a lot of effort and time and focus, so it's hard to take all that constant work and want to do even more work. The world is so large. It's so vast and we're connecting more and more, entangling ourselves more and more. It's beautiful on one hand, because we get to experience and know other cultures and ways of life and learn from them. But the more we entangle, the harder it becomes to find solutions to anything because an already flawed and imperfect system meets new systems with their own separate flaws and imperfections. And they all want to help and fix the others, but can't help and fix themselves.

And I mean, flaws and imperfections are not bad. Nothing is perfect, but what is right? How much can an education do? How much observing and learning have we done over the course of the human race? How many people graduate from college, or earn their masters, or doctorates, or whatever, every year? And we're still facing so many of the same problems. All I do is observe and learn, or try to, and I'm tired of it. I'm tired of fearing that I don't know enough.

I'm tired of thinking I'm going to figure out the right answer. Like if I hold out long enough it'll all make sense. It won't. I need to make choices and take action and do something. But what? I have no idea where to start.

Maybe Rachel is right. Maybe I should look into some of the clubs here at school. At least that's something.

I finally step out of my head and find that we're done watching *BBC* and Mrs. Fitz is handing out our assignment for tonight. When she gets to my desk, I ask her if we can talk after class, "I'm the one who usually asks that," she says. I laugh and she agrees to meet with me for a few minutes before a meeting she has to go to. After the bell rings and everyone leaves the classroom, I make my way up to her desk.

"I'm not in trouble am I?" Mrs. Fitz asks as an addition to her joke earlier.

I laugh politely and shake my head, "No, I just wanted to ask your advice on something."

"Yeah, of course, what's up?" Mrs. Fitz asks, focusing her attention on me and putting a big folder of papers and other things aside.

Now that I'm up here at her desk, I don't really know what to ask. Well, I do, I know what I want to say, but it just seems so stupid now. Like, I could have just found out on my own. Though, I guess, that's what I'm doing now? Why do people think that asking someone else doesn't count as finding something out on your own? I mean if you read about it, or google it, or whatever, that's still someone else telling you. I suppose those other ways may help you retain the information better or something.

"I just wanted to know if there are any good clubs here at school to join?" I ask. I immediately feel even dumber now because I'm aware of the variety of clubs here and even where to find information on them.

"Well, that depends on what you want to do," Mrs. Fitz smiles in a way that validates my fear of asking a dumb question, though I know she doesn't mean it to.

"I want to save the world," I say. More distress in my voice than I mean there to be.

"And how do you want to do that?" Mrs. Fitz asks.

I don't know. My first response is to say, "Save the cheerleader," but I doubt she'd get it. I want to travel the globe and fix problems as they arise, I want to be able to use my powers in public and use them for good, I want to not hide who I am, but I can't say that, so I don't know what to say. I don't know where I want to start with saving the world. I guess saving the planet seems to be the utmost important thing, right? Without our home here, the rest becomes moot.

"I think ... something environmental," I reply, a little unsure.

"So Farson High Green then. That's the one environmental group we have at the school. I can't promise you'll save the world if you join, but you'll damn sure avenge it," Mrs. Fitz suggests with a laugh.

An *Avengers* reference! Nice! Maybe I should have used that *Heroes* one after all. I smile big to show her I got the reference and there's a bit of a pause that we both end up trying to fill at the same time.

"So ..." Mrs. Fitz starts.

"So ..." I begin.

We both look at each other to continue, realizing we cut each other off.

"You first," she says.

I nod, "I was just going to ask ... do you really think they're doing things to save the world? Things that'll change anything."

"Well, they're doing what they can to help," Mrs. Fitz replies. "I don't know what saving the world even entails, but doing nothing until you know exactly what to do probably isn't going to be the answer. If you think this is something that could help you figure out how you want to help the world, I think you should give it a try."

I wish I could say what Mrs. Fitz just said makes me feel any more sure about joining this group, or trying to, but there's still a lot of fear and doubt there. But she's right, I have to give it a try. I have no other ideas or options at this point.

"Thanks, Mrs. Fitz," I smile. "I'll give it a try."

She smiles and I wave goodbye, but then she remembers something. "Oh wait, I have this Farson High Green pamphlet. I'm sure you know where to get them, but save yourself some time." She hands me the pamphlet and I thank her again and then leave the classroom.

I'm not really sure what to do now. I mean, I'm going to contact this group and see about joining. Says the president of the club's name is Sasha Hart. It's a pretty name. I bet she's a pretty girl. Her email's here. I'll write her when I get home.

But it's the home part that has me unsure. I don't know what I'm going to do with the rest of my day. All I do is spend time with Bright and Rachel and everything's all weird. Rachel barely said anything to us on the ride to school this morning. Well, none of us really spoke, I guess, but she's usually one to keep a conversation going.

I don't want any of us to be upset with each other, and overall I don't think any of us actually are upset with one another, but we're all upset. And we all have differing opinions on what we should be doing about the things we're upset about, so … yeah, it's just all weird.

As I'm heading down the stairs to the first floor, I run into Rachel. "Hey," I say.

Rachel barely looks at me as she responds, "Hey," and we continue to slowly make our way through the sea of people all trying to get the hell out of this place.

"Are you seriously this mad at me?" I ask.

"I'm not mad at you," Rachel states, darting her eyes toward mine, but not quite making contact.

"So we're lying to each other now?" I ask, but it comes out as more of a statement.

"Jess, I'm not mad, I'm not lying. I've got a lot on my mind. I'm sorry I'm not in a great mood and that I can't always act how you want me to," Rachel vents. I can almost see the steam rising off of her. She then looks around self-consciously, remembering we're in a crowd of people. "Look, I don't really want to talk about this right now."

"Why not?" I ask as we reach the bottom of the stairs and free ourselves of the horde.

Rachel opens her mouth to answer, but is cut off from someone calling her name. We both turn to see Jason Holi making his way toward us.

"Oh," I respond, understanding now.

"Hi," he says when he finally reaches us. He says this mostly to Rachel, looking directly at her, but then turns toward me just enough to wave and include me in the greeting too. It's not anything mean or petty, it's just clear he's really excited to see her. Rachel and I both put on fake smiles. I'm not exactly sure why I put on mine. I don't really care if he sees that I'm upset. But I'd rather not include him in any of this and I'm sure he'd ask what's up or if everything's okay. And also, part of me doesn't want to mess this up for Rachel. I don't really know how I feel about this happening, but I don't want to fuck it up. I mean, I guess we sort of asked her to end it, but I don't want to have to do that.

I shake my head realizing just how much I sound like my parents with thoughts like that.

I can see that Rachel and Jason have things to talk about that don't include me, so I awkwardly start to back away and wave and say goodbye. "Should we wait for you?" I ask Rachel. "Or, I mean, do you still want a ride?"

"No, that's okay," she replies. "Thanks though. I'll, uh, text you later or something."

I nod, turning toward the door and giving Jason a slight wave goodbye all in the same motion. I want to not be facing them as quickly as I can. I don't want either of them to see the hurt in my eyes. And I don't even totally know what the hurt is. It's not like she's choosing him over us. It's not that dramatic. It's just … for the first time, she's choosing herself over us. She's trying to do what's best for her, what makes her happy. And I don't know what hurts worse, the fact that Rachel's doing something that makes her feel good upsets me, or that even knowing I'm trying to do to her exactly what my parents are doing to me still doesn't make me want to be on her side on this. I'm still worried about me, and about Bright, and about what this will mean if she keeps getting closer to Jason. I still think it would be easier for her not to see him, and nothing has even really started between them yet. I'm trying to change the world, yet I don't want mine to change at all.

When I get outside, Bright is waiting on the steps where we all always meet.

"Let's go," I bark before he even has a chance to notice me. I pass him and head toward the van and he quickly gets up and follows.

"Is Rachel coming?" Bright asks, bewildered at my attitude.

"No, she's with Jason," I say, still feet ahead of him.

"So, we're losing her already," Bright nods, clearly joking, but it just makes me more upset.

"Yup," I respond.

"I was joking," Bright defends.

"Yeah," I answer.

Bright stays quiet the rest of the short walk to our van. When we reach it, I get in on the passenger side, feeling much too distracted to be a safe and responsible driver. I can't tell if Bright stopped talking because he saw that I need space or if I've pissed him off. Probably both. I feel like I should apologize, but he's also a big boy, he can handle it. Though I suppose that's not really fair, downplaying whatever he's feeling because I'm pissed off. Because I'm hurt. I shouldn't reinforce any sort of gender stereotypes. "Just because he's a boy, he's tough" is bullshit. I know Bright's a sensitive guy. I mean, I'd argue all guys, or boys—men, whatever—they're all sensitive. They're human. All humans are sensitive. Some are just more vulnerable than others, whether involuntary or by choice. And I mean, I didn't mean that he could handle it because he's a boy, and therefore he's tough, I just meant that we're not babies, we're teenagers—big kids. Being a big kid comes with understanding that you may need to tough shit out sometimes. But still, "he's a big boy, he can handle it" is generally a lame thing to think. I mean, just about anyone. I've learned that assuming someone is fine or can handle it is dumb. If you think they need to talk or something's wrong ask them how they are and if they want to talk. Check in with them. Just let them know you're there. Often times, they won't want to go deeper into it right away, but knowing you're open to listening will help them talk to you when they're ready.

We're a few blocks from school now and still neither of us has spoken. We hit a red light and Bright pulls out his iPod and plugs it in. He quickly picks out something to listen to, hits play, and sets down the iPod. The light turns green a few seconds before he finishes and a car behind us honks, so he sort of ends up throwing the iPod more than setting it down.

"Don't Save Me" by Haim starts playing and all of a sudden I really want to cry. A big smile comes to my face because I know Bright put this on just for me. Haim is a fairly new band that I love. Bright wasn't as into them as I was at first, but he quickly became a huge fan too. I love their voices! Danielle is lead vocals, but Este and Alana sing as well. They're all sisters. Haim is their last name, pronounced "high-em." I think it's so cool that they formed a band together. Traveling around the world, playing music, doing what you love with your family who are also your best friends, it sounds like a dream come true.

"Bright and I both sing in unison as the second verse kicks in. It's a favorite of both of ours. We smile at each other, easing the tension a bit.

"I'm sorry," I say.

"What happened?" he asks.

"Nothing really, just … Rachel is upset, and she wouldn't talk to me about it. Which is fine, she can talk to me when she's ready. But she's upset, and I don't like that, because I think it's because of me, or partly at least. And she's hanging out with Jason, which is cool, or—you know, I am happy for her about that, but it's also scary. And I feel bad that I can't fully just be supportive of her. I should be supportive of her. But I can't. I can't because we have to be responsible and we have a secret to keep. And saying that just makes my skin crawl because I sound like Mom and Dad. And then she's upset, but she's still hanging out with Jason. Is she just covering up her feelings so she can spend time with him, or is she confiding in him, opening up? Obviously not about us and our secret—I know she wouldn't do that—but she's finding someone new to lean on. And then when she's mad and upset, soon she'll just be going to him or someone else. Maybe she's making more friends. Maybe we'll be left behind. And she'll keep our secret, but she'll see that we're just holding her back. Because aren't we?"

My eyes water and Bright gives me a look that makes me feel like the most pathetic girl in the world. And I know that wasn't his intention, but it pushes me over the edge to actually crying. Not big sobs, not even more than a few small tears, but crying nonetheless. I know everyone talks about how boys don't cry, or feel ashamed to, but I always feel self-conscious about crying. And it tears me up inside, because I know people have feelings and you gotta feel what you need to and express that in healthy ways, and there's nothing wrong with crying. But though it's more "acceptable" for girls or women to cry, I feel like mentally it's still hard for us. Or even socially. It's hard because it's so expected. It's like, if boys cry they get made fun of or told to "man up," but if girls cry it's almost like anything we're feeling becomes void or invalidated. It doesn't really matter. What matters is that we're crying and then the goal is to get us to stop crying. Like we're babies. It's like they know we're going to cry, us crying is a part of the plan, and then when we do they think they have to take care of us. Society doesn't see our crying as something that's natural and a part of being a human being. Society sees crying as a sign of weakness. Someone "breaks down" and cries. Crying means you're not strong enough to keep it in, to keep composure. And since women are expected to cry, since it's a part of the plan, women are viewed as naturally weak. "They're going to cry, and when they do we'll have to take care of them. Some are stronger than others, but they're going to cry. They cry." And so even though people might not necessarily make fun of us for crying, I feel like crying for women isn't as easy as people think it is.

And then of course, being a black girl there's no real place to be. You're a girl, you're expected to cry, you're expected to be weak. But you're also black, you're expected to be aggressive, sassy, tough. You're still seen as weaker than a man, but your weak state is one that lashes out. You're to be placated even more than other women, because you're more likely to do something "crazy." And it's usually assumed that your pain is because of a man. Probably a black man who done you wrong. People fear you and even get mad at you for showing anger with your sadness. Sadness is expected, anger is a problem. Sadness is there to be taken care of, anger shows agency. It shows initiative to solve your own problems. If you're angry, you have an idea for why you're angry, and maybe there's someone to blame. Nobody wants you to be in a position to be able to blame someone. Nobody wants you to be able to solve your own problems. Because that's not expected. That's not a part of the plan. And nobody really wants to change the plan, or so we're meant to think.

"You're right," Bright concedes.

"What?" I ask, sort of lost as to where we left off.

"You're right about Rachel. We are holding her back," he clarifies. "I mean, to an extent. Keeping secrets holds you back. But I think she's just realized that she has a choice in this. She doesn't need to be held back, but that might also mean a bit of distance from us. Not an end to what we have. I don't think we'll ever lose her, but ... distance. And I think we have to give her that if she needs it. I think we owe her that."

I know Bright's right, but I don't want him to be. All I want to do is cling to Rachel right now. I don't want distance. How do I know how much distance to give? I don't want her to think I'm mad at her or that we're mad at her or—I just don't want to give her more reason to pull away. I'm already the reason she's pulled away as much as she has.

"Fuck," I sigh, "Can't we just be like Haim?"

"What do you mean?" Bright chuckles.

"I just want the three of us to travel the world, together, doing what we love. Being ourselves. Loving each other. I just want to ..." I don't know how to continue.

Bright looks at me and maybe starts to say something, but knows it's no use. There's nothing really to say. Well ...

"I love you." I say.

"I love you, too." Bright responds, confused.

He looks at me with a smile that hints at wanting an explanation, but I don't give him one. I don't need to. I love him. He's my brother. He should get it. I'm sure he does. I smile and we jam to Haim all the way home, and when I get back to my room the first thing I do is put on Haim so I can continue jamming and email the Farson High Green president, Sasha Hart. I start with my name, say why I'm interested, and end with saying that I look forward to hearing from her.

A couple of hours go by and I don't get a response, so I decide to also send an email to the club's school account. I basically say the same thing in this email, but I don't know if I'll hear from Sasha and at least this way I know they'll see it. Assuming they check their mail daily.

I've got a bit more homework to do, but dinner will be ready soon, so I decide not to bother starting anything yet. I like to do my homework on the floor, so I'm just propped up against my bed. I slide down and just lie, staring up at the ceiling. I'm not sure if I really want to join any of these groups. I want to push myself to get out of my comfort zone and try things, but I feel like I'm going to feel the same way about whatever group I join as I do about school. They'll have their own agenda, and though I'm interested, I mostly just want to learn from them and then expand on that in my own way. I guess I just don't like being told how to learn or how to explore my interests. I can't just not give it a try though. I owe it to myself.

"Are you okay?" my mom asks. I don't like to close my door unless I really don't want to be bothered or I'm changing or something. That way I give off a vibe of being accessible.

"Yeah, I'm fine. Just a lot on my mind, and a lot of homework," I reply.

"Anything you want to talk about?" Mom takes a few steps into my room and leans against the wall next to my door.

"I'm just wondering what I'm going to do with my life, is all," I say casually.

"Honey, you're only 16. You've got plenty of time to figure that out."

"Not really. Next year I'll have to start looking into colleges. Then I'll be graduating. Then I'll have to decide on a major, and the next thing you know, I'm married! I'll have some job that pays the bills, but I hate, and I'll never feel fulfilled, and I'll get divorced, because my husband will be in the same boat and we'll take it out on each other, and—"

"Jessica! Calm down, everything is going to be fine," Mom comes and lies on the ground beside me. "Where is this coming from?" she asks.

"I don't know, I just ... we have these powers," I say.

"Jessica, we've talked about this. You can't use your powers out in the world. Nobody can know about this," Mom sighs, already trying to end the conversation.

"But they won't have to know!" I plead.

"No! You're only a teenager. It's not your responsibility to save the world, but it is mine to protect you," Mom says.

"I know, Mom, but you can't protect me forever. Eventually I'll have to live my own life, and I know I have to do something to help the world," I assert.

Mom caresses my face and tucks my hair behind my ear. "Your father says dinner will be ready soon, so wash up and head downstairs." She kisses my forehead and gets up to leave the room. She stops at Bright's room to tell him about dinner before going back downstairs.

I've never felt unloved, but I do feel unheard.

RACHEL

Jason will be picking me up any minute now. I can't believe this is happening.
I'm going on a date! Like, actually! I've tried on a dozen different outfits. I'm sure
Jess is about ready to throw her phone out the window with how much I've been
texting her. Well, her phone or me. I know she's not happy I'm going on this
date. Or I guess she's just got her reservations. I know she supports me. Things
are odd with us, but she's still my best friend. And this is my first date and I'd
be throwing myself out a window without her right now.

I've been pregaming by listening to Kesha. Feeling pumped. Maybe
a little too pumped. Whenever I'm getting ready for something I'm really excited
for, I like to listen to music to pump me up. It's not that unusual, rather normal,
but I think sometimes it works against me. I get so excited, and I start to dream
about how I want things to turn out. It usually involves montages and musical
cues that aren't possible in real life, and then I end up disappointed.

I start to scroll though my iTunes to look for something to bring me down
a bit. Nothing depressing, but just chill—relaxing, you know? I end up changing
to Lykke Li. It's not somber, but also not hype. It's just what I need. I think ...

I try to get out of my head. That's the real problem. The music won't
matter if I keep imagining grand things happening tonight. I want to allow

myself to be excited, but I don't want to expect anything. I want to allow the night to flow how it flows and go where it goes. I just want to let go of it all and just be in the moment. But I mean, this is a huge moment for me. I *should* be fucking hyped, shouldn't I? I should imagine grand things. I should see myself being swept away, scooped off my feet—or me doing said sweeping or scooping! I should see myself in Jason's arms as the music swells and the camera spins. The passions growing and the stars shining. I should see myself happy right? Is it wrong to get what you want, just sometimes?

"Time Flies" starts playing and about half way through it the doorbell rings. My heart stops, my stomach flutters, and I notice my palms start to sweat. "Rachel!" Dad calls. "Jason's here!" I hit the shift bar to pause the music and I take a quick look in the mirror. I'm ready. I hope … .

I head down the stairs and my dad is introducing himself to Jason, "David, nice to meet you Jason."

"Nice to meet you as well, sir." Jason responds.

I reach the bottom of the stairs and Jason smiles and says, "Hey." I respond the same. We spend an awkward amount of time smiling at each other in front of my dad before I ask if he's ready to go. Which I immediately think is a stupid question, he's picking me up. He's been ready to go, he's waiting on me.

"Nice meeting you, Mr. Crowley," Jason says as we leave the house. He then mutters something to himself.

"What was that?" I ask.

"Oh, nothing, just me being stupid. I was just saying to myself that it was stupid of me to say that. I already told him it was nice to meet him. I just—that's usually what people say in the movies at that moment, and I guess I'm a little nervous," Jason says. He chuckles as he finishes and it's the cutest little laugh. This is amazing.

"Yeah, I'm a bit nervous too. I've never been on a date before. I've never gone out with anyone, or held hands, or kissed or anything." I quickly wish I hadn't said that. I don't want him to think that I'm expecting all of that to happen now. But he just responds, "Me either," and he opens the passenger side door for me.

I sit down and buckle my seatbelt and he gets in and does the same. "You don't mind that I did that do you?" He asks.

"What?" I ask back.

"Held the door open for you. I just felt like I should. I mean, I know some people have a problem with that sort of thing. Like, I don't think you need me to open the door for you or anything. I know you're very capable and that women are capable and they don't need men to open doors for them or anything ..." Jason fumbles out.

"Um ... no, I know. It was nice. I didn't think you were being ... offensive or anything." I assure him.

He smiles, and loosens up a bit. "So, uh, do you wanna pick something out?" He hands me his iPod and starts the car.

"Yeah, sure," I accept as we pull off. Though I don't really want to at all. This is a lot of pressure. At least I know everything on here is something he likes—it is his music. I just have to find something I also like. I scroll through the options for what feels like minutes and then I get self-conscious that I'm taking too long. What if he thinks that I don't like any of his music and that's why I haven't picked anything? I panic and just pick Blink-182 and play their album *Take Off Your Pants and Jacket*. It's not on shuffle so the first song that plays is "Anthem Part Two."

"Good choice!" Jason nods his approval.

"I love them!" I say.

"Me too! I wish I could see them in concert. You know, Travis, Mark, and Tom still together," Jason fantasizes.

"I know! That would be so awesome. It seems like Tom was kind of a dick, so good for them for moving on, but I love his whiny little voice. It adds so much angst and ... realness? to the music," I respond.

"I know. I'm a Travis guy myself, I just fucking love drums and cymbals and he's amazing at 'em. But Tom's voice is such a huge part of their music. It's weird without him, but I still really dig it."

I nod and I smile big, unable to contain how fucking happy I am right now. Having connection like this with someone other than Jess and Bright is beautiful. We both rock along to the music for a while, just taking in the moment. He bites his lower lip a bit when he's bobbing his head with the music. This is amazing.

"I'm so excited for these burgers!" Jason exclaims.

We discovered that we both love burgers, so we decided to go to this restaurant Doorbell that has really great burgers. "I know, me too! I've been waiting all day!" I reply.

Jason smiles, and he looks like he's going to say something, but he doesn't quite get it out. "First Date" starts playing and we both laugh. "Did you pick this album on purpose?" he asks jokingly.

"I wish. I don't know, maybe I did it subconsciously."

"Well, very well done."

This is amazing.

When we get to the restaurant we have to wait a bit before we're seated. We didn't make a reservation—it's not really that type of restaurant—but I guess Tuesday is date night at Doorbell. Like actually, it's a special. We end up getting a high top table for two. I order a lemonade—my go-to drink—and a California style burger with fries. I'd usually go for a double bacon cheese burger with pepperjack cheese, caramelized onions, and peanut butter on it, but my stomach isn't feeling up to that due to nerves.

Time passes and I don't even know what we really talk about. I focus so much on having to respond to what he says, that I don't really listen. I remember what my mom used to tell me about spiders, "They're just as afraid of you, as you are of them." That always helps me in moments like this. I remember that Jason wants to be here, and he's just as nervous as I am. Or at least that's what I'm going to believe. By the time I really get control of myself, our food is here.

Jason gets a Coke and a regular cheeseburger with waffle fries. He finishes his meal before I'm even half way done with my burger. "I'm sorry, I eat so slow," I say.

"No, I'm sorry I eat so fast. I'm not too great at pacing myself when it comes to food." Jason assures me.

"Feel free to have some fries." I gesture to my plate.

"No, they're all yours. I'm good." Jason declines, rubbing his stomach.

"I think you've told me before, but how many siblings do you have again?" I ask.

"Two. Twin sisters Kate and Mara." Jason says.

"And how old are they?" I ask.

"They're 13." Jason responds.

"Awesome! I always wanted a younger brother or sister. I mean, overall I think I like having been an only child, and really, Jess and Bright are pretty much like my sister and brother, but I think it would have been cool to have, like, actual siblings too," I say.

"Yeah, I know not everybody gets along well with their siblings, but I love my sisters. We get along great," Jason replies proudly.

"That's so cool! I always get kind of mad when people tell me they hate their siblings. I don't really understand how that can happen," I add.

"I dunno, I mean, I suppose it's just like anybody else. Some people are lucky and their siblings are people who are agreeable to them, but it's all chance really," Jason shrugs.

"True," I concede.

I do my best to hurry up and eat. The waiter asks if we'd like dessert, but we both agree that we're too full for that. "Wanna take a walk around?" Jason asks. "We'll come back to the car later."

"Yeah, that sounds great." I nod in agreement.

"Lake Aria's not far from here. We could walk there and make our way around it?" Jason suggests.

"Yeah, for sure," I say.

As we make our way down the block, we see a classmate of ours, Susan McKnight.

"Is that Suzie?" Jason notices her first.

"Yeah, I think so," I laugh nervously.

Suzie is a very nice, very talkative person. I don't mind her, but once she starts talking to you, you're locked in for a while. She also tends to overshare.

"Hey Rachel, hey Jason!" Suzie says.

"Hey," we both reply.

"What are you guys doing—are you on a date?" Suzie asks.

"Yup," I reply.

"That's so cuuuute," Suzie bunches up with excitement.

Both Jason and I smile politely.

"So where are you going?" Suzie asks.

"Well, we just ate at Doorbell, and now we're gonna go walk around the lake," Jason answers.

"Ooooh, sounds nice. I'm just waiting for my bus. My sister was supposed to meet me for coffee, but she never showed up," Suzie says.

"Oh, that sucks," I respond. "Maybe something came up?"

"No, she does this all the time. She's always standing me up, and if she does show up, she's never on time. I think she gets it from my dad, not that I'd really know, just basing it on what my mom tells us. I've only met my dad a couple of times," Suzie tells us. Jason and I don't know how to respond to that, so we don't say anything, but before there's a chance for an awkward silence Suzie continues, "I bet you guys are wishing I'd shut up."

"No," Both Jason and I say.

"Not at all," I continue.

"No, I know, I talk a lot. You can tell me if I'm annoying you," Suzie pushes.

"You're not annoying us," Jason says. The way he says it, I can tell he means it. Suzie doesn't annoy me either, it's just that most of the time I never know what to say to her. She casually shares really personal things, and then usually asks you if she's annoying you when you can't think of a way to respond. I'm glad that Jason isn't one of the people who hates her. Those people are assholes. I mean, I guess I understand being annoyed by her, but they often make fun of her too, which is an asshole thing to do.

"Okay, well you just let me know if I ever start to," Suzie says. There's another almost awkward pause and then Suzie asks, "Hey Rachel, do you think I can borrow some of your notes for Miss Sadler's class sometime?"

"Yeah, that'd be fine. I can get them to you tomorrow."

"Awesome! That's so nice of you!" Suzie smiles.

"No problem," I shrug.

We share another polite smile and then Jason says, "I think we're going to continue on our walk. I hope the bus comes soon and that your night improves."

"Thanks! You two have fun!" Suzie calls out as we make our way down the block.

"See you tomorrow," I call back.

Jason and I look at each other and smile.

"Suzie's a really sweet person," Jason says.

"Yeah," I agree.

The sun is setting and it's starting to get a little chilly. It's fall, so we're both wearing light jackets. I decided to go for a dress, which I probably wouldn't have done if I knew we were going to spend an extended amount of time outside. I try my best not to look too cold, but I'm not sure if it's working.

"Maybe it's not the best night to walk around the lake, it's only going to be chillier down there. Want to just walk around through the neighborhood?" Jason asks.

I want to protest and say that the lake would be fine, I think it'd be really romantic, but he's right, I don't think I'd make it long down by the lake. "Okay," I give in.

We walk in silence for a little bit and then Jason says, "So, I know you don't have any siblings, but do you get along with your parents? I feel like that's kind of in the same wheelhouse as liking your siblings, most people either really don't, or really do get along with their parents."

"Uh …" I begin. I have to think about this for a second. I mean, my dad and I get along fine, but I wouldn't say we're super close. Though, I guess we are. It's just that when I think of "super close" I think of Gilmore Girls or something, you know? I think of being each other's best friends, but we're not that. We just get each other. We understand each other more than anybody else could understand us. And then now I'll also have to bring up my mom's death. It's not that I'm uncomfortable talking about her, it's just that … I don't want people to feel like I expect their sympathy. I'm not looking for anything when I talk about my mom. And people always instinctively say, "sorry," I don't know how to respond to that. Saying, "It's not your fault," sounds weird and a little defensive, and saying "thanks" is also weird. I usually just go for, "It's okay."

"Yeah, I get along well with my dad. I mean, I wouldn't say we're best friends, but we get each other. And ... my mom actually died when I was 10."

"Oh, wow, I'm sorry ... I hope I didn't upset you," Jason replies.

"No, it's okay." I say automatically. I want to say more, but that's all I can get out about that. "So, what about you, do you get along with your parents?"

"Yeah, we're pretty close. It's actually pretty great, as a family we all get along rather well. At least as an immediate family," Jason responds.

"That's awesome," I say. I feel like I've said that a lot tonight. There's another small, comfortable silence and then Jason asks if he can hold my hand. "Yeah, definitely." I say, and I grab his hand. Our fingers interlock and we smile at one another. This is amazing.

"So, I understand if you don't want to talk about it, but are you religious at all?" Jason asks.

The question catches me a bit off guard. "Uh ... no, not really. We used to go to church kind of off and on. My grandma on my mom's side was pretty religious, so she'd want us to go, but my parents were never very into it, and neither was I. Also, we stood out a little bit. I mean people were nice, but my dad and I always felt a little out of place. For one, as I said, none of us were really religious, and two, Dad and I were the only Asian people there. I don't know if you knew, but I'm adopted from Korea. My dad's Chinese, he was born here, but his parents and most of his family are back in China. My mom was white. My grandparents on her side are dead, and she only had one brother, Uncle Mike, and he doesn't have any kids, so I don't have much of an extended family. At least not one that I see a lot."

"Oh, wow, well, extended families are a bit overrated," Jason comforts.

"Do you not get along with yours?" I ask.

"Yeah, I dunno. It's just that my mom's family doesn't really like my dad or his family much, and the same goes for his family with my mom. So we do our best not to be around any of them much. And as I've gotten older, it seems that neither side is very fond of me. I mean, for the most part they're not outright mean to me, but it's clear that they're different with me."

"I understand," I say. "That sucks though."

"Yeah, it's whatever," Jason shrugs.

"So are you religious at all?" I ask, trying to keep things going.

"No, not really. We never did the church thing. But, I guess I'm open to the idea of a God, or some higher being, you know?" Jason replies.

"Yeah, I mean, I don't really know. I don't believe in God, but I won't claim to know for sure that there isn't one."

"Exactly! And doesn't anything ever happen to you that just makes you feel like there's no way it could be just a coincidence, that things came together too perfectly?" Jason asks.

"Yeah, I mean, I don't think I've witnessed any miracles or anything, but I think I know what you mean," I nod.

"I don't really like to believe in fate or destiny or anything, but sometimes things just come together right when you need them to. Or you look back and see that even something you thought was shitty ended up working out for the best in some way," Jason notions.

"Like everything happens for a reason?" I ask.

"Yes, but no. I don't really like saying that. I hate when people wrap horrible things up and say 'It's all God's design' or 'everything happens for a reason'. I don't think that there's one plan, and one end goal or anything. I just think that there's good and bad to everything that happens, you know? Like when someone asks if you'd go back in time to kill Hitler. You instinctively want to say yes, that you'd stop him from doing what he did, stop him from killing millions of innocent people, but at the same time you think about what that would change. The world learned a lot from the Holocaust and the events of World War II, horrible things happened, but it also inspired change and compassion and helped shape the world we live in today. Of course those people weren't 'meant' to die, it didn't happen for some grand reason, but it wasn't all completely bad … if that doesn't sound horrible?" Jason clarifies.

"No, I understand what you mean. Like with my mom, I've thought a lot about what I'd do if I could go back and somehow stop her from dying, but I don't know. I mean, her death affected me greatly, in both good and bad ways. It's shaped me into the person I am today. And of course if she were still around, that would be amazing, but who knows what life would be like? I don't think bringing her back would for sure be a good or bad thing. Like you said, she wasn't 'meant' to die, but there were positive things that stemmed from her death," I concur.

Jason squeezes my hand a bit, and gives me a consoling smile. This is just so amazing. I'm on my first date, walking hand-in-hand with an awesome, very cute, very handsome guy. A guy I think I could really like. A guy I think my dad would like. A guy I think Jess and Bright would like. I mean, it honestly feels like I'm in a movie right now. It doesn't feel real, but at the same time it feels very real. It feels like something I haven't felt in a long time, but I can't quite place it.

We spend about an hour and a half walking around and talking. Holding hands the whole time. Eventually he says he has to get back home, though he'd like to stay and talk to me all night. It'd be a corny line if it wasn't so genuine. He's just so genuine. He's kind of awkward, but not in an off-putting way, in a delightful, endearing way. As we get back to his car Jason asks if I want to grab some ice cream on the way home. "We may not finish it together, but I mean, ice cream is a classic first date thing, right?"

"Totally!" I beam.

So we run by DQ and grab small cones to go. I get a vanilla and chocolate swirl, and he gets a butterscotch dipped cone. When we get back in the car he changes the music to Cults. "You heard of them at all?" he asks.

"Jess has mentioned them before, but I haven't listened to them much," I admit. They're melodic and very calm, definitely a good choice for the end of the night. It makes me wish we were dancing together right now, out in the starlit night.

When we reach my house, he turns the music down. "I had a really awesome time, Rachel."

"Me too," I say, not wanting this night to end.

We smile at each other, he looks deep into my eyes and then asks, "Would it be alright if I kiss you?"

"Yeah," I smile. "I'd like that."

He unbuckles his seatbelt, triggering me to do the same, and he leans forward to kiss me. I don't close my eyes until our lips are touching because I can't get the movie *Hitch* out my head, where he says the kisser is supposed to go 90 percent, the kissee goes the other 10. I want to make sure I go the 10.

There's an initial kiss that's a bit awkward, but we try again, and it comes together much better that time.

"Do you want me to walk you to your door?" Jason asks.

"No, that's okay," I respond. This is perfect. I want the night to end on *that* kiss, and this way there doesn't have to be another goodbye.

"Goodnight, Rachel," Jason says, smiling hard.

"Goodnight, Jason," I reply.

We stare at each other for a few seconds and then laugh a bit. "Goodnight," I say again in an "Okay, I'm really getting out of the car this time," sort of way.

"Goodnight," he laughs.

He waits until I get inside before driving away.

Tonight was amazing.

BRIGHT

It's Wednesday, which is the day new comics come out, so I'm headed to Bleu Comics to pick up my subscriptions. I follow The *Walking Dead, Batman, Daredevil,* and *The Flash* right now. I'd like to follow more, but I don't really have the money for that. It can be expensive. I've had times where I put off buying comics for months and then by the time I finally go to pick them up, I've got so many issues to buy that I'll drop about 70 to 80 bucks in one day. So I try to keep my subscriptions low, so that I'll put off buying comics less, and then I won't have to spend a bunch of money all at once.

Bleu Comics is owned by Ken and Marsha Bleu, who're married. It's a decent-sized shop in Uptown. I started going there a few years ago and they were so nice, I just kept going back. Now we're pretty good friends. I stop in every Wednesday for new comics, but also to catch up with them, and sometimes I go in just to hang. I had tried a few shops before I found theirs and I always felt judged when I went to comic book shops. I mean, some of that was just in my head, but I remember trying to buy an issue of *Kick-Ass 2* from Blaze Comics and the cashier looking at me patronizingly and saying, "Well, we have a *sixth* printing of it." I didn't care what printing it was, or how much it was worth, I just wanted to read it, but I still didn't buy it because I knew if I did he'd know I was an outsider, someone who just *casually* reads comics. Because clearly, in his eyes, nobody who's serious about comics would buy something that wasn't a first or second printing. I never felt like that with Ken or Marsha. They treated you with respect no matter how much you knew about comics. They didn't want to push people away by acting superior. They wanted more people to get into comics and they loved helping people figure out which comics were right for them.

I park the van on a side street and make my way up to the shop. It's a pretty nice day out, a little on the chilly side, but perfect hoodie weather. My favorite. I'm wearing my white Furiosa hoodie. I've never seen any other *Mad Max* film, but *Fury Road* was so fucking awesome. Furiosa was a legit boss. Or I guess is. I'm really excited for Charlize Theron to be in the next *Fast and Furious* movie. I love those films and I think she's great. I get that they're trying to capitalize off of her success with *Mad Max*, but that's okay with me. More badass women in that franchise can only help.

I'm humming, "If It Makes You Happy" by Sheryl Crow as I enter the shop. It was playing on the radio on the way over. "Hey Marsha!" I wave. Ken is helping a customer—or *guest*, as they like to call them.

"Hi, Bright!" she waves back. She's sorting comics, placing them into people's subscription bins.

"Sup, dude!" Ken says as he finishes with the guest.

I can't help but to smile as I watch them. They love this shit so much. Talking with new people every day, getting to know the regulars, guiding the newbies. Sometimes it's hard to believe they actually exist. They're just so genuinely kind. Both of them are just short little angels. They're the type of couple where you have a hard time thinking of either of them separately. That's probably because I only see them together. Well, unless one of them is out sick or something. But it's always weird when I see them apart from each other. I know they're individuals. I know this. They just go together so fucking well. It's ridiculous. They even wear the same style of glasses, but Ken's are orange and Marsha's are purple. Those are their favorite colors, but Marsha's favorite is orange and Ken's is purple. It's so sickeningly adorable.

I walk up to the counter. Nobody else is in the shop now. "Not much, how are you guys today?" I ask.

"Doing alright," Marsha gives a sideways grin.

"Not much business," Ken adds.

"I'm sorry," I say, giving a sympathetic smile.

"It's cool. I mean, it's new issue day so today's busier than normal, and overall we're doing fine, I just wish we could do better than fine, you know? I'd like to feel a little more secure than that, financially," Ken states.

"Yeah, totally," I nod.

"And how are you today?" Marsha asks.

"I'm alright. I dunno … I guess I'm feeling a little weird," I admit, willing myself to open up.

"What's up?" Ken asks.

I look around towards the ground, trying to figure out how to say what I'm feeling. I don't totally know, so I just start talking and I hope to figure it out along the way. "Jessica and Rachel both have other things going on. Rachel's off falling in love, and Jessica is trying to save the world. I'm happy for both of them. It's really cool that my sister is so excited to make a difference, and it's great Rachel is dating and branching out, but they're all I have. Them having lives means I either have to find one or I end up alone."

There's a pause. Ken and Marsha exchange a look, one that shows sympathy for me, but also understanding with each other. "I don't think that's true," Marsha consoles.

"Yeah, you won't end up alone. They're your family, they're not going to abandon you," Ken says, patting me on the back.

I wish I was as confident about that as Ken seems to be. I mean, I definitely don't think Jessica or Rachel would want to hurt me intentionally or anything, but I could see them leaving me. I could see them needing to do their own thing and moving on without me. And not like without me, but just, I don't know what I'm doing, and if they do, they'd have to follow that and not let me hold them back.

Marsha continues from where Ken left off. "Yeah, and I also mean that you don't have to 'find a life'. You have a life. I think people putting themselves down with that insult is bullshit. People seem to equate 'having a life' with going out clubbing, or dating, or being super busy with a job, or school, or something that people deem as important. And yes, the people who do those things have a life, but so do you. You're 16. You're figuring out who you are and what you want to do—and to be honest, pretty much everyone is. You have a life, Bright. You're doing you, and you're not hurting anybody doing it. Now if you want to find something more to do, of course you should, but don't do it because you think it's what is expected of you, or out of pressure."

"Yes, man! You are life! Seriously, think about how crazy it is to even be here. Think about the vastness of the universe and of … everything. Don't knock your life, man. You're an individual. There's only one you. Don't worry about what other people have going on. I mean, in the sense of comparing yourself to them. You have to worry about making yourself happy for you, not for others," Ken exclaims.

I smile, "You guys should start a book of life lessons."

"That's all this place is!" Ken says, gesturing around to all the comics.

"Why do you think Ken and I love comics so much? We love learning from them, we love seeing what others learn from them. We all get something different out of each page, and out of each line of dialogue, and out of each drawn image. It all adds up to something different inside of all of us, and I fucking love it. It's amazing," Marsha smiles big, her hazel eyes open wide.

"It's funny, when I was a kid, it was so simple. Reading comics was fun, but it was clear cut. There were good guys and bad guys. Right and wrong. It wasn't until I got older that I started to realize it's all gray. Well, not all, but the big things. The big events. It's kind of up to you to decide who's right and who's wrong. Both sides will have people who are extreme, but both causes are valid. I miss knowing what's right and what's wrong. Like, 100% without a doubt. As a kid, it's simple. You're ignorant to it all," I reminisce.

"Ignorance is bliss," Ken agrees. "Or so, we'd like to think."

We all take a second to just be, let the moment sink in. I take a look around and fully take in what they said about everyone taking something different away from each comic and each page and each word. I realize how amazing this place is, how much potential there is. There's so many different stories and different characters and emotions and feelings, and you could walk out of here with something that'll change your life. A character who will move you beyond description. I know I've been moved by so many things I've gotten here. There are panels that are imprinted in my head. Images that haunt me. In the best possible way. I'm so happy I have this place, Bleu Comics, and Marsha and Ken.

"So, anyway, Bright, if you ever are lonely or just want to chat, feel free to come here," Marsha says.

"Thanks," I accept.

For some reason "Don't Dream It's Over" by Crowded House comes into my head. It just seems like something that would play at a moment like this, if life were a CW show. It's hopeful melody would carry us into the credits as the three of us laugh. Ken would probably be giving me a one-armed hug, and Marsha would open up an issue of *Archie* to show us. I'm feeling optimistic, but not overtly so, and this song sets a good tone for that. I don't really know what I'm doing, or what will come, but hopefully it'll be alright. Hope. In one of the *Sandman* comics by Neil Gaiman, Morpheus or Dream or whichever of his many names you wish to call him, wins a debate in hell by proving hope is ever-powerful. He argues that hell would hold no power over the souls trapped there if they were unable to dream of heaven.

Maybe not the most inspiring idea, hoping to get out of hell, but I don't know, it means something. Hope is necessary. Hope is ever-powerful. With hope you have the potential to do anything. You can be controlled with hope, but you also can't progress without it. It gives the power for oppression and for freedom.

I get a sense of what Jessica feels now. She sees our abilities as hope. Hope for inspiration. Hope for the potential for change. I get why I can't change her mind on any of this. I still don't know how to help her, but I understand her more now.

I just hope that she's right.

RACHEL

꘎

I'm walking home from school feeling … well, amazing. Last night was one of the best experiences of my life. It was better than any fantasies I've ever had about a first date. I'm listening to "Bombastic" by Bonnie McKee and just feel so pumped and energized. This song makes me feel confident and in control. The way the words "Bombastic" *pop* as the chorus kicks in elicits a feeling of strength and action. But sort of in a way that won't last. Because those things can't be sustained at all times. And the chorus itself loses oomph as it goes on. The last words were slung together rapidly in a jumble. It's like a boost in a video game. I take it and all my stats quadruple and I'm not worried for the time being. I'm just coasting on the moment. Not concerned with the inevitable comedown.

Things are still weird with Jess and Bright. Besides needing help with outfit choices last night, I haven't really spoken with either of them since Monday morning. I don't really know what to say to them. And I know the more things develop between Jason and me, the worse this situation with them will get. But I'm just feeling too good right now for any of that to bother me.

I pull out my phone for no real reason other than needing something to do with my hands and I see I got a text from Jason.

> Hey, I know this is really fast and weird, but my parents have this saying, embrace the awkward, and they want to know if you and your dad want to come over for dinner tonight? Don't feel like you have to or anything, I told them it'd be weird and that we just had our first date yesterday.

My first reaction is to say no. This is too fast, too much. I don't even know what we are. Are we dating? Is he my boyfriend? I feel like parents meeting is sort of something that should happen after those things are decided. But that thought process flashes by and then I think, "Why not?" I mean, they're right, embrace the awkward. I don't really know what Jason and I are, and I doubt he does either. I'm sure his parents must know that. If they want to meet me, I'm game. Or at least I'm gonna try and convince myself to be.

I start to call my dad when I remember that he's got some work meeting tonight. He left a note on the kitchen counter this morning with twenty bucks for a pizza. I guess I could go alone. I assume their main goal is to meet me, not my father. Though, I dunno, maybe they're, like, really into seeing a person's parents and seeing where that person came from? Maybe that's how they're planning to decide if I'm good enough to date their son?

No, that's stupid. I need to calm down. I should text Jason back with something. I'm sure he's feeling rather anxious about this too.

> Hey, I think I'm up to "embrace the awkward," but unfortunately my dad is working tonight. Is it cool if I just come alone?

Jason's response comes a minute later, if that.

> Haha, yeah of course it's still okay if it's just you. But I was thinking, what if you ask Jessica and Bright to come?

I'm taken aback with that one. I start a response, but Jason sends a follow up before I get too far.

> I mean, you've said they're like family to you. Family is family.

I don't think it's a good idea. I mean, I know it's not. At least not before we get a real chance to clear the air. But I would really like someone there in my corner. Going alone sounds scarier the more I think about it.

> I don't know what they're up to, but I'll check and get back to you. What time should I/we be ready?

> Great! I'll pick you up around 6. Just let me know if they're going or not.

I start to think about how I want to compose this text to Jess, but I then decide my first priority should be getting home. If Jason's picking me up at six, that gives me about an hour and a half to figure this all out and get ready. It takes me about five minutes to run the rest of the way home and rush through the door and then burst up to my room.

Once there, I throw my backpack to the ground and plop down on my bed and text Jess the whole situation. As I wait for a response, I get up to put some music on. I can't decide on anything before getting a text back. Jess tells me that she's going to some potluck thing for Farson High Green so she can't go, but she tells me to text Bright.

I don't want to waste anymore time so I just opt to call Bright. It takes a few rings for him to answer.

"What were you doing?" I ask.

"Hi, Rachel."

"Were you screening my call?" I ask.

"I'm sorry I didn't rush to the phone," he says sarcastically.

"Like it wasn't right next to you."

"Whatever," Bright laughs. I'm glad that we're still able to joke easily. "What do you want?"

"I need to you come to Jason's house for dinner with me tonight," I propose hopefully.

"What? Why?" he asks.

"Becauuusseee, his parents invited me and Dad over for dinner, but Dad's at a work meeting tonight and Jason told me to invite you and Jess, but Jess is going to some stupid Farson High Green meeting, so you're the only family I have left."

"Damn, they must really want Jason to lock in a girlfriend. Wasn't yesterday your first date?"

"Yes! It's weird right? Which is why I don't wanna go alone," I plead.

"I dunno," Bright says. I can tell by the sound of his voice that he's decided to do it though.

"C'mon, Bright. Pleeeeaaasssee," I give one last push.

"Fine. I'll run it by my parents, but it should be fine. What time? And what should I wear?"

"Wear whatever," I tell him, but then rethink it. "Well, like, something nice, but casual nice," I add.

"Okay, that helps somewhat I guess," Bright chuckles.

"Great! Jason's going to pick me up at six. I'm sure he can pick you up to, but I'll text you when I know those details for sure."

"Sounds good," Bright says.

"Okay bye!"

"Bye."

I throw my phone on the bed and start flinging my clothes off so I can hop in the shower. But halfway through I remember I need to text Jason that Bright is going, so I do that, shedding the rest of my clothes while I wait for a response. He tells me that we can pick up Bright on the way back to his place and that he'll see me around 6:00.

I'm so excited, and nervous, and I run to the bathroom and start the shower. But then I remember that I need to feed Rebel, so I run downstairs naked and put her water and food in their respective bowls. She looks at me and meows rather sassily. "Shut up, Rebel. It's not like this is the first time you've seen me naked. Grow up," I yell. I run back upstairs, almost get in the shower, but then remember that my phone is on my bed and I should have it in the bathroom with me in case Jason or Bright calls or something. So I run and grab it, place it on the bathroom counter, and then finally hop in the shower.

Jess is always on me and Bright to make sure to take short showers. "You don't need more than five minutes," she says. My amendment is that you don't need more than five minutes *unless* you're doing sexy things with yourself o r someone else, or you're sad and want to just stand under the hot water like they do in dramas all the time—especially medical dramas. So I usually don't spend more than five minutes in the shower, but this time I spend even less— maybe about three minutes. I rinse my body down and I'm out. No need to wash my hair, I already did that with my shower this morning.

I start to dry myself off and I remember that I still haven't put any tunes on, so I go out to do that. I turn on Matt & Kim's album Sidewalks. They're super fun to move to and they're just feel good music. They also put on a fucking amazing live show. Jess, Bright, and I saw them in concert and it was bananas! Definitely in the top five concert experiences of my life.

Their song "Cameras" comes on, which is one of my favorites on this album. The song is about pushing back against social media's insistence that we need to capture every moment in a picture or video. It tells us to put the cameras away and use our eyes. That it's okay that not every moment is recorded. Some memories are just for you. This has generally been my motto. I don't take a lot of photos, well I didn't, I kind of do now because of Snapchat, but those "go away" after you look at them. Overall, I don't really take a lot of photos. I think it's better to just be in that moment and experience it. You'll remember it if it's meaningful to you. Hopefully. Unless you get Alzheimer's or something. That would be awful. I can't imagine what it's like to go through that or have someone you love go through that. Ah! Just the thought of slowly losing all my memories and losing myself and there's nothing I can do about it, that's too much. My mind's going to dark places. Gotta focus on here and now. Isn't that what I was just saying?

I head back to the bathroom to finish drying. Then I set out to pick something to wear. I toss a bunch of shit out of my closet and onto my bed. After a little more than half an hour, I think I've got my attire for tonight ready. I'm going to wear this purple dress that I love and these black wedge heels. I'm not 100 percent about it, but I've got to just choose and be done with it.

Rebel makes her way into my room and makes herself comfortable on my bed.

"Whattaya think?" I ask.

I don't really get an answer, because she's a cat, but I like to think that she's too stunned by my good looks to respond. "UUUHUAAAAAAAHHH!" I scream out.

Rebel looks at me wide-eyed.

"I'm just so excited!" I tell her.

I really am. This is crazy. I'm going over to dinner to meet the family of a boy I'm dating. Me. *ME*. I've never dated anyone. I never even really thought anyone was interested in me. I think I'm decent looking, but there are gorgeous girls at our school. There are girls way smarter and cooler and funnier than me. There are girls who do things. I don't do anything. I just never thought I'd be dating anybody. At least not until later in life when I've figured shit out and have a life and do things. This just feels so surreal.

I've just got too much energy. I've got to do something with it or I'm going to go crazy. I just want to dance. I need something I can dance to harder than Matt & Kim right now. Something a little clubby and just pure dance. I decide to listen to "Burn" by Ellie Goulding. It's not really more dancey than Matt & Kim, but I just love it so much and it'll pump me up more right now.

The song starts and I close my eyes and just let my body flow how it flows. I just do whatever I feel in that moment. There's this character Karolina Dean from the comic *Runaways*—the one comic I found out about on my own and not from Bright. She's from the planet Majesdane—or her parents are—and Majesdanians natural form is luminous, being composed of pure light and energy.

Visually changing from second to second. In that form, Karolina can fly, create light blasts, force fields, and emotionally bond people together. She flows freely. When I'm dancing, eyes shut, I feel like Karolina Dean. I feel powerful and iridescent. I feel like I'm on equal playing grounds with Jess and Bright.

In those moments of dancing, everything makes sense. I may still have problems on my mind, but as long as the song keeps playing, as long as my body is still moving, they don't matter. I'm free and nothing can stop me.

I start to cry as I'm dancing. I'm just feeling so many emotions right now. Different levels of joy. And that reminds me that I should put on some eye liner and do my makeup. I've got about 20 minutes before Jason will be here to get me. It takes me about 10 minutes to get my makeup on and then Jason texts me saying that he's on his way.

Now I just play the waiting game. I try and go over everything and make sure I'm completely ready. I've fed Rebel. I've got myself together. I didn't do any homework, but none of it is that hard so I can tackle it when I get home. I think I'm good. Everything should be taken care of.

I spend a few minutes walking around, just trying to not let myself freak out. I've turned off the music because I don't want it to influence me in any way right now. I decide to turn my lights off and go wait downstairs in the kitchen. I grab myself a glass of water and just walk around the island, looking out the window every time I pass it to see if Jason's here yet.

All of a sudden I have to pee, so I run upstairs to the bathroom, and of course as soon as I sit down, Jason texts that he's here.

I text him that I'll be right out. I pee as fast as I can, grab my purse off the counter, and start to run for the door when I see the note Dad left for me this morning. I need to tell him where I'll be. I write a quick note in different color ink and place it next to his, and I also send him a text just to be sure. And I'm out the door.

I speed walk to the car, open the door, plop down in the passenger seat, and let out a quick sigh of accomplishment. "Hey!" I say.

"Hey," Jason says back, laughing a bit.

"What?" I ask.

"You seem a bit frazzled."

"I was just rushing a bit to finish some last minute things," I reply.

"Alright well, you look amazing. I love your hair! And tonight will be amazing, so just take some deep breaths," Jason tries to comfort me.

"Thanks," I say. I don't even remember what I did with my hair.

"So, is Bright ready?" Jason asks. "Also, you'll need to direct me to their place. I assume it's not too far."

"No, it'll take like maybe 10 minutes. And he should be ready, I told him that you were on your way to get me and that we'd be picking him up after. But I'll text him and tell him we're on our way."

I direct Jason to the Walker residence and it doesn't even take us 10 minutes to get there. I text Bright that we're out front and he's coming out of the house less than a minute later wearing a Pokémon T-shirt—green with Bulbasaur on the left side over his heart, gray jeans, and a navy blue zip-up sweater. I guess that will do.

Bright gets in the car and sits in the middle back seat.

"Hey, guys!" Bright greets us.

"Hey," both Jason and I say together.

"You buckled up?" Jason asks as he pulls away from the curb.

"Yup," Bright responds.

We spend a minute or so in silence and then Jason asks Bright what kind of music he likes to listen to.

"I dunno, I listen to a lot of different things I guess. I guess things of the rock persuasion are what I listen to most, but really I can like anything," Bright answers.

"Well here, find something you like." Jason hands Bright his iPod with the audio jack plugged into it.

Bright ends up playing Girl Talk. It's just one guy who's like a big DJ mash-up and sampling artist. Just snippets of songs, placed over snippets of instrumentals of other songs. He does it very well though. I don't listen to Girl Talk often. I have to be in the right mood for it. I think this is a good time for it though.

By the time we reach Jason's house, my excitement has turned into pure nerves. I'm just so nervous. What if this all goes wrong? His parents could hate me—or his sisters! I could say something offensive and stupid. I don't know what, but it could happen. Maybe they're racist and they don't know I'm Korean or that Bright is black? What if I can't control my stomach and I vomit all over the place? I'm not getting out of this car. There's no way I'm getting out of this car.

"So, you ready?" Jason asks.

I imagine I must look crazy as I nod. I can't bring myself to speak. He'd know I'm terrified and then him trying to make it better would just make me more terrified. We get out of the car and as we're walking up to the house, Bright walks up beside me—both of us a little behind Jason.

"I know you're freaking out."

"Shut up," I whisper.

"Look, just relax, Rachel. I know you're going over everything that could go wrong, but you're no more likely to do anything embarrassing now than you would any other time. You're just psyching yourself out. And plus, I got your back, sis. It'll be fine," Bright whispers back.

I know it's only been like two days, but I was getting so worried things between me, Bright, and Jess weren't going to get better any time soon. There's still a lot to talk about, but I'm so glad that there's still love there. I'm glad I've still got them in my corner. Or at least Bright, that is.

Jason gets to the door and then waits for us to catch up. I smile at Bright and mouth thank you. Jason takes my hand as he unlocks the door, "We're back!"

"Hey!" Jason's father greets us, coming out of the kitchen.

"It's very nice to meet you, Rachel." Jason's mother says, following his father. "My name's Sharon," she takes my hand in both of hers and shakes it.

"I'm Frank," Jason's father puts a hand up and does the wave without actually waving type of thing.

"It's very nice to meet you both!" I reply. Then I look over to Bright, feeling the sudden urge to explain him, even though I know they've been told the situation. "This is Bright. He's like a brother to me. I've known him his whole life. I was there when he and his sister, Jess—who's also like a sister to me—was born. I'm sorry my dad couldn't make it, but I'm sure you'll get to meet him soon. Or I hope. I mean, I think that'd be nice … for you all to meet."

I blurt all of that out very rapidly and now I feel very silly.

"Well, we're very happy that you both could make it," Sharon smiles, politely ignoring my word vomit.

"Dinner's running a little late, but it shouldn't be too much longer," Frank announces.

"Why don't you show them around the house, Jason?" Sharon suggests. And then she yells for Kate and Mara to come meet us and she and Frank go back into the kitchen.

They leisurely come out of the living room, I can't tell if they're shy or just playing it cool. They're identical, except one is wearing a striped black and white turtle neck, and one is wearing a white turtleneck with gold polka dots. Both have sporting medium length, brunette, Rose Byrne-esk bobs.

"Hi," the one wearing stripes says.

"Hi," the one with gold polka dots says.

"Names?" Jason presses.

"I'm Kate," the first one waves.

"I'm Mara," the second one smiles.

"It's nice to meet you," I respond. "I'm Rachel."

"I'm Bright." Bright waves.

Kate and Mara don't say anything else and we stand in silence for a second.

"So, you wanna see my house?" Jason asks, trying to keep the moment from turning into an awkward silence.

"Yeah, sure," I comply with a smile.

He first takes us to the right of the entry, which leads into the living room where Kate and Mara are now back to watching TV. From there leads into the dining room which leads to the kitchen, which leads back into the front entryway. It's all got a very "at-home" vibe. Sharon and Frank have clearly spent time molding their house into a place that people would feel comfortable in. I could feel it when I first walked in. You know how there are some places you instantly feel connected to? This felt like that. It felt right. It felt like I was supposed to be here all along. And I don't know if that's just me being wrapped up in the moment, or if it's something more, but I'm really happy.

"Yeah, that's pretty much it. Upstairs there's just two bathrooms, and then all of our rooms," Jason tells us, completing the tour.

"We don't get to see your room?" I ask.

"Yeah … not today. It's a bit of a mess, I'll spare you two of that," Jason eludes.

"I really don't mind," I push.

"Me neither," Bright adds.

"Not gonna happen," Jason declares and then starts walking back towards the living room. "Let's watch some TV until dinner's ready."

"Actually you can help set the table," Sharon orders from the kitchen. "We're just about ready."

"I guess we're setting the table," Jason claps his hands together and about-faces.

The three of us head into the kitchen to grab plates, forks, knives, and glasses. I set out the plates, Bright sets out the glasses, and Jason does the silverware.

"It's amazing what 3 people can do," Jason jokes.

"Teamwork makes dreamwork," Bright chimes back.

I think Bright must feel the same vibe I do. Normally he's more withdrawn in situations like this. He definitely wouldn't be joking around. This makes me feel good. I can feel my nerves slipping away. The excitement is coming back.

Dinner is ready a few minutes later and Sharon tells everybody to go wash up beforehand. Kate and Mara run to the kitchen sink first and Jason and Bright form a line behind them. I have to use the bathroom, so I ask Frank to direct me which way to go once I get up the stairs, and I step out of the handwashing line. I think I mostly just need a second to get myself together. It's dinner time now. Questions will be asked. I'll be in the spotlight. Oh, man, and the nerves were just settling …

After I pee, I wash my hands and stare at myself in the mirror. I tell myself that everything is going to be fine—because it will. I'm 17 years old. I have conversations everyday with people I don't know that well. This is nothing any different than that. I can do this. The Disney Channel Original Movie, *Gotta Kick It Up!*, pops into my head. America Ferrera grabbing her teammate and proclaiming, *¡Si se puede! Yes we can!* At least I think it was America Ferrera who said it. I don't remember. I never actually saw the movie. I just saw the promo for it a lot. I should watch that movie.

I take one last look at myself in the mirror and fluff my hair and I head back to join the others. As I'm walking down the stairs I see everyone smiling and laughing, passing the food around and loading up their plates. Family dinners like this are not something I have often. I understand why TV parents are always trying to get their kids to sit down and eat with them. They just want nice moments like this. Time to just be with each other.

I take a deep breath and make my way over to the table and take my seat. Whatever happens, it'll be great.

JESSICA

I'm walking down the block to Sasha's house for the Farson High Green potluck. I didn't meet her yesterday. The FHG VP was the one who invited me to the potluck. I wish I had just gone to the meeting yesterday like I was going to, but I figured this would get me out of my comfort zone, and I guess the "past me" thought that would be a good thing. Present me isn't so sure. There's so much going through my mind right now. I'm wondering if this is the right move, I'm worrying about what's going to happen with my friendship with Rachel. Bright is with her right now at Jason's for dinner. I guess I shouldn't say I'm surprised, but I kind of am. Bright's the "let's always be as responsible as we can" guy. We agree that Rachel may need room to grow, but we can't go along with her for that ride. Bright can't get closer to Jason. But then, here I am, outside of Sasha's house, ideally about to expand my friends list as well.

I make my way up to her door, 3336 3rd Avenue South. Lots of threes. I ring the doorbell and wait. It's kind of chilly out today, so I do a little dance while I wait. After a few seconds, a boy my age answers the door.

"Hi! Jessica, right?" The boy asks, greeting me.

"Hi, and yeah, I'm Jessica nice to meet you—"

"Sasha," He replies.

I try to hide my surprise. I feel stupid for assuming he was a girl just because his name is Sasha. I mean, there's Sacha Baron Cohen, and ... I know I've watched a show with a guy named Sasha. It's not like I've never experienced that.

Sasha motions for me to come in the house. I make my way through the door and he closes it behind me.

"Nice to meet you, Sasha. Thanks for having me over," I say.

"Thanks for coming!" Sasha responds.

I take off my jacket and slip off my shoes. Sasha takes my jacket and hangs it in the closet with everyone else's. It looks like there's a lot of people here. A lot of people I'm going to have to socialize with. A lot of people I'm going to have to work to hide myself from. This was a dumb idea. This whole thing makes no sense. Why am I even doing this? Because I want to help the world. Because I want to promote understanding and respect and love. How can I do that if I'm always hiding?

"Everyone's in the dining room," Sasha leads the way. "They're all a fun group of people, really nice." He must be picking up on my hesitation.

We enter the dining room and I'm greeted by at least 20 people. I don't do social interaction well. I hate going over to other people's houses for school projects. Why did I think I'd like to do it tonight when there's not even a set objective other than to talk and get to know each other? None of them can really get to know me even if I wanted them to.

I wave and introduce myself, and then everyone goes around the room saying their names. I shake the hands of a few people who are close to where I'm standing. I'm happy that there seems to be a good balance of boys and girls, and also that I'm not the only minority—though I seem to be one of five out of 20 or more. It's funny how no matter the situation, I'm always doing a minority count.

"There's tons of food. It's all local and organically farmed, and it's all delicious. There's plenty of veggie and even vegan options if you are either of those," Sasha encourages me to grab a plate.

"Awesome!" I comply.

I care a lot about helping the environment, but I've never been really knowledgeable about where my food is coming from. I really should be, and I should try and eat healthier, and locally, but my parents don't really pay attention to that and they buy our food. I can do my best to eat better when I'm fending for myself though, and I guess I can talk to them about it. I'm sure they'd make an effort if I brought it up, especially if they think it would ease a bit of my needing to save the world angst.

I head around the dining room table and I load a plate up with as much delicious looking food as I can. There's music playing, coming from the other room, and this song by the band Interpol comes on. It's a song I haven't heard in a long time, but it brings back very vivid memories of Bright, Rachel, and I playing around the house on Sunday afternoons and my mom and dad hanging around just relaxing, or doing the things around the house they didn't get to do during the week. My dad really likes Interpol and this song would play all the time. I completely forgot about it, but I remember really liking it. I really like the singer's voice and the melody and vibe of the song. It's actually kind of heartbreaking. The way this song builds is beautiful, but sad. It's like it wants to reach a more epic climax. It wants something it can't obtain. But the passion and angst and energy—the feeling—it's all there. It's all pushing for the big ending. But it doesn't come. In the end it's almost like they give up. Or more so accept that it's not going to be like they want.

All of a sudden I just don't want to be here at all. The song has hit me with a wave of nostalgia and I just feel the urge to be somewhere private, somewhere I can experience this alone and not be bothered. And it's nothing they've done obviously. It's just this song. This feeling. I'm reminded of a time when things were much simpler and I was generally carefree. I'm only 16 and I'm already reminiscing on the "old days."

I finish loading my plate, and I make my way over to Sasha—I need to know what this song is called.

"Um, I always forget. Hold on a sec," Sasha says. He walks into the other room and comes back a few seconds later. "Obstacle 1."

"Thanks. I know it's Interpol, but I don't think I've ever known the name. My parents used to play this song all the time," I explain.

"Yeah, I really like Interpol," Sasha responds.

"I've only really listened to them through my parents, but I should definitely check them out more," I express.

"Yeah for sure!"

There's a lull in the conversation and then Sasha comments on how packed my plate is. And that's about it for excitement. The rest of the evening at Sasha's is rather uneventful. I find out more about the club. I learn a few names. I mostly sit in silence and listen to others' conversations and try not to be too awkward, like I usually do at parties. I want people to know me. I want them to see me and understand me. I want to go to a party and fucking be confident and just be myself and not worry about saying the wrong things or being judged. I mean, I don't need everyone to love me, but I want to be confident in myself regardless. I'm a good person. I'm an intelligent person. I have opinions and a viewpoint that I know people would find interesting. Not because I'm special, but because nobody can have my viewpoint but me, and if I shy away from conversations and socializing, nobody will know that viewpoint.

And if I don't talk with others and share ideas, how can I hope to save the world, or change it, or help it? I can't.

Before I leave the party I do my best to genuinely open up with some of the people there. My ambition proves to be larger than my actual ability to achieve this goal, but at least I try. At about 9:30, I call Bright to see if I can get a ride home. He tells me that he's still with Rachel at Jason's, but they're just about to leave and then he'll come get me.

As I wait and continue to mingle with the people who are still lingering, I decide that I'm going to give FHG a real chance. I have to. I can probably learn a lot from them and figure out a way to direct my passion of helping the world, of doing more. This could be the start of a new me. A stronger me. A more confident me who's not afraid to show my vulnerability to those around me. This feels right. I feel good about this. I'm deeming this "The Beginning of Jessica's New Life."

It may just be bravado for now, but they don't say "fake it 'til you make it" for nothing. I've got to believe it for it to happen, so I'm going to believe.

This night is my catalyst.

BRIGHT

Jason drops us off at home. My place is closer to his and Rachel decides to be dropped off with me and go with me to pick up Jessica.

I'm glad I went with Rachel tonight. It was a lot of fun. Jason and his family are very welcoming people, and his parents are rather good cooks. It was one of the best meals I'd eaten in a long time. Not that my parents aren't good cooks also, but I'm just used to their style. It was something new.

I call Jessica while Rachel and Jason are saying their goodbyes to tell her that we'll be on our way in a few minutes. I also tell her to text me the address. After I hang up with Jessica, I spend a few awkward seconds deciding if I should wait by our van for Rachel or just get in and start it up. I don't want it to look like I'm trying to hurry them, and I can't decide which way will look the least like I'm trying to.

I end up choosing to get in the van, but not start it. As I'm opening the door I hear Jason's car door shut and look back to see him driving away. Rachel has a huge grin on her face. I'm happy she enjoyed the night too. She deserves this.

I get in the van and start it up. A few seconds later Rachel hops into the passenger seat. We both buckle up and I pull out of the driveway.

"You look really happy," I observe.

"I am really happy," Rachel smiles.

"I know I really wasn't your ideal choice, but thanks for inviting me tonight."

"No, thanks for coming. I'm really glad you did! It seems like you really had a good time. I don't normally see you open up to people so easily," Rachel remarks.

"I know, right? I don't know, there's something about that house. It's just so … at home. You know what I mean?"

"Yeah, I felt exactly the same way. It was very welcoming and so were they. Tonight was amazing." Rachel agrees.

It really was …

As we're driving, it starts to rain. I turn on the windshield wipers, and for a while, we just drive listening to the rhythm of the wipers, the hum of the engine, and the beat of the rain hitting the roof of the van. Eventually, Rachel plugs her iPod in and puts on Childish Gambino's album, *Because the Internet*. It's one of my favorite albums ever. I'm always finding new meanings to his lyrics. Donald Glover—his real name—is a very talented writer and just a talented man at that. He's also on one of my favorite shows, *Community*. He's had a big influence on me. He's spoken out a lot about not putting people—more specifically black people—in a box. He has a *ton* of great lyrics. My favorites are when he speaks about how black people telling other black people that they're not black enough is the same as white people saying we're all the same. Or when he says that he doesn't act black, he acts himself. I hate being put in a box. I hate it when other black people tell me I'm an "Oreo"—black on the outside, but white on the inside. Or white people tell me that they're "blacker" than me. What the fuck does that mean? Are all black people the same? What is being black? We're all just people. There isn't *one* way all black people think. There isn't one type of movie or music all black people like. We don't all live the same.

And I'd be lying if I don't have to remind myself of that too. Sometimes when my extended family asks me about my interests, I'm afraid to tell them. I think they won't like what I like because a lot of things I like are seen as more "white people things." I have to remind myself that they can also like them, or if they don't, there's no reason they can't. It's not because they're black, they simply have different interests. And when I'm walking down the street at night, and there's a larger black man walking towards me, for a split second I get afraid. I quickly remind myself that he's just a person, but there's still that split second of fear. That split second of the brainwash of constantly being told from the media that black men—and black people—are aggressive and dangerous. I hate it. I *know* the black man walking down the street towards me is just a man walking down the street, yet the fear is still my initial reaction because that's what I've been told my whole life. *I hate it.* I hate being judged and I hate judging others. Racism scares me, but the internal racism scares me more.

I'm surprised Rachel put this album on. It's kind of a downer.

"Don't you want to listen to something happier?" I ask.

"Eh, I'm just relaxed, this has a good blend of relaxation and hype," Rachel declines.

I nod and we continue to drive in silence. In a few minutes, we're pulling up to where Jessica is. I text her and it takes a few minutes, but she eventually comes and hops in the back seat behind Rachel.

"Well, this is a rare occurrence," Jessica prompts.

"What do you mean?" Rachel asks.

"Me being in the back seat. I'm always either driving or in the passenger seat," Jessica says.

"Well, you can drive if you want," I offer.

"Nah, I'm good," Jessica concedes.

She buckles up and I pull away from the curb.

"So how was it?" Rachel asks Jessica, turning down the music.

"It was good. A little awkward at first, but eventually it was fun. There's some cool people in the club, and Sasha was really nice, and also a boy."

"Really?" I ask.

"Yeah, I felt stupid for assuming he was a girl because of his name," Jessica admits.

"Assuming does make an ass out of you and me. Though mostly just you in this case," Rachel laughs.

"Yeah, well, anyway it was cool. I think I'm going to join!" Jessica announces.

"Awesome," Rachel says.

"Yeah, that's great!" I congratulate.

"Indeed, indeed. But, what I really want to know is what your night was like?" Jessica prods.

"Really?" Rachel asks.

"Yes, Rach," Jessica says. "I have my reservations about you and Jason. I've realized some of that is just me not wanting to lose you. But I'm still happy for you. I still care about you and your life."

Rachel smiles and then begins to recap the night to Jessica—the dinner consisting of a Greek salad, oven-baked chicken, grilled cheese (for the people who didn't eat meat), and broccoli with rice, followed by a brief session of figuring out what we wanted to do next, which led into everyone playing Wit's End—men vs. women, and eventually Jason, Rachel, and I just hanging in the living room watching TV with Kate and Mara until we left.

It was a really fun night. It was great to see Rachel so happy. Not that she normally isn't happy, but I've never seen her like this. It's like her aura is completely different. And Jason seems like a really great guy. I've never really tried to be a protective older brother when it came to Jessica or Rachel and boys, but I am glad that Jason's not an asshole.

I ask, and both Rachel and Jessica say they're fine if I take the long way back to Rachel's to drop her off, so I take the parkway. It's really beautiful this time of year—all the leaves changing colors, the beautiful houses. It's dark now, but the street lamps illuminate enough for it to still be worthwhile. And I really like the style of street lamps along the parkway. It's all a bit magical, especially in the rain, but a bit more like Neil Gaiman than Disney.

Jessica asks me something, but I don't hear, so I turn my head back for a quick second to ask what she said.

"I said, I totally told you about swamp boogers, like, *months* ago," Jessica repeats.

It takes me a few seconds to register what she's talking about, and then

I remember Jason telling us about the horribly terrifying taxidermy creations that are swamp boogers. I quickly whip my head back around toward Jessica again, "There's no way you told me about them months ago! I would not forget something like this!"

"Maybe you just—"

Jessica is cut off by Rachel screaming.

I turn my eyes back to the road just in time to see myself hit a woman.

RACHEL

Bright slams on the brakes, but there's no way for him to avoid hitting the woman. He does lessen the impact though. She was running across the street, so the van hit her from the side. Her body bent over and her head whipped against the hood and she fell to the ground. At that point the van was at a stop, so it didn't roll over her.

I look over to Bright. He's gripping the wheel with both hands and he's shaking fervently. He's in shock. I don't bother snapping him out of it, I just rush out to see if the woman is okay. She's on her side and her body is in the type of position I've only really seen cats lie in—ones that look impossibly uncomfortable, but in which they somehow sleep. She's bleeding from the head, but the rain is washing a lot of it away and toward the curb.

I go to check her pulse, but stop myself. All the crime dramas I've watched come to mind and the thought "Don't get your prints on anything," runs through my head. I quickly shut that thought down and I check her neck for a pulse, but I can't find one. I look over and see that Jess is standing next to me. "I think she's dead," I manage to muster.

Jess acknowledges what I said with a nod. I think she's crying, but I can't tell because of the rain. I know I'm crying. My chest is heaving, and I feel as though I could maybe pass out at any moment. "What are we going to do?" I ask. I scan the area and see that there's no one else around. I can't tell if that's good or bad.

Jess doesn't answer me, but instead goes over to the driver's side and opens the door. She's talking to Bright, but I can't quite tell what she's saying. Whatever it is seems to wake him from his stupor though. He gets out of the car and they both walk over to me and kneel down, placing one hand each on the woman's body. "What are you doing?" I ask. Neither of them answer, so I repeat myself. When they don't respond, I start to get angry. "Why aren't you guys fucking answering?"

"It's not working," Bright groans, more to Jess than to me.

"What's not working?" I press.

They both look at each other and take their hands off the woman. They glance at each other. "We can heal people," Jess responds.

"What?" I ask.

"We can heal people," Jess repeats.

My breathing gets quicker and shallower, "Since when?" I ask.

"It doesn't really matter right now," Bright cuts in.

I don't like that answer, but maybe he's right. "Okay ... so what are we going to do?" I ask.

"I don't know, I guess just try again," Bright suggests.

"Maybe we should think about this a bit." Jess cautions. "I mean the last time this happened—"

"*Last* time this happened?" I ask.

Neither of them say anything. They just look at each other nervously again.

"What the fuck is going on? What happened?" I demand.

"Well, the way we learned we could heal ..." Bright trails off.

"It was the same day we discovered our powers," Jess says.

My mind goes back to that day—Jess knocking me out, learning she had superstrength. "So did you guys heal me after knocking me out or something? Fix a gash on my head? Make me wake up sooner?" I ask.

"Well, sort of ," Jess says.

"Okay, well why would you keep that from me? Why wouldn't you tell me about the healing powers?" I ask.

"Because … Jessica didn't just knock you out that day. She killed you," Bright confesses.

"What?" I ask.

"I didn't knock you out. When I hit you that day I snapped your neck and you died." Jess explains.

"But …" I start.

"We didn't tell you because … we didn't know how. But we brought you back to life that day," Jess says.

"And I know we can bring this woman back, we just have to try harder," Bright adds.

"But when we brought Rachel back, she didn't remember anything about what happened, and it took her a while to get her bearings. What are we going to tell this woman, Bright? What are we going to do once she wakes up?" Jess asks.

Bright and Jess seem to have forgotten that they just told me that I died when I was 13. That Jess killed me. I want to yell at them, but I can't work my mouth. I can't seem to move my body at all. It's as if gravity is laughing at me—pinning me still and whispering, "Fuck you."

"Okay, so we'll try again, and we'll just get her breathing and—we'll check her wallet to see where she lives, and we'll get her breathing, and we'll teleport her home and find a way to get her inside before she wakes up," Bright stresses.

"There are so many flaws in that plan. What if she lives with someone? She looks to be in her 30s. She could have a husband or kids, or just a roommate. And we can't just leave her there. We should take her to a hospital," Jess puts forth.

"We can't do that, Jess. There's no way to do that without getting caught," Bright warns.

"It's what's right. We hit someone, we can't just leave them here," Jess stands her ground.

"We're not going to, we're going to heal her!" Bright yells.

"Okay, well, whatever, we have to heal her! We don't have time for this! We'll heal her, and we'll just have to figure it out after we get her breathing," Jess orders.

Bright looks as though he wants to argue more, but he just nods and they attempt to heal the woman again. They close their eyes this time and grip her tightly. After a minute or so, color starts to return to the woman, and not long after that, her chest begins to rise and fall—she's breathing! She's alive! "She's alive!" I yell.

Jess and Bright open their eyes.

"Well, what now?" Bright asks.

"I don't know. I don't know. I guess she's fine. We'll move her to the side of the road, out of the street, and we'll drive off a bit, and … someone can hang around out of sight and make sure she gets up alright," Jess suggests.

Bright doesn't answer, but he nods and Jess picks the woman up.

Once Jess gets her out of the road, Bright runs over to check out the van. "There doesn't seem to be any real damage," he says, wiping away what I assume is blood from the hood. He uses his sleeve, and once he finishes, he looks to the ground, he takes off his hoodie, and wipes away the blood from the pavement. Most of it has been diluted due to the rain, so there's not a lot of clean up. "Come on guys! We gotta go!" Bright calls out.

It takes everything in me to will myself to move. I'm pretty much moving on autopilot now. I make my way to the van as quickly as my body allows me to move. Bright is already in the driver's seat, but when I look back, Jess is still standing by the woman. "I'm going to stay with her," she calls.

"What? No—come on, let's go!" Bright yells.

"No. I'll stay and say that I came across her passed out here. Say I was just about to call 911, when she started waking up. Maybe help her back to her house. This way we'll really know she's alright. You guys go. I'll call you when you should come get me," Jess relegates.

Again, Bright seems as though he wants to argue, but he just starts the engine and we take off. I look back and watch as Jess and the woman fade from view. Nothing makes sense right now. I don't know what to think about anything.

My best friends just resurrected a woman whom one of them killed. That's a monumental mind-fucking event all on its own. But they brought me back to life years ago. I was dead. Jess killed me. I died and they revived me.

I feel like I'm going to throw up.

"Rachel? Are you okay?" Bright asks.

All I can manage to do is shake my head, but even that is very slight and pathetic.

"I'm sorry we never told you, Rachel. We didn't mean to lie to you or hurt you. I hope you know that," Bright pleads.

Bright saying that reminds me of the last time I can remember feeling like this. The day my mom died. I was at Bright and Jess's house when I found out and Jess said something similar, along the lines of, "Rachel, you know I never wanted anything to happen to your mom." I was 10 at the time, and Jess was nine. There was no way she knew how to process my mom dying any better than I did. She just wanted to find some way to comfort me. But I remember in that moment I was so angry she said that. Of course she never wanted anything bad to happen to my mom. Why would she feel the need to say that? It was pointless, and it didn't change anything. It wasn't going to bring my mom back or make the sinking feeling in my chest go away.

I wasn't mad at Jess longer than a millisecond. I very quickly realized it wasn't logical for me to be upset at her, that I was just upset that my mom was dead, but that memory, that split second of intense anger is one of the most vivid memories I have of that day.

I don't respond to what Bright says. I just ask him to drop me off at home. He tries to apologize a few more times before realizing it's useless. Nothing's getting through, so he shuts up and we ride in silence, once again just listening to the sound of rain hitting the roof of the van. Neither of us know what to do or say.

Lost.

JESSICA

Bright and Rachel drive away and I'm standing here next to a woman who was dead moments ago. I can't believe I'm in this position again. Bringing someone back to life and lying to them about how it happened. Though at least this time it's not my fault.

I know it's not fair, but I can't help but be a small bit relieved that I didn't kill this woman. This time the death isn't on my hands. Though I know Bright must be feeling terrible, and I can't even imagine what Rachel is going through. Not only did she see a woman die and be brought back to life, but she also found out that she herself died years ago, and it was I—her best friend—who killed her.

It was also I who brought her back to life, but I don't know if that's going to matter. I don't know how much damage this is going to do to our friendship. The whole Jason situation already made it rocky. Tonight felt like it was a healing force for us all. Not anymore. That small amount of relief I had of not being guilty fades quickly, and all of a sudden, I realize I'm freezing cold—wet in the rain and alone.

I bend down to check the woman's pulse. I can feel her heart beating and as I pull my hand away from her neck her eyes start to flutter and slowly begin to open. As she sees me for the first time, I think she recognizes me as someone else—someone familiar. Someone safe. But when she sees that I'm indeed very unfamiliar, panic sinks in.

"Whu—where am I? Who? ..." Her voice is weak.

"My name is Jessica. I was walking by and I saw you passed out here. I was just about to dial 911 when you started waking up. Do you feel okay? Do you remember what happened?" I ask.

She shakes her head, "I was passed out?"

"Yeah. You don't seem to be hurt from what I can tell. I think you might have fainted," I try to reassure her.

"I don't understand. I was jogging home. The last thing I remember is coming down this block and ... nothing after that," she says.

"Do you remember your name?" I ask. It's what they always ask in movies and shows when someone takes a hit to the head. Though it's not like I'll know if her answer is correct or not.

"Sarah, Sarah Murdock," she answers.

"Well, I mean, I'm not a doctor, but I think that's a good sign. Can you tell me where you live? I can help you back there, or I can still call 911 if you want me to," I say and then I immediately regret it. I don't want to have to explain anything to anyone.

"No, I think I'm fine," Sarah insists, trying to get up. I take her by the arm and assist her.

"So how far away from here are you?" I ask.

"Not far, like two blocks," Sarah points, her voice still weak.

"I'll help you back there. Do you think you can make it?" I ask.

Sarah nods. She tells me the address, and we begin our way to her place. The insecure part of me feels like I have to be the one to keep a conversation going, but I opt not to. I really have no idea what to say, and it's probably better for her to reserve her energy anyway.

I wish I had an umbrella. We're both soaked and I don't know how strong her body is. I don't want her to catch a serious cold or anything. We brought her back to life, but I don't know how long it will take for her to be at 100 percent.

I'd walk faster, but I don't think she can, so we just continue on incrementally.

I listen to Sarah's deep breathing as we walk. She keeps her head down, looking only at the ground, never making eye contact. I think she's afraid, not necessarily of me, but of the situation. Her trembling is getting worse.

"I think I remember a car," Sarah claims. "Like, a big one. A van. Or a truck."

My heart stops. It feels like it almost erupts through my spine. I catch myself early enough to not completely come to a stop. "You mean, you think you were hit or something?" I ask.

"I don't know," Sarah tries to remember.

"Well, you're not hurt in any way are you? You don't feel any pain?" I try to dissuade her.

"No, besides being a little lightheaded, I feel physically fine," Sarah concedes.

"Well, I don't think you'd be up and walking if you were hit hard enough to knock you out. And you'd definitely feel some pain," I assert.

"Yeah, it's nothing." Sarah agrees. "I'm just trying to make sense of this. I don't remember feeling wrong in any way leading up to passing out. Don't you usually feel it coming?"

"I don't know, I suppose you would, but I've never passed out," I tell her.

"How old are you?" Sarah asks, as if she's just now taking notice of who she's been talking to.

"I'm 16."

"This is so weird," Sarah says to herself.

I don't respond. I don't know what to say. It is weird. It's beyond weird. It's fucked up. Sarah is never going to know what really happened. I mean, I could tell her, but she'd just think I was crazy, or trying to mess with her. I could prove it to her, but what would that do? She'd go to the police. She'd be frightened. I don't think it would help anything.

I still feel terrible though. I don't like lying. I sometimes have to, but I don't want to. Sarah deserves to know what happened to her. She deserves to know the truth. It's her truth. It's her life. But it's also Bright's life, and

Rachel's, and mine. It involves more than just me and Sarah. It's not just my secret to keep.

"My house is coming up. The blue one with the light on," Sarah directs.

"Is there anyone home to help you?" I ask.

"Yeah, my husband Mark will be home," Sarah assures.

I hope Mark doesn't want me to stay and answer a bunch of questions. I hope he's calm. I have a feeling that this could be a long night. I picture him calling my parents to come and get me, not wanting me to go home alone at night in the rain. He'll probably want to take Sarah to the hospital just in case. I know my parents, they'll want to be kept informed of how she is to be polite and because they'll genuinely care. And then they'll have questions for me. *Why was I alone? Why didn't I call for a ride?* What if they talk to Bright and Rachel? Will our stories match up? All of a sudden I'm terrified. This could all go so terribly, but there's nothing I can do now. The only option I have is to play it cool and to do my best to make sure Sarah is alright.

Sarah pulls out her keys as we walk up to the house, but Mark opens the door having seen us coming.

Marks is smiling, about to say something witty I assume, but then sees that something is off. "Sarah? What's wrong?" he asks.

"Everything's fine," Sarah tries to calm him. "This is um …"

"Jessica," I wave. "I found Sarah passed out on the side of the road. I stopped to help and she woke up soon after."

"What?" Mark exclaims.

"I think I overdid it jogging. I don't know, I don't really remember," Sarah says.

"Well, come sit down. You too, Jessica. I'll get some tea for you, Sarah. Jessica, is there someone I should call to come pick you up?"

"I can call my brother. I know he should be on his way home from a friend's house," I respond.

Mark goes into the kitchen to turn the kettle on. He comes back and sits down on the couch next to Sarah. I'm sitting in a chair across from them. Their house is really nice. It's quite modern, but … earthy. Lots of plants and pictures of nature, but up-to-date appliances.

"So you say she was just lying on the side of the road?" Mark asks me.

"Yeah, I was walking by, and I dunno, I saw her there and ran over to help," I answer.

Mark lets out an anxious sigh. "How are you feeling?" He caresses Sarah's head, brushing her hair behind her ear.

"I'm fine. Really," Sarah assures.

"I think we should take you to the hospital, just to make sure," Mark insists.

"I'm fine, I promise," Sarah asserts.

"Sarah this isn't normal. Something could be wrong," Mark pressures.

Sarah just shakes her head. "We don't need to go to a hospital. I know my body. I feel fine. Like I said, I must have just pushed myself too hard."

Mark lets out another sigh, this one of frustration. He turns toward me, "Did your brother get back to you?"

"Oh, sorry, I haven't asked yet. I'll call him now." I take out my phone and dial him. My phone volume is usually loud enough to be overheard by others so I turn it down as soon as it starts ringing.

"Is everything okay?" Bright answers.

"Yeah. Hey can you come pick me up?" I ask.

"At the … the place?" Bright asks.

"I'm at …" I glance up at Mark and Sarah, who are still bickering over if they should go to the hospital. "What's your address again?"

"1729 Winchester Ave South," Mark responds.

I relay the information to Bright and he says he'll be here in a few minutes. After I hang up, I just watch Mark and Sarah talking with each other until they notice that I'm just staring at them.

"Is he on his way?" Sarah asks.

"Yeah, he'll be here in a few minutes," I say.

"Thank you so much for helping me," Sarah expresses.

"Of course, I couldn't just walk away," I assure her.

"You could have," Mark states. "Thank you."

I nod and I look around the room, not wanting to maintain eye contact for long. "I like your house," I say.

"Thanks, we built it ourselves," Sarah replies.

"Really?" I ask.

"Yeah I build houses for a living. I figured I should make myself one while I was at it," Sarah smiles.

"That's pretty awesome!" I tell her.

"I thought so, too," Mark says grinning.

I suddenly realize that I'm soaking wet and I'm sitting on their big comfy cushion chair, and I jump up. "Oh my god, I'm sorry."

"What?" Sarah asks startled.

"I'm dripping wet. I shouldn't be sitting on your furniture," I explain.

"I invited you to sit, and it's just water. It'll be fine," Mark insists.

"Well, my brother will be here any minute anyway," I say and continue to stand.

"I can't believe I didn't ask if you wanted a blanket or something. Are you cold?" Mark asks.

"I'm fine," I assert.

"Were you just walking alone in the rain? How far are you from home?" Sarah asks.

"Not too far, I was coming from this group meeting thing. And yeah, I like walking in the rain. I find it kind of cathartic. Freeing," I admit. Which is true. I do love rain walks. Now would actually be the perfect time for one.

My phone rings and it's Bright. "My brother's here," I announce.

"Alright. Thanks again, Jessica," Sarah praises.

"Get home safe," Mark adds.

"Bye," I say, not really feeling worthy of their gratitude .

Sarah and Mark watch from their doorstep until Bright and I drive away. Sarah gives one last wave as we pull off. I wave back.

"So what happened?" Bright asks.

"Nothing. I just said what I said I was going to, and I helped her back to her house," I respond.

"Did they have any questions?"

"Yeah, but nothing we need to worry about. She did say she thought she remembered a van, but I shut that down quickly saying she wasn't physically hurt in any way, and I'm pretty sure her husband will say the same thing if she mentions it to him, as well as any doctors."

"Are they going to the hospital?"

"Her husband wanted her to, but she says she feels fine. I wouldn't be surprised if they go though."

Bright doesn't say anything for a moment, it seems like he's focusing hard on keeping his eyes on the road. "What was—is her name?" Bright asks.

"Sarah Murdock," I respond. "And her husband's name is Mark."

"Like *Daredevil*." Bright says, eyes still glued to the road.

"Yeah. How's Rachel?" I ask.

"I don't know. I don't think she knows," he responds.

"Did you just drop her off at home?"

"Yeah. We didn't talk much. I tried apologizing, but I don't think anything I was saying was connecting."

I don't respond. I lean my seat back and look up at the street lamps, wishing I never had to get out of this car again. That I could just stay here, looking up, and not have to deal with whatever shit events were coming next. I want to help the world. I want to help people. Yet, all Bright and I seem to keep doing is kill them. At least we can fix the mistakes we've made. Maybe fixing mistakes is what I'm good at. I don't need to know how to start saving the world, I just need to start fixing the mistakes we've made as humans. If there's one thing this night has made clear, it's that I can at least do that.

Things are going to change. Tonight really is my catalyst.

RACHEL

Bright drops me off and I get out without saying anything to him. He says my name in an attempt to apologize one last time, but I just don't want to talk right now. I close the van door and I make my way up to my house. I don't hear Bright drive away until I've unlocked and opened my front door.

I kick my shoes off and head up to my room. You can get to the stairway from both the kitchen and the living room/front entryway. My dad's in the kitchen washing dishes and has a clear view of the front door from there. I try to move quickly so he won't see that I'm crying, but it doesn't work. "What's wrong?"

I don't respond.

"Rachel?" He calls out.

"Nothing, I'm fine! Just … don't worry about it," I brush it off.

I get to my room and I slam the door. My dad knows me and knows I just need some time to myself for now, so I can count on him not bothering me.

I don't even know what to do. I don't know what to feel. I'm angry, but I also understand. I probably would have done the same thing if I were them. I wouldn't know how to tell me that I died and they brought me back to life. But they lied to me for four years. We're supposed to be best friends. We're supposed to be family. And tonight had nothing to do with their powers. My death was a mistake—Jess didn't know she had superstrength—but Bright hit someone with their van. That's completely different. Yes, still an accident, but there's no excuse. If you're driving, you're responsible for driving safely. You're responsible for not killing the people sharing the road with you. They're supposed to be more responsible than this. Though is saying "they're" fair? Bright was the one behind the wheel. Jess had nothing to do with that. And if Jess does deserve any of the blame, I deserve some too, because I didn't tell him to keep his eyes on the road. I was just as wrapped up in reliving our night at Jason's as he was. Fuck my life.

I go to sit down on my bed, but then I hear Rebel clawing at my door. I crack it and she saunters in, rubbing against my leg and purring. I pick her up and sit on the floor, leaning against my bed.

"Fuck the world, Rebel. Why is there always something, you know?"

I nuzzle my nose up against hers and release her. She rubs up against me a few more times and then hops up on my bed and settles in up there.

"Gosh, can't even just sit with me for a sec?"

I check my phone and see that Jason texted me saying that he had a lot of fun tonight. I don't know how I should respond. I don't want to start a conversation, but I also don't want to blow him off. I type out that I had an amazing time and that I'm really happy to have met his family. I also add that I have a bit of a headache and that I think I'm going to turn in—which isn't a lie. There's a dull headache threatening to do real damage that I should probably just sleep off. If I can get to sleep.

I notice that I'm still sitting in soaking wet clothes, which is probably why Rebel wasn't thrilled to cuddle with me. I strip down, throwing all of my clothes in a pile by my door. I'll take them to the basement before I actually go to sleep.

Jason texts again and says his family really liked me and that I'm welcome there anytime. And he says that he hopes I feel better and that he'll talk to me tomorrow. It makes me really happy that his family is so inviting. It's like something out of a movie or a show. In fact it reminds me of the episode of *Malcolm in the Middle* where Malcolm starts dating a girl and then ends up having more in common and bonding with her family more than her. I hope that isn't the case here, but my point is it's just really nice.

I text him goodnight and he responds the same, but adds a smiley face. It's so stupid that a smiley face at the end of a text can elicit such a positive feeling—or maybe it's amazing, probably a little of both. I smile because I realize I'm naked in my room with a big cheesy grin on my face looking at a goodnight text from a cute boy. A cute boy who I think might be my boyfriend? Or at least is on the way to being one.

I lie down on the floor, still smiling, close my eyes, and hold my phone against my heart. Life is amazing.

Except for the fact that my best friend killed me years ago and lied to me about it. I owe Jess my life, but my life would never have been taken if it weren't for her also. So maybe I owe her nothing. Though, I mean, she's still my best friend. She's still my sister. She still cares about me. Like right now, she'd be telling me not to hold my phone over my heart because of the radiation. She's always looking out for me. Even with her not wanting me to date Jason, that's her way of looking out for me. She knows I'll have to keep secrets for her and Bright, and that having to keep secrets from someone you're dating is hard and adds more complications to an already pretty confusing situation. I mean teen dating is full of lots of fucking emotions. I'm sure all dating is. But especially teen dating. I could fall in love with Jason. That alone is crazy to me. But what do I do then? How do I not let him in on everything?

I move my right arm, which is holding the phone, and lie with my arms spread open for a minute. I can't bring myself to fully be mad at Jess or Bright, but I can't quite let this go either. I don't want to see them. I just don't know what to do. I want to vent, but I can't explain this to Jason, and the only other people I'd go to are them. I honestly just wish I could talk to my mom about this. I wonder if I saw her when I died. I hope not. She'd have been so heartbroken. The thought of my mom's spirit seeing mine enter the afterlife is too morbid. I try to think about something else, but then I just land on my dad. What if they hadn't been able to bring me back? What would my dad have done?

I start to think about how broken my dad was when Mom died. How hard he tried to be strong for me. I remember the hurt in his eyes that never fully went away. He lost the love of his life and I don't think he ever fully recovered. Well, I don't know if you ever really do fully recover from these things—I know I haven't—but I can't imagine what he'd do if he lost me too, or what I'd do if I lost him.

I wish I could say that the way I responded to him trying to talk to me when I got home tonight wasn't a normal occurrence, but it is. Like I said, he knows me, he knows to just give me my space, because him trying to talk to me never works out.

I start to cry because I realize how mean to my dad I've been over the years. I don't intend it—at least most of the time I don't—but that doesn't make it any less shitty. The more I think about it, the more I cry, and the more I just want my dad.

I get up and throw some pajamas on and head down the stairs. He's still in the kitchen, but now he's reading *The Atlantic* at the counter. "Hey, Dad ..." I murmur.

"Hey, Rach." He looks up from his reading.

"Dad ... I'm really sorry that I was so mean earlier. I'm really sorry that I'm mean a lot. I don't know why I lose my patience with you so easily. I mean, I guess that's normal for teens and their parents, but I feel like it shouldn't be this bad. It's like a switch goes off in me, or on ... or whatever ... ."

"Where is this coming from Rachel? You don't need to apologize, I know you don't intend to hurt me—at least not always—but I just chalk most of it up to 'parents annoy their children,' you know?" Dad smiles.

"I know, but that's what I'm trying to say. It's more than that. It's like, I want to talk to you. I'll be headed home or downstairs with the intention of talking to you, but then once you ask me something, I completely retreat inside myself and put up this barrier. All of a sudden I don't want to talk to you anymore. And it doesn't even make sense to me. I'm not mad at you. You're not even really annoying me, but all at once there's this ... urge to get away. And I don't know why."

I start to cry even harder and my dad gets up to comfort me. He wraps me in his arms and I bury my face in his chest. We embrace for a while without saying anything. I can feel that he's crying now also. He kisses me on the forehead, "Everything's alright, Rachel."

"No it's not Dad. It's not. I've been so unfair to you all these years. You lost Mom too, and I always knew that, but I never really grasped it, you know? You were dealing with all the same shit I was and probably more, but you had nobody to take care of you. Then you had to lose me too in a way, because I wouldn't let you in. I wouldn't really be there. How don't you hate me? You have to hate me a little bit. I hate me."

"No, Rachel. Of course I don't hate you. I love you immensely. I couldn't ever love anyone more than I love you, and you shouldn't hate yourself either. That would break my heart. Look, all that matters is that we're working on this together now. We both could have tried harder." Dad looks me deep in my eyes "I love you. I'm always going to be here for you, and I will never hate you. Okay?"

"Okay," I reply as I wipe the tears from my face. "So, any good articles?" I ask motioning toward the magazine, in an attempt to lighten the mood.

"The fighting going on in Syria," Dad says. So much for finding a lighter subject. "You know, it was your mother who got me into reading *The Atlantic*. I don't know if you remember, but she was big on keeping up on world events, and she was a big activist."

I shake my head, "I don't really remember that much. Well, I can kind of remember her going to a lot of community meetings."

"Yeah, she participated in a lot of community events. She cared about people a lot. I always meant to keep at it after she died. I know she'd have loved it if you followed in her footsteps, but it was just hard, you know?" Dad says, a look of remorse in his eyes.

"Yeah, well, I mean I care about the world. I want to help. Maybe I should give it a try?" I respond.

"If you want to. I didn't mean to imply that you should, I was just … reminiscing."

"Yeah, I know, but I dunno, Jess has been talking a lot about getting more involved with the community and … worldly matters. So it's been on my mind.

I think that maybe it'd be good to look into. Help me keep my mind off of some things," I add.

"Like boys?" Dad jokes.

"No, the boys are staying," I assure.

"So tonight went well?"

"Yeah, it was great."

"You don't seem so sure," Dad says, concerned.

"It was great. Really. I just, it's all moving kind of fast. It feels like everything in my life is changing."

"Well, there's nothing wrong with slowing down," Dad advises. "In fact, I might prefer it."

I laugh and slap him on the arm playfully, "Well, I think I'm going to try and sleep. I think I'm starting to get a headache."

"Oh, do you want some aspirin?" Dad asks.

"No, I think I'll be fine. Goodnight, Dad. I love you." I go over to give him a hug.

"I love you too, Rachel. Feel better, okay?" He gives me another kiss on the forehead.

I smile and nod and head back up to my room. I think more seriously about what Dad said about slowing down. Everything in my head seems stunned and crazy right now, but I don't think I want to slow down. Especially not with Jason. I want to ride this with no preset ideas about how it should go. Let it roll how it rolls. When I get back to my room Rebel is still lying on my bed. I start to get in, but then think to fill my water bottle, so I go to the bathroom to fill it and then climb into bed.

I think I'm going to focus on trying to spend more time with my dad. I didn't realize how much I miss him until tonight. It sounds silly to say— I mean, I live with him—but it's true. I'll see if he wants to go to a movie and dinner soon, maybe tomorrow night. I don't know what to do about Jess and Bright. I don't know when I'll be ready to face them. I'm sure I'll see them at school, and I'll have to figure out something to tell Jason, but I really just need some space from them for now.

I pull Rebel closer to me and she lets out a meow of annoyance, but doesn't pull away. "Get used to this," I tell her. "I have a feeling I'm going to need a lot of support in the coming weeks."

I turn off the lamp next to my bed and just stare into the darkness for a while and start thinking about too many things. There's this old—I dunno, meditation trick I guess—that my mom taught me. She told me to start at my toes and just focus on relaxing that part of my body and relaxing my breathing, and to slowly work my way up the rest of my body. "If you ever catch yourself getting off track," she said, "just start back at the toes. It all goes back to the toes." That was a sort of inside joke between us—*it all goes back to the toes*.

"Fuck, I miss her." I don't know if I say this to myself or to Rebel. I let out a sigh and then I focus on my toes. Letting relaxation creep over me. Soon my body and mind are at peace, and soon after that, I am asleep.

BRIGHT

Everything has been pretty fucked up since that night. I mean everything between Jessica, Rachel, and me. When I picked Jessica up from that woman Sarah's house, she barely said anything other than catching me up to speed on the situation. She hasn't said much to me since then. It's been a few weeks and we just don't know what to say to each other. Jessica has been hanging out in the backyard and has been out alone a lot, just being pretty antisocial. Not that antisocial is really unusual for her or anything. But as I said, she's not talking to me, and Rachel's not talking to either of us, and that's pretty much all of the social interaction she had. I dunno what she's doing about Farson High Green. I think she stuck with it for a while, but from what I can tell, she's not going anymore.

   I tried talking to Rachel a couple days after the incident, I wanted to give her some space for a while, but she just told me that she needed more time. She didn't know what to say or how to be around us right now and she was going to focus on herself and strengthening her relationships with her dad and Jason. And then she walked away. I wanted her to tell me that she still loves Jessica, and she still loves me, and that we're still family. I wanted her to say that it would all be fine. But I don't know why I even hoped something like that. How would everything be fine? There has to be some fear there. There has to be some major distrust. We've killed twice now. Sure, maybe she still loves us, but we're killers now. I'm a killer. There's no separating that from me now. No matter what I do, I'll always be a killer.

Since I have no other friends, I've just been spending a lot of time at Bleu Comics, which is where I'm headed now. No Jessica and Rachel means I also need to figure out a new social life, and Ken and Marsha have been a big help with that. I guess it's a little weird that I'm hanging out with people in their 30s, but honestly, talking to adults usually gives me less anxiety than talking with people my own age. I think it's just because most adults I talk to aren't going to be around me much. I'm not going to be socializing with them often, so the thought of saying or doing something embarrassing in front of them isn't too terrifying. And I know it should anger me, but sometimes it's comforting that older people don't take you seriously as a teenager. Takes a bit of the pressure off in the right setting.

"Well, look who's back," Marsha smiles as I enter the store.

"Fifth time this week," Ken adds, "I think he likes us, Marsha!"

"Hey," I greet them, shaking my head, "How's it going?"

"It's going well, nothing too special going on," Ken responds. Marsha nods, indicating her sentiments are the same. "How are you? I take it you still haven't made up with your sister or Rachel?"

I shake my head, "I tried. Sort of. And maybe I just like coming here," I protest.

"Yeah, you've always liked coming here, but it's pretty obvious why you're here so much lately," Marsha claims.

"Avoidance," Ken adds, Marsha nodding again in agreement.

There's a few people in the store pretending not to listen as we talk. Talking about anything when other people not involved can listen always makes me uncomfortable. I just feel like they're going to judge me without understanding the full context of everything. Though really I shouldn't care, but I do. But it's just, being black, I'm always afraid that I'm being judged or deemed lesser in some way. Like here at the comic shop, I'm afraid other comic fans—who are mostly white—see me and think I'm a poser or something. A fake fan. Aside from Marsha and Ken, whenever I'm talking to comic fans, I get the feeling that I have to prove my knowledge or prove that I'm a fan. Being black—or nonwhite in general—and a comic fan is similar to being a woman and a comic fan. By default it's assumed you know nothing. And of course women face a whole different slew of harassment and prejudice, but we're in similar boats. We're striving for the same ends.

Anyway, I told Ken and Marsha about having a falling out with Jessica and Rachel, but obviously not about the specifics. "Well, maybe. Yes. But I'm not the only one avoiding. And Rachel said she needed time. I have to respect that," I defend.

"True, but that was like a month ago. You can try again," Marsha pushes.

"Well, maybe I need time now," I insist.

"If you say so. But hey, so we've been talking, and Ken and I would like to know if you wanna work here? I mean, you're here all the time anyway, and we could use a little help, or at least, we'd think it'd be cool," Marsha proposes.

"Uh … wow, yeah, I think I could swing that. I mean, I don't know a ton about comics, I mean, I do, but you know, like histories of everything, and artists and writers, and all that. I feel like I should have more knowledge of things," I shy away from the idea.

"Well, I really don't think you'll need a super in-depth knowledge of everything. I mean, you can always come to us if there's something you don't know, and we have this fancy contraption they call a computer here for looking up specific writers and artists and whatnot," Marsha presses further.

I nod and mull it over for a second. "Also, I feel like I wouldn't have a ton of time for actual working. At least not on the weekdays. I'm in school until four, probably wouldn't get here 'til around 4:30, and you close at six."

"We know. We've thought about that, but we still think it'd be cool. I mean, it'd give you some work experience, something to put down for future jobs, and you'd get paid to hang out where you're hanging out anyway. Also, we still have to take inventory and place orders and—there's still work to do after we close, so you'll definitely be useful," Ken assures.

"Okay," I concede. "When would I start?"

"How about on Monday?" Marsha suggests. "Start you off with the new week."

"Cool. Thanks you guys!" I exclaim.

Marsha is now helping a guest so she just gives me a smile. Ken raises his hand for a high five, which is a little embarrassing, but I do it. And then he also helps a guest and I just start to browse around the store. I think it'll be really cool to work here. I love it here. I've gotten a lot closer with Marsha and Ken in the last month, and it'll be really cool to get to learn more from them and work together. I wasn't sure at first, but thinking about it more, I'm getting really excited. This could be something awesome for me. Maybe this is something I'd like to do. Run a comic shop. Just be around the stories and art that I love and being with people I love. One of the reasons Jessica and I have had such a hard time talking with each other is not only because I killed a woman, but also because it seems like ever since that night, Jessica has had an even stronger urge to help and a stronger passion and sense of what she wants to be doing. And I still don't have that. And I'm not just talking about with saving the world or activism, but just in general. I still don't really know my passion or where I think I want to head in life. Most of the time I just don't care. I don't want to do anything. Okay, I care, but I just want to be able to do the things I enjoy. Be with great people. Read. Watch cool shit. What I do for money doesn't really matter as long as I don't hate it. I just need to be able to afford to do the things I love with the people I love, and most of that is fairly cheap.

So with the weirdness and tension about what happened with Sarah, and Rachel being upset with us, and Jessica's desire to do more, there's just nothing we're connecting on. I live with her, but I miss her. I miss Rachel. I miss us, the three of us. But I wasn't lying to Marsha—I do really think I also need some time and space.

Maybe this is what's right for all of us right now.

JESSICA

·/~·

In my time alone, I've been doing some things. Fixing stuff or plants and whatnot. I've been regrowing small plants around the neighborhood. I know fixing things is what I've realized I can do, but I don't really know where to start or what all to fix. I don't even really know if "fixing" is what I'm doing. For all I know I could be introducing new DNA or whatever into the ecosystem. I have no idea what my powers do to the genetic makeup of the animals, plants, and people I use them on. I don't even know what my powers are.

I chose plants because for the most part, it's really easy to see when they're dying, and nobody is really going to notice if I bring a few plants back to life. It's been helping me hone my healing powers and it makes me feel like I'm helping the earth—albeit in a small way, but one that means something to me. Plants give us oxygen, and life, and I don't know for a fact, but I've read that they can have a big impact on our mental health. And I'd believe it. When I'm out in nature, surrounded by trees, and flowers, and bushes, and lying in the grass— I feel empowered. I feel truly alive. I feel happy. Free of worry. Content. And not like I'm settling, but truly okay and willing to be where I am. It's one of the reasons why climate change is such a big concern of mine. The more we hurt our world, the more we hurt the trees, flowers, ferns—all of it, the more we hurt ourselves. Not just because we are destroying our only home. But because we're damaging the air we breathe. We're slowly killing our bodies. We're fucking up our minds. What we do to our environment affects our mental and physical health more than most of us would like to realize or accept. I just hope I'm not damaging it even more. I've damaged enough.

I miss Rachel. I haven't even tried to speak to her. Bright told me he did to no avail, but even without him talking to her, I knew it was no use. At least not right now. And it's probably good for Rachel to get away from us. I know how much she's had to sacrifice for us trying to keep our secret. And with the experimentation I'm doing—planning to do more things she'll have to keep secret—it's best she keeps her distance.

Right now I'm sitting in Branson Park, not too far from that woman Sarah's house. I can't stop thinking about her. I feel connected to her. It's a weird feeling to bring someone back to life. You get this feeling of … responsibility—like you have to keep an eye on them. I imagine it's similar to what you feel like after having a child. I don't know how my parents do it. Having superpowered teens must be hell.

Bright and I didn't tell them about what happened with Sarah for the same reason we didn't tell them about the original incident with Rachel. Though this time, there's more of a sense of shame connected to it.

I'm never going to hurt anyone again.

I get off the bench I'm sitting on and I tilt my head up to the sky. I sigh and I wish I could just take off and fly. I mean, I know technically I can, but part of not hurting any more people means I should try and be more responsible, so that means no flying around in the middle of the day. No bringing unwanted attention to myself and my abilities if I can help it.

As I look around the park, trying to figure out what I should do with the rest of my day, I get an idea that goes against my just founded vow of being more responsible. I get the urge to go to Sarah's house. I just want to check up on her. I don't think that'd be too weird. I mean, it's normal for someone to be curious about another someone, right? Especially if you supposedly saved their life.

I make my way to her house, and the closer I get, the more nervous I get. I stop multiple times to debate whether or not to keep going, ultimately ending up outside of her house. I don't walk up right away, I just stare—creepily, I assume—as I try to work up the nerve to go knock on the door. I walk away from the house once or twice, but I can't leave. I have to talk to her. I have to see her. I have to know that she's okay. I slowly walk up to her house and I can't decide if I should knock or ring the doorbell. I go for the knock. There isn't an answer after 30 seconds or so, so I knock again. This time I hear footsteps walking up to the door, the clank of it unlocking and then, it's her. Now that I'm looking her dead in the face, I have no idea what I'm doing here.

"Hi," Sarah says.

"Hi," I say awkwardly, stretching out the "i."

Neither of us knows what the next step is, both of us wait for the other to make a move first. Me: Waiting for her to show that she remembers me and hopefully invite me in. She: Waiting for me to explain why I'm here on her doorstep.

We both end up trying to speak at the same time.

"Wou—" Sarah starts.

"I—" I begin.

We both smile and stop, "Go ahead," Sarah nods.

"I just wanted to say that—I mean—I wanted to see how you were doing," I explain.

"Jessica, right?" Sarah asks.

"Yeah."

"I'm doing well." Sarah answers. "Thank you again for helping me out that day. I'm sure everything would have probably been fine, but who knows, right? You didn't have to help, but I appreciate that you did."

I smile and I look for the words to respond, but I don't find any. After a few more moments of silence Sarah opens the door wider, "So uh, would you like to come in?"

"Yeah, sure," I say appreciatively. I enter the house and stand in the doorway, awaiting my next instruction. "Should I take my shoes off?"

"Whatever you feel like."

I'm not sure what I feel like, but I decide to leave them on in case Sarah doesn't feel like having me here for long. I don't want it to seem like I'm making myself too comfortable. I take off my jacket though and hang it on the coat rack by the door.

"Please, sit down," Sarah gestures.

I pick the same spot I was in last time I was here, and so does she.

"So, everything was alright?" I ask, after we've both seated.

"Yeah. Mark persuaded me to go to the hospital, but they said nothing was wrong, said I probably overexerted myself and to get some rest."

"That's good. I was just … I guess I was just worried about you. I mean, I figured everything was fine, but I didn't really know for sure, so I wanted to come and see," I say.

"That's really nice of you," Sarah smiles and tries to keep the conversation going once it's clear that I'm not going to. "So, tell me about yourself Jessica. How old are you again?"

"I'm 16."

"Oh, I think I remember you telling me that. Some stuff is still a little hazy from that night," She says, tapping her pointer finger on her head. "But yeah, what are you into, Jessica? What's your story—You have a brother right?"

"Yeah, his name is Bright. He's my twin. Um …" I pause, trying to process my answer for the rest of her questions. "I go to Farson High." I shrug, "I don't know. I guess I don't do a lot. I mostly hang with Bright and our best friend Rachel. Or I did. We've all kind of been doing other things lately. I've been looking into how to help the environment as much as I can. You know, trying to save the world," I give a little laugh, indicating that I'm not taking myself seriously, but then feel dumb because she doesn't laugh and I quickly stop.

"So Bright and Rachel don't want to save the world?" Sarah asks.

"I wouldn't say that. It's mostly that they don't feel it's their responsibility."

"And you do?"

"Yeah," I say a little too indignantly.

"Sorry, I didn't mean to offend you. I mean, I guess it's obvious you've got a bit of a hero complex. You saved me, after all," Sarah ribs.

"Isn't that a good thing?" I ask.

"Yeah, for me."

Sarah laughs and she locks eyes with me and we stare. I feel like I need to prove something to her, but I don't know what. It's like all of a sudden I'm on the defensive. I can't look away from her. I feel like if I just gaze long enough, I'll figure out what she means. I'll figure out what I owe her. Eventually she looks away, but I still feel as if I'm the one who gave in.

"You know, Mark—my husband—and I are pretty into that as well. The environment. He teaches environmental science at the community college downtown, and I help build and develop passive houses. Do you know anything about passive housing?"

I shake my head. I feel like I missed something. Her mannerisms and conversation skills are so graceful.

"Well, there's a lot to it, but a passive house is a house made to be as self-sustaining and energy efficient as possible. It's very well insulated. We make sure there are no thermal bridges, or work to eliminate any if we're working on an existing building," Sarah explains.

"What are thermal bridges?" I ask, feeling like I need to ask something. I need to do my part in this conversation.

"Thermal bridges are just any pathway, any beam or rod or anything that's in the house that may lead to the outside of the house. Or basically, materials that are being used in the structure of the house that are poor thermal insulators. Heat will run through these materials and escape outside. So if you are heating your house in the winter and there are thermal bridges, you'll have to use more heat than you would if there weren't because it's escaping. We also search for any airways or holes that are in the house to make sure that there are no air leaks."

"That sounds really cool."

"Yeah, I'd say so," Sarah agrees and then stands up, "I'm in the mood for some tea, would you like any?"

"Yeah, sure," I accept. "What kinds do you have?"

"Tons." Sarah laughs, and motions me into the kitchen. "I don't remember them all, but we keep a big shoebox full of tea." Sarah goes over to the fridge, picks the box up from on top of it, and hands it to me. "Choose whatever you want."

I riffle through my options, not wanting to take too long, and I end up choosing a type of tea called African Skies. I hand the box back to Sarah. She chooses a tea and fills the kettle with water to boil.

"I've never used loose-leaf tea before, how do you do it?" I ask.

"Well, there's multiple ways, but we just have tea sacs. You basically put the loose tea into the sacs and put them in the water like you do with normal teabags."

"Cool," I say because I don't know how else to respond.

There's a small silence before Sarah starts the conversation back up. Just long enough for me to recognize it as silence, but short enough for me to question it. "We also try to utilize the sun as much as possible with passive housing. Using solar gain to heat the house. And what that means is to design the house—or building—in a way that keeps heating and cooling efficiency in mind. So the placement of windows and materials of the walls and floors are arranged to absorb, hold, and disperse heat throughout the house. This makes it so that the house stays well heated in the winter, and helps control the heat in the summer, reducing cooling costs."

"It sounds like it's pretty complicated, " I say.

"Well, a lot of thought has to go into it, but it's not too complicated. Most of it is the cost. It's expensive to do. The placement of windows and walls, as well as the materials used to construct the house, are all important, so it's easier to do starting from scratch. Making an existing home into a passive one is challenging because it's hard to do without a fair amount of reconstruction. It's something I think every home should be, but obviously most families or homeowners could not afford this. Germany and Sweden have made huge strides on the passive front, but their governments are also more invested in being sustainable and environmentally friendly. If we were to put our minds to it here as much as they do, well, it'd be amazing."

"Man, it's so cool you're so passionate about this," I admire.

"Yeah, it's awesome. It just makes so much sense, you know? Why wouldn't we want to be as sustainable as possible? Why wouldn't we want to reduce heating and electrical costs and make our way to using solar, wind, and geothermal energy? Even if you don't believe in global climate change—which I hope you do—you do, right?" Sarah asks.

"I do." I laugh.

She smiles with her eyes more than her mouth, "I'm testing you. But yeah, even if you don't believe, it doesn't make sense to use finite resources instead of renewable, sustainable ones." Sarah pauses and lets out a big sigh, one that usually leads into more on the subject or a segue into something else. But she doesn't say anything. That's all she had.

I watch her as she watches the water boil. This woman is so majestic. The way she smiles is so knowing. It's like she can see all of you. She can see your intentions and your fears, your doubts. And it kind of pisses me off. She doesn't know me at all, but I feel like she knows me better than I know myself. And I feel like if I were to say that to her, she'd simply say, "You know yourself." The silence has lasted too long now and so I tell her that I really like listening to her talk.

Sarah looks up at me and smiles that smile with her eyes, but remains silent. In the next second her attention is back on the almost boiling water. "Well, I'm glad you dig it. I've got one more cool thing to show you, and then let's really talk about you more. Maybe I can help you figure out how you want to help the environment."

"Yeah, okay," I shrug.

"Cool. So, after we've got the house constructed, we also try to supply it with as many energy efficient appliances as we can. One of my favorites is this." Sarah points to her stove. "Have you heard of induction stoves?"

I shake my head, a little embarrassed to have another thing I know nothing about. "Nope."

"It's okay, a lot of people don't know about most of this stuff, especially not kids your age. An induction stove heats with electrical induction, and this process makes it so that only certain types of metals are heated on the surface of the stove. You have to have special cookware, but it means that no excess heat is lost, making it more efficient."

"So only the special pot or whatever is heated?" I ask.

"Yeah, look," Sarah lifts the kettle from the stove and puts her hand right on the heated area.

I walk over to the stove, "It doesn't burn you at all?" I cautiously move my hand to the stove, placing my hand on the surface grinning big. "How does it do that? I mean, I know you kind of just told me, but like, what makes it do that?"

"Well, the easiest way to explain it to you is that the cooking pot, or whatever you use, reacts with wire in the stove surface, and through magnetic process the pot becomes the heating element, not the stove itself. The induction area on the stove gets a little heat from what the pot puts off, but it's not enough to burn or cook anything, including your skin," Sarah answers.

"Awesome! I totally want one!"

"I know! I love this stove! I love this house," Sarah says looking around longingly.

"So this is a passive house? I mean, I guess that makes sense," I admit.

"Yeah, the best way to fully know the benefits and challenges of a passive home is to live in one. And really, there was no way I was going to go around making awesome houses like this and not live in one."

"I totally feel you on that one."

Sarah smiles and checks the kettle, "I think the water is warm enough. Ready for tea?" She turns the stove off.

"Yeah," I nod and I take a seat at the kitchen table.

Sarah pulls out two mugs and hands one to me full of steaming water. She grabs some tea sacs from the tea box and puts the teas we chose into two. She hands me mine and I begin dunking it in and out of my mug. Sarah puts the kettle back on the stove and the tea box away before settling down across from me at the table. "So, have you looked into any clubs at school? I'm sure you have an environmental club?" Sarah asks.

I take a small sip of tea and nod, "Yeah, I have. I was in this group for a little while, but I wasn't too into it."

"Why not?"

"I don't know." I take a minute to think. "I guess I just wanted to be doing more. Like real protests and bringing about real change."

"And you don't think they were making real change?" Sarah continues to pry.

"Not really, not anything big. I want to be showing the world things like this." I motion towards the house as a whole. "People like you. And experts on climate change should be heard more. Our country should care about this stuff—the world should!"

Sarah nods, "I understand. And I don't mean to imply that teenagers can't make a difference, everyone can, but you're only 16, Jessica. There are tons of adults whose whole lives are dedicated to changing the world. To making it a better place. But is that really what you want?"

"Yes!" I answer impatiently, knowing that she had more to say. "Yes, because I can't imagine not doing everything I can. I'm only 16, but shouldn't we be out having adventures? Getting lost? Making mistakes? We should be encouraged to—yes enjoy life—but also to follow passions, to be involved in the world. I'm so tired of people telling me it's not my job, that it's not my burden, because that's not true. It's all of our jobs. Unfortunately, it is my burden. It's my home. Our home."

Sarah looks at me and I can't tell if it's sympathetic or patronizing, both or neither, "Jessica, there are a lot of problems in the world. Climate change is just one of them. And they're all connected. They all intertwine and involve one another. You can't fix them all."

"I can try," I say.

Sarah shakes her head, "There is no fixing them all. I think a lot of the problems come from people assuming we can."

"What does that mean?" I ask. I can feel my body tensing up. I don't even know this woman, but it feels like I'm arguing with family.

"I just mean that I think there are ways of living that benefit us all as well as the earth, but we can do that in many different ways, and there are always going to be problems."

"So we do nothing to fix the problems?" I ask.

"No, but not everyone's way of that will be the same. Assuming we can fix all problems assumes that there's one blanket solution to solve one problem in every area. It also assumes that everything one person views as a problem is also viewed as a problem by everyone else," Sarah responds.

"So? I just don't get it still. If I have a group of people who are against racism, but there's another who isn't, you're saying that we what?"

"I'm not saying I have an answer for that. What I'm saying is, I think most big problems like that are issues for everyone. Racism, sexism, sexual assault, any form of discrimination or harm. If there is someone dealing with those things, they're not going to stand for it. We have to fight for change in our lives personally. We can't decide how everyone makes that change or how they implement it."

"But real change in my life personally, and in many lives, comes from implementing vast change. Either citywide, statewide, nationwide, or worldwide. Like you said, it's all connected and intertwined," I retort.

"Yeah. I get what you're saying, Jessica. I don't really know what's right, I think it changes from case to case and from time to time, but do you understand what I mean? That it's not up to us to decide it all? We can't."

I nod, not so convincingly. Because I'm not convinced. Bright has said this to me, and Rachel, though not in the exact way, but it still doesn't convince me. I still don't see how we can just not get involved. If there's injustices being done in another country and we have a way to help, isn't it our job to do so? Or even if it's just in another part of the country that we're not connected to? As humans, we should help other humans. I understand that we can't always know what's right, that we shouldn't assume we do know what's right, but how do you set out to make a difference and help people without assuming you know what's best for them? I'm not saying I know what's best, but how do you make change without having your own idea of "better" in your head?

Sarah reaches out and places her hand on mine. "I know it's a troubling thing, we all—or most of us—want to help, to do good, and we should. We should help, we should try, but ultimately we need to listen to those we're helping. We need to listen and understand that sometimes the best way to help, is to know when it's not our place to."

I look Sarah deep in the eyes, and I wish I could say that it all made sense in this moment. I wish that I could say I understood. Maybe it would if she wasn't her. If I was hearing this from someone who I didn't bring back to life ...

I *have* to do something to help. Not everyone is going to agree on how something should be done, but does that mean that nothing should be done? I mean, I think I understand what she's saying, I just don't know how to bring about change in that way.

Once again, I just don't know ... .

BRIGHT

It's weird. For the first time in probably forever, I feel like I'm doing something I feel strongly about. Hanging out at the comic shop with Marsha and Ken has been great. I love talking to people about all the different stories, and art, and characters, and—all of it. I like it here. I'm happy. But I feel like there's something missing.

It's always been me and Jessica and Rachel. I thought it'd be good to not be spending all of my time with them, to explore myself more, and it has been, but it's weird to go home and not talk to Jessica about my day. It feels wrong not knowing how Rachel and Jason are doing. It's such a huge thing for her, and whatever our feelings about the relationship are, Jessica and I should be along for the ride. I feel like we've failed Rachel beyond measure. It feels like there's no going back. Whatever that means.

I think I was more okay with the space away from Rachel and Jessica at first because I was running. Maybe I still am. I killed a woman. I ended someone's life, and the only people who know are Jessica and Rachel. The only people who can be ashamed of me. The only people who I can't look in the eye. Besides myself. I've started to feel like Bloody Mary a bit. Like if I look at my own reflection, it'll destroy me. My sins will consume me. I had to find myself, because after that, after being responsible for someone's death—whether I brought them back to life or not—I lost myself. I don't know who I thought I was or what I thought I was doing, but all of it evaporated after I hit Sarah. I don't know if I'll ever see her again—I kind of hope I don't—but I'll never forget her name. Or the sound of her head smashing against the hood of our van.

This is probably something people get counseling for. I wish there were someone I could freely talk to about this, someone not connected to me or anyone, who wouldn't lock me away in an insane asylum. Maybe that's why people talk to God. It's too bad I don't believe in any, and even if I did, from what I've seen in life, gods seem to stay on the sidelines anyway.

I've been sorting through back issues of *Wolverine*, and I decide that it's time I move on to a cheerier subject. Wolverine and I actually have a little bit in common. We're both surrounded by wonderfully complex women. Or at least I used to be. And I suppose we both also have dark past. He can't remember his, and I wish I could forget mine. And he's a mutant and I'm black, so we're both snubbed by society. We both have powers. Right now you could say that we're both broody, lonesome men. But what I wanted to focus on was the powerful women in our lives. Thinking about the women in Wolverine's life makes me realize that I don't read any female lead comics. I spend a few moments beating myself up about it, but then figure there's no point in that, I work in a comic shop, this is an easy fix.

The shop is closed. Ken is setting out some new action figures on display for tomorrow and Marsha is handling the money. I walk to the back office where Marsha is, not totally sure of how I want to frame my question, "Hey Marsha?"

"Yeah?" She answers without looking away from her work.

"I was wondering if you could give me a list of awesome female-lead comics to read. I just—I realized that I don't really read any comics with women as the core character, and you know way more about comics than I do, and you're a woman, so I figured you'd know of ones that are good. You know, like not just men writing shitty story lines about women in tight-fitting outfits."

Marsha looks up at me and laughs a bit. "Bright, first of all, I've spent enough time with you to know that you know how to analyze and critique things to know a well-developed and thought-out character when you see one, whether they're male or female. But I understand being cautious about it. Ken's the same way. He's always trying to sneakily find out how I feel about whatever new woman hero he likes, or a new story line revolving around one—trying to make sure that it's actually progressive. Like, if I think it is, it means it is. Don't get me wrong, I think it is important to find out what women think of women characters and listen to their critiques. However, just because you ask one woman in your life what she thinks and she likes the character or story, doesn't mean it's a good story or character—she (meaning I) don't—doesn't? ... speak for all women."

I open my mouth to say something, but Marsha continues, "I know that you weren't implying that I speak for all women, but the point I'm trying to make is that you wouldn't need to come to me asking for advice on well-developed men superhero comics would you? You'd just read, and if you didn't like it or you found issues with it, you'd make a judgment. It's the same thing. You use the same guidelines you'd use for yourself to find any other good story or character. Don't overthink it. But yeah, I'll come up with a list I'd think you'd like and I'll get back to you."

"Thanks, Marsha. And sorry if I was being a bit of an idiot," I say, embarrassed.

"Not at all." Marsha smiles and returns to her work.

I walk out of the office with a smile on my face. I really do overthink things all the time. I'm really happy Marsha checked me a bit there. It's something Rachel and Jessica definitely would have done. My mom too. All in their own ways of course, but ... I miss them. With everything that's happened, I've sort of isolated myself from my parents as well. I can't really tell them anything without telling them everything.

The women in my life are incredible. My mom packed up and drove away from her home when she was 25. She came to Minnesota knowing no one. She had no plan, no job, and no place to stay. All she knew was that she wanted to work with the youth, and that it was time for her to branch out. To be somewhere new, where she could be anybody she wanted. And she made it work.

She created a life here. She worked hard at her goals and is now a school counselor. She took a chance on herself and it paid off tenfold.

Jessica accidentally killed her best friend at a young age. She's been sheltered, encouraged to tone down her passions and beliefs, but her heart is still wide open. All she does is think about how to help the world. A world that doesn't know her, and maybe won't ever get the chance to. A world that looks down on her for being black, and a woman. A world that doesn't even want to give her a voice. I remember when we were younger, Jessica used to have this saying, "Choose to trust." It was a line in some song, I think. I can't remember, but what I do remember is how taken she was with that saying. Trust is a choice to her. Most people—including myself—think that trust is earned. That other people's actions control if you trust in them or not. But from an early age Jessica chose to trust in people. In individuals. She believed that it's up to you to decide to trust. It has nothing to do with anyone else. And that's what she continues to do. She chooses to trust.

And Rachel? I once saw Rachel hold my mom while she sobbed. Rachel was 10. It was just after her mother's funeral. She had just said goodbye to her mom for the last time, her eyes raw from all the tears, yet she was the one to comfort my mom. And that's who Rachel is. She's incredibly tough, but still vulnerable. Even when she has nothing left for herself, she'll listen.

I miss the strong and amazing women in my life. It's clear that they're what's missing.

RACHEL

Dad and I are in the car on our way over to Jason's. We're having dinner there. I'm pretty nervous—very nervous. I don't really know why, I know my dad will get along with Mrs. and Mr. Holli well, but ... we're just different. My dad can be a little awkward, and sometimes I think he's a little ADD. I dunno, I know it'll be fine. I'm sure it'll be fine.

My dad tends to either overdress or underdress for things like these. Tonight he went over, which works for me. At least they'll know he's trying to make a good impression. I wanted him to wear his favorite turquoise turtleneck he wears to family dinners, but I'm also digging the James Bond imitation he's got going on.

"So is there anything big I should know before we get there?" Dad asks. We're about a block away.

"Like what?" I respond.

"I don't know, I'm just looking for ways not to put my foot in my mouth," he laughs.

"I'm sure you'll be fine," I say, both to him and myself.

"Well, I've always got embarrassing stories of you to fall back on if I need to," he jabs me playfully with his elbow.

"Well, it wouldn't be a successful meeting of a girlfriend and boyfriend's parents if there weren't embarrassing stories involved," I say as we pull up to their house.

Dad parks the car, and I step out and open the back door to pull out the blueberry cobbler we brought for dessert. After I've secured it, I join Dad on the sidewalk and we make our way to the front door. Before we can get close enough to knock, Jason pulls the door open. We lock eyes, and instantly I can see that he's as nervous and excited as I am. In my mind, we have an anime moment where our eyes are glittering and huge, and the background blurs into an assortment of bright colors, but mostly hues of pink, and we float into the air, both our legs kicked up behind us. We grab hands and spin in circles staring into each other's eyes.

Thinking about this makes me smile even harder, and seeing my smile, Jason's increases too. "You've got perfect timing. We're just setting everything onto the table now." He directs his attention to my dad. "Nice suit, Mr. Crowley." He stretches out the "i" in nice, emphasizing the coolness.

"Thanks!" Dad smiles, but then looks concerned. "We're not late, are we?"

"No, not at all," Mrs. Holli assures as we step into the house, Jason closing the door behind us. "We just got done a little early." She extends her hand to my dad, "Hi, I'm Sharon."

"David," he replies, shaking her hand.

"Here, take your shoes off and let me take your coats," Mrs. Holli insists.

"I got it Mom," Jason says, grabbing our coats from us before his mom can. "You and Dad already made a huge dinner. Why don't you and Mr. Crowley go sit down, we'll be in in a sec."

My dad removes his shoes and then follows Mrs. Holli, who takes the cobbler from me, into the dining room where I hear he and Mr. Holli introduce themselves.

"I'm really excited this is happening," Jason says, giving me a hug.

"Me too! It's amazing."

We look into each other's eyes for a moment, smiling.

"Well, let's join 'em in there," he motions with his head, holding my hand in his as we walk, going through the kitchen to the dining room. Before we fully get into the kitchen, I have the sudden urge to kiss him, so I pull him back and do so, out of range of our families.

During the kiss Jason moves his hands up to my face, and after it's over, he holds them there for a moment, leaning his forehead onto mine. We look into each other's eyes yet again, but it's funny because looking into eyes this close up makes them meld together to form one big cyclops eye, and we laugh. We hold hands again, my right hand in his left, and we join our parents and Kate and Mara in the dining room.

"Come on and sit down, I'm starving!" Frank hurries us.

I sit next to my dad. We're across from Kate and Mara. Mr. Holli sits at the left end of the table and Mrs. Holli is at the edge right next to him on Kate and Mara's side of the table. Jason sits next to me at the right end of the table.

We all take turns dishing out food onto our plates. There's burgers—some of them veggie for Kate and Mara—as well as homemade mac and cheese, Greek salad, cornbread, and baked beans. I can see my dad's mouth watering as he picks up his burger to take a bite. "Mmmm, this is so good," he says, mouth still half full of burger. He then apologizes for talking with his mouth full.

Mr. Holli laughs, "No, we encourage it." He thinks for a minute, "Well, maybe not encourage it, but we definitely don't mind." And this time we all laugh.

"Rachel told us you loved burgers, and I knew she was rather fond of mac and cheese, so I let my parents know," Jason confesses.

"Yes, he set us up for success," Mrs. Holli admits.

"Indeed he did. Again, this is great," Dad says.

There's a moment of silence, or rather non-talking. There's still the scrape of forks against the ceramic plates, the swig of beverage being swallowed, the crunch of lettuce and bun being bitten into; the sounds of eating a satisfying meal. I've always loved this time. There's an energy that surrounds you when eating a great meal. Even if you don't like each other, you can all shut up and just be in the moment. When it's a great meal, you don't want to rush it. You plan the last bite of your favorite dish because you want that taste to last in your mouth forever. And if you're with people you love, it's even better. You get to look around the room and see them in pure bliss. Just lost in the joy of sharing a delicious meal with beautiful people. I get so wrapped up in it all that I don't totally realize that conversation has started back up again.

"So what do you do?" Mrs. Holli asks my dad.

"Like, job-wise?" He asks.

"Yeah," Mrs. Holli clarifies.

"I'm a film editor," Dad answers.

"That's pretty cool, work on anything we would have seen?" Mr. Holli asks.

"Possibly, but nothing exciting. I've done some work for some friends of mine who've made small local movies, but mostly I just do work on commercials and training videos for businesses and stuff like that."

"So is it just job to job?" Mr. Holli asks.

"Not for me. There are freelance editors out there, but I work for an editing company. I don't always get to choose what I work on, but I have a steady income, which is really nice," Dad responds.

"That's really cool. Some friends and I were thinking about making some highlight reels for ourselves. Maybe you could help us out?" Jason asks.

"Yeah, sure, I could probably do that. Just let me know when you've got it all figured out," Dad offers.

"Yeah, for sure!" Jason says.

This is amazing. My dad and my boyfriend just made plans to work on a project together. What is life? I'm actually not sure if it's amazing. It could be really weird. Though they probably wouldn't even really work together in the same place. Jason would just give my dad the footage, and he'd work on that on his own. Whatever, I love it either way.

"So, do you do any editing, Rachel?" Mrs. Holli asks.

The question caught me off guard. I was off in my own world. I open my mouth to answer, but Kate speaks before me, "Just because her dad does it, doesn't mean she does, Mom."

Mrs. Holli smiles, "I'm aware, Kate. I was just curious." She turns her attention back on me.

"No, I don't do any editing, but I guess I have a bit of an amateur eye for it." I point my thumb over at my dad, "He's always pointing out bad editing when we watch stuff together."

"I point out the good stuff too!" Dad exclaims, nudging me with his elbow.

We get some laughs from everyone before Mrs. Holli continues, "So, do you watch a lot of movies and stuff?"

"Yeah, I love movies and shows. I get really into the characters, I sometimes call myself a TV-aholic," I joke.

"She's gotten a lot better though. I used to have to fight her and her friends to go out and do something, but now she's always out and about," Dad adds, attempting to talk me up.

"Well, admittedly, I'm usually going out to see a movie, or going to Jess and Bright's house to hang and watch something," I laugh, but then cringe a bit because I realize I haven't been to their house in over a month. Which is crazy for us. Depressing even.

"Well, I'll pretend the wool is still over my eyes," Dad says. He chuckles a bit, but it's kind of uncomfortable because he's noticed my demeanor has changed.

"Did you ever see that movie *Bridesmaids*?" Mr. Holli asks. "Sharon and I recently rented it, and we loved it!"

"Yeah, I was really surprised. The trailers didn't make me want to see it at all, but I had only heard great things about it," Mrs. Holli admits. "Though, it's rather raunchy, I definitely wouldn't let Kate and Mara watch it yet."

"We've totally seen it," Mara shrugs.

"When?" Mrs. Holli asks, shocked.

"We were at Heather Samlee's house for a sleepover and they had it," Kate replies.

"Why would you tell her that?" Mara demands.

"Why would you tell her we saw it at all?" Kate retorts.

"Whatever, we'll talk about it later," Mrs. Holli scolds. "So yeah, have you two seen it at all?"

"I actually haven't," my dad responds.

"I have. I also watched it at my friends' house—Jess and Bright," I reply, looking at Kate and Mara. "I didn't see it right away, but everyone hyped it up so much. When I finally saw it, it didn't quite live up to the reputation. I mean it was funny and I liked it, it just wasn't amazing, you know?"

"I get that. I just loved that it was a comedy with an all-woman cast. You don't really see that a lot," Mrs. Holli defends.

"Yeah, not with comedies or anything really. I actually came across this website through Twitter called Bitch Flicks. It's a feminist website dedicated to film and media. And since I've started following them and reading their articles and such, I've been looking at everything I watch and read though a … sort of feminist lens, I guess. Like looking at the number of women in films and the way they're portrayed. Are they simply a damsel in distress? Are they killed off to further the plot of the male protagonist? Are they just sticking to gender roles and stereotypes? Like, have you heard of the Bechdel Test?" I ask.

"No," Mrs. Holli shakes her head. "What's that?"

"It's this test you put movies to—or anything really. I think the rules are: Does it have more than one female character? Do you get to know these characters' names? If so, do they talk to each other? And if they do, do they talk about something other than a man? If the movie meets these qualifications then they're at least at a good start."

"Why is it called the Bechdel Test?" Mrs. Holli asks.

"Well, I don't know all the details, but Bechdel is the last name of a cartoonist whose characters talked about these requirements for the films they watch. And so people took the idea and named the test, or set of requirements, after her," I explain.

"Well, yeah, that's pretty cool. I'll have to start checking the things I watch for that. Though I'm sure I probably have been, just not actively," Mrs. Holli replies.

"Yeah, I realized that that's just something I had already sort of been doing, looking for roles with female leads and not just things about women looking for guys. A lot of movies don't really fair too well on the test though. And I mean, I don't dismiss a movie if it fails, and not every movie has to have women in it, but I do like to just take notice and I definitely give more points to a movie that passes even if I don't like it a lot. I also look at movies and see how many minorities there are and how they're portrayed as well."

"Wow, it looks like you might have a social activist on your hands," Mr. Holli says to my dad.

My dad nods and turns his attention towards me, "Yeah, just like her mom."

I smile, not knowing what to say. I don't really want to talk about mom in front of everyone, but it is nice to think about. I guess I have been following in her footsteps in a way. With my own interests, and with my friends. Jess, Bright, and I are pretty much always talking about morals, and how to better the world, and I mean, they have superpowers and they look to me for advice. They trust me to help them make responsible and moral choices. That has to mean something. I don't remember a lot about my mom's activism, but I do remember that people came to her a lot for advice. They knew she would be there for them. They respected and admired her, and a lot of people loved her. I always knew she had a lot of friends, but seeing the turnout at her funeral was amazing. Seeing just how many people came to show their love for her and support for me and my dad. I always feared that I've let all those people down. They always talked about how they saw a lot of my mom in me, and that was a lot of pressure. It still is. How do you live up to that image? Someone who's always there when you need them? Someone who's that loved and charismatic? My mom definitely wasn't the best person in the world. She had her faults, but she was one of the best friends a person could have. I just hope I can be like that.

The rest of dinner was wonderful. I did my best to stay in the moment and take it all in. It's a hard thing to do, especially when it feels like a million butterflies are running through your body, emerging, and lifting you away.

By the time we finish dessert—our cobbler with some salted caramel ice cream of the Hollis'—it's getting to be late. My dad suggests that it's time we head out, seeing as it's a school night. Mrs. and Mr. Holli agree, making it clear, though, that they had a wonderful night and that we're welcome back anytime.

Jason walks my dad and me to the door once we've got ourselves together. He gets our coats from the front closet as we get our shoes on.

"Thanks," Dad says as Jason hands him his coat. "It was great seeing you again, Jason, have a good night." My dad shakes Jason's hand and then turns to me, "I'll see you out in the car."

After my dad leaves, it's just Jason and me in the room.

"I had a really good time tonight. I'm so happy our parents get along so well," Jason says.

"Me too," I respond. "It's amazing."

"You're amazing, Rachel." He doesn't say anything more, but I can see he wants to. He wants to say something, something that I think I want to say. I can feel it. I can see it in the way he's looking at me right now. There's a strong chemistry between us, a real connection. I open my mouth to say it, it's on the tip of my tongue, but I don't get it out. I bite my lip and we continue to gaze into each other's eyes, and then we kiss. It's not the sweeping, 360-camera-spin kind of kiss you see in movies, but more intimate and honest. Definitely supercharged.

"I think I'm falling in love with you," he says.

I don't know if he's looking at me, because my eyes are closed, still leaning close to him from the kiss. "I think I'm falling in love with you too," I say back.

I open my eyes and he's looking at me with the most sincere smile. I kiss him again and then slowly pull away. "I should go, my dad's waiting."

Jason just nods, still smiling.

"Goodnight," I say.

"Goodnight," He responds.

"Well, I think that went well," My dad says as I get into the car.

I nod, "Yeah, me too."

"Didn't even need any embarrassing stories," Dad chuckles.

"I'm sure there'll be plenty more chances for that," I say.

My head is turned toward the window, but I can see that he's smiling at me. I lean my head on the window and just close my eyes. I think this smile is going to be stuck on my face forever.

JESSICA

It's been a few days since I had that talk with Sarah. I'm still lost as to what I should do. What she said makes sense. I shouldn't think that I can solve all problems. I can't. I know I can't, but I have the power—multiple powers, in fact—to solve *some* problems. And I think that I should.

But I don't know *what* I should do or how I should do it.

I've gotten pretty good at healing plants. I even went into some heavily wooded areas and tested restoring trees. It was simple. It worked like a charm. Though I guess it kind of was … .

Healing trees and stuff is awesome, but it's not a big enough impact. It's not doing anything, really. I should be healing the Amazon or something. Re-growing a whole forest!

Seriously, I should be doing this. What would happen if I just healed forests around the world? I can actually think of a ton of good and bad things that can and probably will happen, but ultimately the state of our planet would be vastly improved. I think. I mean, I don't know if rapidly re-growing trees hurts an ecosystem, but I can't imagine it'd be terrible.

Whatever, I just have to act. I have to just do this. Pick a weekend and just teleport somewhere and get to work healing forests and jungles and meadows and whatever needs healing!

My immediate urge is to run and tell Bright, but we still haven't really been talking and he'd shoot the idea down anyway. He'd think too much. I just need to act. That's that. I bet Rachel would be up for it. Maybe, I dunno. I wish I could talk to her about it too. I really miss them both.

I'm listening to Ellie Goulding's album *Halcyon* and the song "In My City" just came on. The song starts with Ellie singing about how if she had one wish, she would have used it to listen more to her brother. For a second I doubt myself. I doubt it all. I shouldn't try this. I shouldn't attempt any of this. It's stupid.

But then in the next few lines she talks about how she was given wings, which represent a freedom. And about how she has used, and will continue to use this gift. The confidence in her voice as she proclaims that she will not lose or give up these wings replaces all my doubt. I've got to use my wings. I've got to use my powers, and I've got to do this. I'm going to do this. Whatever mistakes happen, and whatever trouble comes, I *know* I fully believe in this. I know I won't regret it.

I laugh at myself. It's pretty ridiculous that I just decided on a huge life decision based on lines from an Ellie Goulding song. I mean, I love Ellie Goulding. I'm not knocking her in anyway. But it's probably best not to make decisions based on lyrics in general. I'm just so in love with this song right now. I want to live in this song. I want it to be my world. I want to live in a world that feels like this. It feels corny, and hard, and inspired—or maybe ambitious—but most of all hopeful. Like overall it's a bright world. Ha, Bright. I can never think that word without thinking of my brother. I sometimes forget how awesome a name he has. Sometimes I'm jealous. Bright is so unusual, uncommon. Jessica is great, but not special.

Sometimes I just want the real world to feel like music. To actually feel hopeful. It's hard to feel hopeful. And though maybe being inspired by lyrics is dumb, if something inspires you, hold onto that. Let yourself be fueled by it. Guide it and use it. I walk over to my computer and tweet those words out. And then I go back over to my bed and just lie down. I close my eyes and imagine all the change that will come from what I do. I imagine the look of all the forests coming back. The feeling swells inside me and it feels good.

I jump up and rush to my computer. I decide I should research places that have had the most deforestation. I also actually should look into what a rapid recurrence of trees in an area would do. I should be responsible. Just have to step back, weigh the options, and make a calculated decision.

Soon "Lights" comes on and I turn it up and dance in my chair. There's something magical about this song. Something unifying. Rachel, Bright, and I usually dance around to this song with all the lights off. I'm going to do this. I'm going to go out and heal our planet. And then I'm going to work on healing my relationship with two of the most important people in my life.

RACHEL

It's been a few weeks since Dad and I had dinner with Jason and his family. Things have been really great as of late. Dad and I have been talking a lot more, and I really feel like our relationship has been improving. And things with Jason are going well, but he can tell something's up with me.

I'm headed over to Jason's place now. I need to be honest with him, let him know what's going on with me. I mean, I can't tell him everything. Obviously I have to keep Jess and Bright's secrets, but I have to let him know some of the things I've been feeling and I have to try and explain why.

I'm just getting off the bus, and I've got a few blocks to walk to get to his house. I'm listening to Britney Spears' album *Femme Fatale*, the deluxe edition. It's probably not the first thing that would come to mind when you think of preparing for an emotional conversation, but it's a beautiful day out and it's just a fun, clubby album. I don't want to be bogged down with emotion before we even start talking. Also, the upbeat music pumps me up and makes me less afraid of expressing myself. And this album is all about that. It's basically just about having a good time and expressing yourself sexually, and not being ashamed of that, but proud. Britney Spears is really inspiring. She's gone through so much shit, and all publicly, and she's still going. She's still making music and doing what makes her happy. She's still expressing herself how she wants and not letting society's views of her past, being a woman, or being a mom shape her. She's fucking boss, and I love it.

I pause the music and take my headphones out as I approach Jason's house. He's sitting on his front steps waiting for me. I put my iPod in my bag and wave, "You didn't have to wait out here for me."

"I know, but I thought I'd meet you out here and we could just go for a walk. It's a little more private than my house right now, Mara and Kate have a few friends over," Jason says, standing up to greet me.

"Sounds good to me," I say as I give him a hug and a kiss.

"Do you need to go inside for anything, or you wanna just go?" Jason asks.

"I'm good to go if you are."

"Yeah, let's do it," Jason takes my hand and we begin walking down his block.

"Do you have anywhere specific you wanna go, or just kind of walk?" I ask.

"Let's just see where we end up."

I nod and we walk in silence for a little bit, our hands gripping tight and our arms swinging between us.

"So what did you want to talk about?" Jason asks.

I take a moment to respond, trying to think of how I want to say this. "Well, a lot, I guess. I mean, I know you can tell there's been a lot on my mind lately and I haven't talked to you about a lot of it. But I want to open up. You're always so open with me, and I want to be the same with you."

"Well, for the record, I think you've been pretty open with me," Jason says. "And you don't owe me anything. When I open up with you and tell you things, I don't want you to feel pressured to do the same with me. I know you care about me, and I know you'll open up when you're ready."

"You're really sweet, Jason. You're so amazing. And I'm not feeling pressured to share with you, I just want to. You're who I want to tell things to. I love talking to you," I say, smiling. Jason smiles too, but he stays silent, allowing me room to continue. "As you know, Jess, Bright, and I haven't really been talking. And I told you we were having issues, but I haven't really said why. Some of the reason for that is because I can't. It's not only my shit, it's theirs too, and I can't share it all." Jason nods, indicating that he understands, but again stays silent.

"I found out they've been lying to me about something pretty big. They've been lying for years, and the way I found out wasn't really ideal. And I just haven't known how to feel. I completely understand why they lied, but that doesn't make it hurt any less. I still love them, they're still my family, but I just don't really know how to talk to them right now." I pause as we come to an intersection. We wait a few seconds for a car to pass before walking to the other side. "So yeah, that's been rough. They're my best friends, I really want you to hang with them and get to know them, but … I dunno."

"I didn't want to pry," Jason says, "but I definitely want to hang with them and get to know them too. Have they tried to talk to you at all?"

"Not in a while," I say. "They tried when it all first went down, but I told them I just needed space."

"Do you think you're maybe ready to at least talk a bit?" Jason asks.

"Maybe … I just still feel like I'm going to be too angry. Like, I'll say something that'll just make things worse."

"I think it'll be a tense conversation for sure. At least based on what you're telling me. But I think you need to express that. If you get a little angry, that's okay. They should know how you feel. I think you'll know if it goes too far, and if it does, then you just deal with that as it happens," Jason responds.

I nod, "Yeah. I'll try and reach out soon."

"I mean, do it when you're ready, but I just think that if you wait too long, it'll be harder to bring yourselves back together."

"Yeah, for sure," I agree. We walk in silence for a while before I speak again. "Jess and Bright aren't the only thing I wanted to talk to you about." Jason looks at me expectedly. "The stuff with Jess and Bright also sparked stuff with me and my dad. I realized that ever since my mom died, I had kind of shut him out. I mean, our relationship has never been bad, but I don't think it's grown for a long time. But I've been working on that a lot lately, and I feel like we're becoming a lot closer."

"That's really great, Rachel," Jason smiles, squeezing my hand tighter.

"Yeah, I'm really happy about it," I nod. "It's just ..."

"What?" Jason asks.

"I told you my mom died when I was 10, but I didn't tell you everything. I was at Jess and Bright's house when it happened. Their parents were having a barbeque that day and I had stayed over the night before. I remember my mom and I had been arguing with each other a lot. Or really just disagreeing on things. I was starting to question her more, always giving her a hard time. Instead of me going over to Jess and Bright's the night before, she really wanted me to go to the Uptown Summer Festival with her. She was disappointed because she had really been hoping to go to Illinois that week to visit some old friends, but the timing just didn't work out. Money was an issue, and Dad also had a lot of work to do. He can do his work on the road, but really didn't want to, and he and Mom were a bit annoyed with each other at the time as well. Looking back I can see my mom just really needed a break and wanted to have some fun, but when I was younger I just always thought the festival was for older people. I remembered going and being bored, so I fought her on it. She tried to make it fun, tried to appeal to me, but I just didn't care. I wasn't even a teenager yet, but I remember even though I did think it would be boring, I more so didn't want to go just to spite her. Just because she wasn't letting me go over to Jess and Bright's. I went over there pretty much every weekend—and in the summer even more—but I couldn't just give her this one day. I was such a little shit." I stop because I'm getting angry with myself all over again. Jess and Bright are the only people I've told this story to, so it's been a while since I last spoke about it. I think about it a lot, but saying the words out loud is a whole other thing.

Jason gently pulls us to a stop, "Rachel, you can't beat yourself up about that. Thinking back on it feels worse because now you're thinking about it being the last day with your mom. Kids are shitty sometimes, and in the grand scheme of things, that isn't really that shitty a thing. You probably wouldn't even remember it if there wasn't so much attached to it. You have to find a way to be okay with it."

"I know. I know it doesn't make sense to hold onto this grudge against myself, but it's hard. It's hard to dissociate this event with what happened after. All she wanted to do was hang out with her daughter, to be with family, and I couldn't even give that to her."

"Rachel …"

I don't know if he was going to say anything more, but I continue with my story before he does. "I kept fighting her on it until she gave in. There was a little while where she sent me to my room, told me we weren't going to the festival, but because of my behavior, I wasn't going to Jess and Bright's either. So of course I cried a little bit and pouted in my room. I don't know what changed her mind, but after a while she came and told me she called Marion— Jess and Bright's mom—and that I could stay the night over there. And then I of course played the grateful child act, hugging her, and thanking her, and promising if we couldn't get to the festival, we could do whatever else she wanted to do sometime soon. I don't know why kids think that acting appreciative after throwing a fit makes everything okay. Anyway, I gathered all my things and we went to the Walkers' place. My mom stayed for a while. She and Marion were really good friends. And before she left I remember I made a point to hug her. I don't remember if I said 'I love you.' As a family we always said it to each other when departing from one another, but I can't remember if I said it then, and I've tried a lot.

"But I know I hugged her, and that was the last time I did. It was the last time I saw my mom alive. I've often wished that I could just go back and say more to her. Just be with her, soak in the moment more, ask her all the things I've wanted to ask her since. But I did get to talk to her one last time. She called Marion to talk about any last minute things she should grab. My mom was a great cook and she had been preparing a lot of food for the barbecue. Probably more than the Walkers were. She and my dad were going to head over after dad got off work. And before she got off the phone with Mrs. Walker, she talked to me. I could tell she was still a little upset, but I was having fun and I didn't want to deal with that, so I ended our conversation short, without saying 'I love you.' I *know* I didn't say it that time. The last time I spoke to my mom, I was too stubborn to tell her I loved her. I've been trying to forgive myself for that one ever since." I start to cry and Jason wraps his arms around me and holds me close.

"You don't have to keep going if you don't want to, Rachel. You can stop whenever you want. We can talk about something else, or just not talk at all, whatever you want."

I don't respond at first. I just let myself cry. I let it all out. Eventually I pull myself away from his shoulder, "I want to keep going. I want to tell you all of this, if you want to keep listening."

"Of course I do. I always want to listen," Jason assures.

I nod and try to smile. "So later, Marion tried calling my mom, there was something she forgot to ask her to get. But she couldn't get ahold of her. It started to get late in the day and she called a number of times, but never heard anything back. I remember having this gut feeling that something was wrong, but I tried my best to ignore it. I told myself I was just being paranoid. So when I saw our car pull up, I was so relieved. But my Uncle Mike—my mom's brother—got out of the driver's seat, and my dad got out of the passenger seat. Both of them were crying. I remember immediately thinking that my grandma Sue, who's my dad's mother, had died. She was in bad health at the time, and it was just the first place my mind went. But when I saw that my mom wasn't with them, I knew something else was wrong and my heart sank.

"'Your mom passed away' is what my dad said. I remember tears streaming down his face. This was the worst I had ever seen him cry. This was the worst I had ever seen him period. He looked absolutely miserable. The first reaction I had was to smile. For a split second, I thought it had to be some kind of joke. I remember seeing that in shows as a kid and thinking that nobody would respond like that if they were told somebody they loved died, but in that moment, it doesn't feel real. In that moment, the only thing that feels logical is that they must be joking, at least when it's unexpected. But that faded quickly. I knew it was real and I immediately started to weep. I remember I had to walk away. I went and sat on Jess and Bright's back steps and I cried for a long time. They sat with me and held me until eventually we moved inside and ate and cried in there." I'm still crying, and I need to take another minute to gather myself.

Jason is grasping both of my hands in his. "So ... how did she pass away? You said it was unexpected?"

"Yeah," I nod. "I guess while she was home alone, she had a seizure. She was convulsing and there was no one there to help. The swelling in her brain was too much and ... she died. She was loading things in the car in our driveway and so she fell right next to the car on her side. I guess at first glance people just thought she was looking for something under the car, or fixing something, but when people finally noticed something was wrong, it was too late. They contacted my dad and my uncle and ... yeah."

"Did she have any history of seizures or anything?"

"No. I didn't really attempt to find all the details then, but my dad said the doctors didn't really know what caused it, but it could have been a number of things. It never really mattered much to me—what caused it I mean. My dad was worried that it could have been genetic and that I'd be prone to it somehow, but the doctor's said they couldn't find anything to indicate that. But yeah ... I had been thinking about all this stuff with my mom, and that made me think a lot about my dad and our relationship. I got really upset with myself because I had pulled away from my dad so much. I was always there, but most of the time there was no real substance to any of our interactions or conversations. I felt really shitty because not only did he lose the love of his life, his best friend, his partner, but then he also had to lose me in a lot of ways."

I'm not looking Jason in the eye. It's a combination of not wanting him to see me cry, and being ashamed of myself. Being ashamed of how I treated my dad for so long. Being ashamed of what my mom must have thought of me her last day alive, and what she'd have thought of me during the years after her death, if somehow she was watching.

I can feel Jason's eyes on me. I can feel his empathy. I know he's trying to find a way to express that. When he speaks, his voice falters. I look and he's crying too. "Rachel, you shouldn't feel guilty. You were dealing with your grief. We all do that in different ways. You weren't actively trying to hurt your dad."

"I know. We talked and I told him that I felt all of this, and he told me what you're telling me, but it ... it still just breaks my heart, you know? I don't know how he did it. I don't know how he managed to hold himself together—how he managed to hold both of us together."

"Well it was probably hard, but I'm guessing he was grateful to have you to look out for. You kept him going. You kept him from giving in to sorrow. I'm sure you gave him joy, even if you were a little distant," Jason tries to comfort me.

"Yeah …" I say looking away from him.

Jason holds my face in his hands and looks deep into my eyes. "I don't want to tell you how to feel, but you shouldn't feel bad about this. When you start to feel upset at yourself for this, just remind yourself that though you feel remorse for the way you grieved, you will not feel guilty about it. You apologized—even though you didn't really need to—and you're moving on. Your dad forgives you. I don't think he was ever upset with you about it, but he forgives you. It's time to forgive yourself, Rachel." He smiles big trying to get me to smile. "Okay?"

I smile, "Okay."

"Good," He says, and he begins to pull his face away from mine, but I thrust forward and kiss him passionately. This time it *is* one of those sweeping, 360-camera-spin kind of kisses. When it ends, I quickly wrap my arms around him and nuzzle my head into his chest. "I definitely wasn't expecting that," he says.

"Thank you for being so wonderful, Jason. I really, really, appreciate you for listening and being so understanding."

"Always. You know, I am quite fond of you, Rachel Crowley. I care about you a lot." His smile is tender, but his eyes are fierce. Passionate.

"I care about you too," I say. And my heart starts to race. I need to say it before my mind comes up with a millions reasons not to. "Jason …"

"Yeah?" he asks. The way he says it, I know he's feeling exactly what I'm feeling. I know he knows what I'm going to say before I say it.

"I love you," I say. I don't totally know what love is, or what that means completely, but I know I love him. It hasn't been long, but I feel so close to him. I trust him. I'm comfortable with him.

"I love you too, Rachel."

We kiss again and then I take his hand and we continue our walk. For a while, we look only into each other's eyes, wrapped up in the moment, but eventually Jason puts his arm around my shoulder and brings me in close to kiss my forehead. "We should probably watch where we're going," He laughs, letting go of my shoulder, and grabbing my hand again.

"Yeah, friends don't let friends stare into each other's eyes while walking … or something, I dunno," I say. I feel my cheeks start to get hot, feeling silly.

Jason laughs and squeezes my hand tight. "You're fucking amazing," he tells me. I smile. I'm thinking the exact same thing about him. We walk along in comfortable silence for a while before Jason speaks again, "Hey, so tell me about your mom. Give me some fond memories you have of her. Or … I mean, if you want to." Jason retreats from the idea a little. He caught me a bit off guard with that, and I'm sure my expression made it seem as if I don't want to talk about my mom. I mean, I guess part of me doesn't. It hurts a lot. But I do want to share with him. I want him to know her too.

"No, I think that's a good idea," I say, pausing to think for a moment. "I don't really talk about my mom a lot. It'll be good to do some remembering. Well, she was really nice. She had an amazing smile. A lot of people tell me I have her smile. She had a lot of friends. All of her friends would go to her for advice or for help. She was always there for everyone. Always reliable. Or at least that's how I remember her. Her name was Catherine. She allowed my dad—and my dad only—to call her Cat. She hated for people to call her Cathy. Sometimes when I was feeling rather snotty, I'd call her Cathy to get under her skin. But yeah, she preferred Catherine. She was really into the outdoors. She always talked about going on some huge camping trip. She said I'd love it. But we never seemed to find time to go. She loved to take walks and just sit and watch the various animals in a park. We also had a very well-kept garden. Well, we still do. My dad helped her with it, and he continued to work on it after she died. I suppose it was a way to keep himself busy, and to retain some connection to her." I hold for a second, getting lost in the wave of memories of my mom. It's like being in a place you haven't been in for a long time.

Thinking of one thing I haven't thought of in years, sparks another memory, and another. It's beautiful and sad. I smile and continue, "She actually really loved to go fishing, which surprised a lot of people. Most people thought she was a vegetarian. She didn't eat a lot of meat, but she wasn't against it or anything. Her dad took her and my Uncle Mike fishing all the time when they were kids, and she used to take me from time to time. I never had much patience for it though. Whenever she went, she'd bring back enough for dinner. As a kid I didn't like fish all that much, *except* for when my mom would make it. Her fish was the best. She was just an amazing cook in general. I really wish I had gotten a chance to learn more from her. Well, both cooking-wise and life-wise.

"She was very intelligent and strong. She was sure to tell me not to let anyone push me around, 'especially not any snot-nosed boys,'" I say, imitating my mom, pointing my index finger sternly at Jason. We both laugh and walk along giggling with each other, soaking in the moment.

"It sounds like your mom was really awesome," Jason says. "I'm sorry I'll never meet her."

The smile on my face fades as I think about that fact. "Yeah m—"

"Wow, I'm sorry!" Jason cuts me off. "That maybe didn't come out right, I dunno … I'm stupid, sorry."

"No, it's fine, Jason. I'm sorry you won't get to meet her too. I think she would have really liked you. I mean, I don't think I've ever even seen snot in your nose, so …"

It takes Jason a moment to get it, but when he does he beams a huge smile. "Did I mention that you're fucking amazing?" he asks.

I brush my hair behind my ear and turn my head, blushing. "Thanks, you're pretty amazing yourself."

"Well, thanks." Jason replies, also blushing. "So hey, you wanna go to the park? It's not too far away, and we can sit on a park bench and be all cute and romantic and watch the various animals and whatnot."

"That sounds absolutely wonderful." I kiss Jason, and we walk off, hand-in-hand, toward the park. Both of us the happiest we can ever remember being.

JESSICA

·↶·

It's a little after five in the morning, and I'm standing in the middle of a forest in Madagascar. A forest that just a half hour ago was barren. A forest that I brought back to life. I spent weeks researching forests, looking for what needed help the most, but also seeing what I should be careful not to do.

I discovered that too many trees is indeed a bad thing. It can lead to drought and limits the growing space of other plants and animals in the area. Too many trees means that the trees absorb too much of the water that other plants and species need to survive. It also means that there isn't much runoff, so lakes and rivers lose volume too.

So when restoring this forest, I made sure to try and stick to the guideline of a few dozen trees per acre. I mean, I obviously am no expert, but that's what I found out through researching on the Internet. I guess we've noticed the damage too many trees can do, which is only a problem because of human interference. We stop forest fires, which are a way for forests to keep themselves in balance. We do that for protection of the forests we're trying to preserve because of massive deforestation (also our fault), but also to protect the life of the inhabitants of the forests and the areas around it. The ironic thing, though, is that a forest having too many trees actually makes the forest fires we can't prevent even more harmful and dangerous because there's more fuel, which emits more carbon into the air. Humans have done a lot of damage, but we've also done a lot of good, or at least a lot of trying to make up for what we fucked up.

I've got a plan for today. I'm going to start here in Madagascar, healing what I can, and then I'm going to move on to different places all over the world: Africa, Australia, China, the Philippines, South America, and the U.S., just to name a few. One of the reasons I chose Madagascar first is because it was one of the first I came across when searching endangered forests, but also because of learning that many of the species found on Madagascar, or at least specific variants of species, are endemic. Meaning they can only be found on Madagascar. Because of the specific climate and environment, as well as it being an island, these species have developed and evolved to survive within the unique conditions they're in. Most don't have the option to migrate to another area because there's no other land around, and even if there were, many rely on the other species specifically found there to survive. Losing one species could easily result in losing another. So I wanted to come here and get to other areas in similarly urgent conditions first.

I sit down to appreciate my work. It's a really beautiful area. So many of the plants here I had never seen in real life before. Pictures really don't do them justice. I feel so empowered and proud of what I've done. It's an amazing feeling, but it's still a little empty. I really wish I wasn't doing this in secret. I mean, I don't want world recognition or anything, but I wish Bright and Rachel were here. I wish I could have told them about this all, but I didn't see any way to do that before talking about a lot of other things, and I didn't want to wait. It's really boring doing all of this by yourself, though. I should have at least brought my iPod or something. I opted not to. I figured I should stay as aware of my surroundings as I could, but it's going to be a long day.

It only takes about an hour and a half more to get Madagascar to a condition that I think is good. I see a lot in that time, though. Fossas, lemurs, tomato frogs, satanic leaf-tailed geckos. Comet Moths, and Darwin's bark spiders. The baobab tress may have been my favorite. And the people—so many people.

I make sure I'm not seen, but I just watch the people and how they interact with each other and the land. From what I can see, they know the land better than I can ever hope to. They live and breathe it. Well, I guess they do literally, but what I mean is that they're experts on it. I know ultimately they need to do what they have to in order to survive. They have to provide for themselves, but I wish they weren't in a position where they had to choose their lives over their land. Because in the long run, what are they going to do without the land? I wish nobody was in that position, but we all are.

So I'll just make sure we at least have land. It's trying to fix a bullet wound with a Band-Aid, but at least it's something, right? At least it'll hinder the effects of our pollution and deforestation, and give us more time to really come up with a solution. Or really, to convince everyone that we need a solution.

It takes me all day to restore things. I mean, I obviously don't do the whole world, but I hit a lot of places. Places that are impossible not to notice. I don't know what it will do, really. But it'll keep the world talking. It'll hopefully elevate the conversation. It has to.

"Where have you been all day?" my mom asks when I get home.

I shrug. "Just walking around. I spent some time at the park. Nothing much."

"You didn't care to tell anyone you'd be out late?"

"I just needed some time to myself, I'm sorry," I retort.

"Is something going on? I swear you're never around anymore. And I can't remember the last time I saw Rachel, or even saw you and Bright hanging out," Mom questions.

"Everything's fine."

She walks over closer to me. "You don't have to lie to me. You can tell me if something's up. Did you guys have a fight?"

"I told you, everything is fine. I'm not lying to you," I defend, getting rather irritated. Both at the fact that she's pressing so much, and that she's right.

"Sorry, 'lie' was the wrong choice of word. I just—I get it, I'm the parent, but something is obviously up."

I don't like lying to my mom, but I don't really know what else to do. I can't tell her about Sarah, or about what happened with Rachel all those years ago. I can't make her understand. "There's nothing to tell you, mom. Rachel's just been busy with her new boyfriend, and Bright's got work at the comic shop, and we're just doing our own things right now." I try to play it off and be aloof about it, but I don't think she's buying it. "I'm sure it'll all come to an equilibrium in time," I add.

"Okay … Well there's some lasagna in the fridge if you're hungry." she tells me. We make eye contact and she holds it for a moment, giving me a chance to really tell her what's going on.

"Thanks, I think I'll heat some up quick," I say, still choosing to avoid telling her the truth, making my way to the fridge. My mom joins my dad in the living room, and I put a piece of lasagna in the oven. I usually try to use the oven over the microwave if I have the patience for it. When it's ready, I plate it, grab some carrots from the fridge, fill my water bottle, and head to my room.

Bright is home. His door is closed, but I can hear him watching a show in there. I almost go knock on his door and ask if he wants to talk, but I don't. I just go to my room, close the door, and look for something to watch myself. I know the only way for things to get back to normal is for someone to take the first step, but I've done enough for today. I just want to relax.

I go to my desk and put my lasagna and water down and I pull up Netflix and Twitter. It only takes a few moments of looking through my feed to see that my actions today definitely didn't go unnoticed. There are a bunch of before and after pics surfacing of areas I restored, showing heavily deforested areas in one image and then lush and beautiful areas in the next. It's only a matter of time before news sources get hold of this. And I'm sure it won't take much longer for my family to catch on. Bright will definitely suspect me, and with us being in a disconnect, I don't think he'll lie for me. The only thing I have going in my favor is that if he tells Mom and Dad, he'll also burn himself because he'll have to tell them we have the power to heal, which we've been keeping from them. I don't know. I'm sure he's tired of lying, and this might be just the push he needs. All I can do is wait and see.

I don't really know what's coming next. I don't know if I've done more good than bad. I'm not going to lie, I'm scared. There's no going back now. I have to be all in. I've made my choice, now I've got to live with it. Or at least try to the best I can.

BRIGHT

Well, I told Mom and Dad. Not about killing Rachel and Sarah and then bringing them back to life, just the fact that we can heal. I didn't really think it through. Once I had seen the unexplained restoration of the world's major forests, I knew it was Jessica, and I knew she was in over her head. This is being noticed, and noticed a lot. Ultimately, I don't really know what telling our parents will do, other than get us both in trouble, but it was the first move I thought of and I made it. Which is kind of probably exactly what Jessica did, so I guess we're pretty alike in that manner.

Now we're all in the kitchen. Mom and Dad didn't believe me at first, but once it was clear I wasn't kidding—meaning I sliced my palm open in front of them and then healed it—they summoned Jessica down to join us. It's morning and we're all in our pajamas, spread around the kitchen island. Mom and Dad are on my right, standing with their backs to the stove and inner kitchen. Jessica is to my left. I'm sitting at the far end of the table in between both factions. There's a ray of sunlight peeking through the curtains and stretching across the countertop. It ends just to my right, dividing the group into parents and children. Husband and wife, and brother and sister. Though I don't think Jessica is really on my side. I'm not sure I'm on hers either, but we're definitely still keeping secrets from our parents, so neither of us is on theirs.

"I want you both to explain yourselves, right now," Mom demands.

"What did I do?" I ask, but immediately feel stupid for doing so.

"Well, assuming what you're telling us is true, you've been lying to us for years," Dad answers, sternly.

I turn my eyes away from his and look toward Jessica for a moment, who's clearly pissed at me, before fixing them down to the countertop.

"So, you've known about the healing since the beginning?" Dad asks.

I wait for Jessica to answer, but realize she's not going to. I'm the one who's lead she needs to follow. She doesn't know if I'm going to tell them about what happened with Rachel or not. I do my best to think of an explanation quickly. "Yeah, pretty much since the beginning. It was some time when you weren't home. We were goofing around and Jessica hurt herself pretty bad. I was freaking out, trying to see if we could handle it ourselves or if we needed to call you. But then suddenly, she was fine. There was a gash on her head that completely sealed itself in seconds. We cleaned up the blood, and it was like it never happened. Neither of us wanted to tell you because we didn't want to get in trouble for roughhousing, but then we kept testing our powers. Hurting ourselves on purpose to see how much we could heal. And we knew we couldn't tell you that. We knew you wouldn't approve. So we kept it from you."

I look over to Jessica and we share a brief moment of understanding. I told just enough truth so that Jessica could work with the lie, and I kept our big secret from them. But I still outed her and she definitely hasn't forgot that.

"You were hurting yourselves on purpose?" Mom yells. "What if it didn't work? What if you actually did irreparable damage?"

"Did you think about the consequences at all?" Dad asks.

"Not really. We were kids," Jessica responds.

"Yeah, and you're clearly still acting like that now," Dad shoots back. I was thinking the same thing. "Jessica, was all of this happening now really you? Were you the one who healed the forests?"

"Yeah ..." She responds.

"Jessica, the reason we don't want you to use your powers in public is so shit like this doesn't happen! This story is on every major news station. It's in every paper and magazine. This isn't going away," Dad spells out.

"Exactly, that's the point!" Jessica yells back at him. "I don't want it to go away. I did this so I could help. I'm so sick of not doing anything with my powers, with all the ability I have. And I'm sick of hiding! We can't make any new friends. You won't let us on any sports teams because you're afraid we'll hurt the other players. You keep us so sheltered and I hate it! All I want to do is help. I'm not trying to go to parties or get drunk and stoned like most the kids my age. All I'm asking is for a chance to find myself. For you to stop hindering me from living my life, because you're afraid of what will happen."

"We're your parents. It's our job to protect you," Mom says.

"At what cost?" I ask. "Overprotecting is going to do us no good. In two years we'll be 18 and either going off to college or starting a life of our own. You can't hold rules over our heads forever. At some point, you have to start trusting us."

"And should we be trusting you right now? When you've been lying to us?" Mom asks, and then turns her head to Jessica. "When you've recklessly used your powers without thinking about the outcome?"

"I wasn't being reckless. I took a risk, but I was careful," Jessica defends. "Nobody saw me. Nobody's going to know it was me who did it. How could they? Nobody's even going to suspect it was a human at all. As far as the world is concerned, what happened is out of the realm of human ability."

"Okay, so say you're right, they won't ever find out it was you. What's your next move?" Dad asks. "What good did this do if no one has any answers to how it happened?"

"It will keep the conversation going. Like you said, it's everywhere. People will be seriously talking about the effects of what we're doing to the world, and while the conversation is going, I've given the world a little more time," Jessica clarifies.

"Honey, I think you've got too much faith in the world," Mom cuts in. "Yeah they'll be talking about what happened, but most of it will be about how it happened. And if anything, it will go against what you're trying to do. People will see this as a means to not do anything. 'If the world is miraculously healing itself, then why should we worry?'"

Jessica doesn't say anything for a moment. "So you just want me to do nothing? Just like Bright and Rachel. Since there's a chance it won't go my way, I shouldn't even try at all?"

"Does Rachel know about your healing powers?" Dad asks.

"What does that have to do with anything?" Jessica retorts.

"So she's been lying to us too?" He demands.

"No," I assure. "She only just recently found out. That's part of the reason she hasn't been around, because she's upset we lied to her."

There's a pause in the conversation before mom asks, "So you had nothing to do with this, Bright? You didn't know this was going to happen at all?"

"Seriously?" I ask. "I know you two like to think of us as conjoined twins most of the time, but I think it's time you realized I'm not responsible for her, nor should I be."

"Watch your tone, Bright. We know that, okay?" Dad chides.

"Do you really?" Jessica cuts in. "Anytime I do something you two disagree with, you immediately turn to Bright for answers. *Did you have any idea this was going to happen, Bright?' 'Where were you?' 'Why didn't you stop her?'* It's like he's my gatekeeper. Fuck, let me take responsibility for myself. I did this. I did it, and I'm proud of it. I don't go to Bright before every move I make," Jessica pauses. "But I guess he still thinks I should. Since he came to you and ratted me out before he even tried to talk to me about it."

I'm not sure what to say, and from their faces, I don't think Mom and Dad are either. I'm still upset with Jessica, though I don't have any right to be. I'm mostly just hurt she didn't talk to me about this. We pretty much tell each other everything. I'm happy this all came out in the open though. We're still lying to Mom and Dad, but at least we're getting closer to telling the whole truth. I hope in time, we'll be ready to. And I'm also glad that Jessica is standing up for herself with Mom and Dad. But maybe part of me does see myself as responsible for us both. Maybe part of me liked it.

After another long silence, Dad nods and looks to Jessica. "You're right." He then looks to me. "You both are. We don't know how your powers work. You're our only kids. We're just trying to do the best we can, and since you two are twins and always seemed to do things together, it's easy to assume you always know what's going on with each other. I know we always deemed you big brother, Bright, but it's just because when you were kids, you were always so protective of Jessica. And I guess as you two got older and we couldn't be with you everywhere anymore, we sort of forced that role of protector onto you. And that's not fair to you or Jessica. "

"Like your father said, we're pretty much winging this. It's all we can do. We realize we were pressuring you and giving you responsibilities we had no right to give you, Bright. And in doing so, we were taking away from your sense of agency, Jessica. So we're sorry." Mom pauses for a moment to let this sink in. "In the spirit of recognizing your independence and letting you take responsibility for your actions, you're grounded."

Jessica rolls her eyes, "For how long?"

"I don't know. But I don't want to hear about you using your powers outside of this house. You are both to go to school and come home. That's it. Bright, you can still go to work, but you are not to hang out afterwards."

"Wait, what? I thought Jessica was getting grounded." I complain.

"Yes, she is getting grounded for the stunt she pulled, and you are getting grounded for your part in lying to us about your powers," Dad explains.

"Are you both clear on this?" Mom asks.

"Yeah, it's not like that's any different from what we already do. You won't let us have a life," Jessica says and she teleports away. A second later, we hear her bedroom door slamming.

"I guess you can be dismissed too," Dad says.

I head up to my room and close my door. Though there's still some obstacles to overcome, I think that hopefully this made a step closer to Jessica and me reconnecting. Just probably not today. I walk over to my bed and allow myself to fall face first on the pillows, my feet still dangling off the bed a bit.

Life is hard.

JESSICA

When I get to my room, I don't quite know what I want to do with myself. I make a move for my bed, but I don't want to be that high up. I want to be low. I feel low. So I take the floor.

I don't even know why I feel so low. I believe in what I did. I just ... I'm alone. Everyone is mad at me, and I get it. They all have reason to be. I broke Mom and Dad's rules and lied to them, I've shut Bright out, I lied to Rachel for years. The more I try and do what I think is right, the more I seem to fuck up.

I don't even know what's going to happen with all of what I've done. Though honestly, probably nothing. What's it really going to change? Why do I even have these powers? I can't do anything with them. I can't make people change. And if I could, what would I have them change to? What do I know, really?

I ponder that for a second, and I keep coming up with, "You know nothing, Jon Snow." That's the truest shit I've ever heard. I am Jon Snow. We're all Jon Snow. What the fuck do we know? So, I know nothing, but I'm trying to do what's responsible. I'm trying to take responsibility for the human race. We've fucked up the planet. We've fucked up each other. I just want to undo some of that.

I'm so tired of feeling like this. I just wish the world would take a second to realize what is happening. To feel for one another, not just hear about it. Not feel sad, or sympathy for, but to empathize, to feel the connection. To embrace not knowing. Not being ignorant, but being open.

All I do is question. It's a gift and a curse. Always asking "why" can lead to great discoveries not only about the world and what's around us, but what's inside us, what is us. The big question I can't seem to stop asking is, "What should I be doing?" You know, the best moments come when my answer to that question is, "Nothing." I'll come to this realization that I don't need to be doing anything. There's no right answer.

But then, how can I sit by and watch people suffer? How can I do nothing? I don't know.

"Whatever," I say to myself. I'm just so happy I'm on the floor. Nothing makes sense, but it doesn't seem to matter down here. Life would be good if I never had to leave the floor.

I just need a movie or something. I need to escape. I guess I could just teleport somewhere, but I don't want to risk making things worse with Mom and Dad, and besides, it's not like I can go somewhere to escape my thoughts. At least not any physical place.

I let out a long sigh, and even after it finishes, it takes me at least another minute to will myself onto my feet. I walk over to my computer and start a random episode of *Scrubs* on Netflix.

I've heard the theme song hundreds of times, but this time it really seems to make sense. I'm no Superman, and I most certainly can't do this all on my own. And more importantly, I don't want to.

RACHEL

‿

"Hey Rachel, can I talk to you for a moment?" Mrs. Holli asks me. I'm at Jason's house hanging with him, Kate, and Mara.

"Yeah, of course." I get up and follow Sharon into the dining room. I'm a little nervous. I can tell Jason is too. He's in the living room trying to act like he's not eavesdropping.

Sharon smiles, "You don't need to look so nervous."

"I'm sorry," I say, smiling back.

Sharon shakes her head. "I just wanted to talk to you about this organization a good friend of mine told me about. I know you're maybe looking to get more active in the community."

"Yeah, definitely. What's the organization do?" I ask.

"Well, it's called Low Income Sustainable Neighborhoods. L.I.S.N. for short, pronounced like 'listen.' Their main goal is reaching out to lower-income communities and speaking to them about the environment, starting community gardens, farmers' markets, making them care about their environment, and the environment overall. And they also fight against environmental discrimination. Which I think would be increased degradation of low-income neighborhoods due to more polluting factories being placed near them, or waste sites, or just the fact they receive less care because they don't get a say on these being put in their neighborhoods, or they're not informed on how harmful they can be."

"Wow, yeah, I think that sounds like something I'd be interested in. I mean, I'm a little intimidated, it sounds like there's a lot I'd need to be informed of myself," I admit.

"Well, don't not do it because you're afraid you don't know enough. I'm sure they train you, and I'm also sure you know more than you think you do."

"Yeah, I know, I just … I think too much."

"Yeah, I think we all do," Sharon consoles. "Hold on." She heads into the kitchen and goes to the drawer she keeps her keys in and pulls out a card before coming back to me. "Here, this is the card of the director of the organization. Shoot him an email and get some more information, and if you like it, give it a try."

"Yeah, thanks. I'll definitely do that."

"Good. And maybe you could get your friend Jessica to go with you. You've mentioned before she was passionate about helping the environment. Could be good for you both," Sharon suggests.

I hesitate before nodding, "Yeah, I should talk to her … Thanks, Sharon."

"Of course! I hope it's a good fit!"

"Me too," I respond. I stand around for a moment, not sure what the polite way to walk away is.

"I'll let you get back to Jason," she smiles. "I'm going to try and get some work done."

I nod and walk back into the living room. I envy people who are good at diffusing awkward moments. I think it's a very underappreciated talent. Jason, Kate, and Mara are watching a news interview about the recent sudden restoration of the world's forests. I haven't talked to Jess or Bright, but I know they were involved somehow. There's no way they weren't. If Jess and Bright can heal, I know Jess has had to come up with a way they can heal the environment.

"What did my mom want to talk with you about?" Jason asks as I sit down next to him.

"Like you weren't listening?"

"Yeah, I may have heard some of it, but tried my best not to."

"Right," I reply sarcastically. "She just told me about this organization that she thinks I might want to get involved with. They work on helping low-income neighborhoods become environmentally sustainable."

"Cool, you think you're gonna do it?" Jason asks.

"Yeah, I think," I say. "She also suggested I talk to Jess about it, so I might do that too."

Jason nods, "I think that'd be good."

"Yeah. So when did you start watching the news?" I ask.

Jason accepts my change of subject, "Well, there's just a lot of interesting discussions happening." He points toward the TV. "This Valeria Franklin woman seems pretty awesome."

On screen there is a woman who, from the info bar under her, appears to be a scientist on the IPCC. "Do you know what the IPCC is?" I ask Jason.

He shakes his head, but Mara answers, "They said it stood for the … something Panel for Climate Change."

"Intergovernmental," Kate answers.

I pull out my phone and google "IPCC."

"Intergovernmental Panel on Climate Change," I clarify. "It says the IPCC assesses the scientific, technical and socio-economic information relevant for the understanding of the risk of human-induced climate change." The three siblings nod and we all listen to Miss Franklin's interview:

"I don't know how this happened. Nobody can explain it. We've got our top scientists trying to figure this out. Not only in the United States, but every big brain in the world is working on this. One thing that is agreed upon is that this change is good change.

"What I want to see now is if our world leaders will work on creating a united front for making sure this miracle wasn't in vain. I know we can't get everyone on board. I'm not asking for world peace, but I believe that we could do a lot of good if we take this opportunity to make changes of our own.

"For whatever reason, the world gave us a redo. Global climate change is real. The evidence is irrefutable. Even if you don't believe it's 'global climate change,' it's impossible not to see that our world is not what it used to be. Or at least it wasn't before this mass restoration.

"Our forests are back, but that doesn't mean the world is fixed. Our waters are still polluted; there are places in the world where they literally have no viable water to drink. We're still polluting our air with billions and billions of toxins daily. We're running our natural resources dry. The amount of oil we consume is appalling. Those resources are not here forever. We're running on fossil fuels. Our energy source was created by a process that takes billions of years! If we run it dry, we will not be able to just create more. And we shouldn't be using it as our main source anyway.

"We need to be doing hard research on renewable energy sources. Clean energy sources. Wind power, solar power, hydrothermal energy!

"No, because of the way our world runs, we wouldn't be able to just drop our bad habits cold turkey. We're far too dependent on fossil fuels right now. We can take this opportunity to really make a change though.

"If the President commits to this, I'm sure we can get our allies behind it too. Now is the time to make it happen. If we let this opportunity slip through our hands, it will be an even greater tragedy than what we've already done to the world."

"I hear you loud and clear, Miss. Franklin, but what I, and I think many of the citizens of the world are wondering is, if nobody can explain what happened, how do we know it's not a natural process of Earth? I mean, your average science class will explain to you the checks and balances nature has to make sure there's an equilibrium. How do we know this isn't one of them?"

"Well, I understand how you could come to that hypothesis Mike, but there is no evidence in our history that shows anything like this happening. Yes, there are 'checks and balances' set in place, but if something goes beyond those checks and balances, it will either run its resources dry and move on until it falls back into equilibrium, or it will die out. We have not been checked. We haven't found equilibrium. We are still consuming far more than what our environment can keep up with, or even ourselves, and we're all paying for it. Like I said, this is not a time to relax and claim victory, this is a time to be thankful for this miracle and to take the time to reflect upon what we are doing and find a way to remedy our behavior."

"Well, I think we'll leave it at that. Thank you, Miss Franklin."

"My pleasure, Mike."

The half of the screen with Miss Franklin goes away, and the half with Mike, the news anchor, grows to take up the rest of the space.

"Powerful words from Valeria Franklin. She's got an extreme viewpoint, Let's see if the president heeds her warning.

"We're now going to turn to Rebecca Easton for some other views on the matter. Rebecca." The screen turns to Rebecca, who's sitting in a news studio with three other people. A woman, and two men.

"Thanks, Mike. I'm here with minister Miranda Taylor, Senator Jim O'Malley, and journalist Matthew Mitchell. Let's start with you, Miranda. You think that this was all an act of God?"

"Yes! Absolutely, Rebecca. How else did this happen? There's no way this was a natural scientific act. The scientists can't explain this, and they know there's no 'logical' explanation. This was intended. It was on purpose. This was grand design."

"Just because it can't be explained doesn't mean it's not a natural event. Scientists are not able to prove what did it, but you can't prove it was God either," Matthew, the journalist, retorts.

"My faith is my proof. It seems rather clear to me that this was a miracle," Miranda defends.

"And I respect your faith, Miranda, but you can't claim your beliefs as fact," Matthew states.

"Well, they are facts to me," Miranda says with certitude.

Matthew begins another retort, but Rebecca stops him, "Alright, we don't want to get too far off track. Jim, let's hear from you."

"I don't know how to explain it, Rebecca. I honestly don't think we'll ever really know how this happened. I don't know if it was natural or if it was grand design, but I do agree with Miranda in that it was a miracle. I know that some people are saying that we should take this as a warning. That we're polluting our Earth and killing it and this miracle gave us another chance. I don't see it that way. I think that whatever did this is looking out for us. Earth is meant to survive. I know I just called it a miracle and this may take away from that statement, but I actually think that it's adaptation. I think the world is always going to find a way to fix itself, and maybe God intended that or maybe it's just the way the world is. I don't know, but I don't think we need to go into panic. I don't think we need to drastically change our society and ways of life. This happened so we can continue living well and keep moving forward."

"I definitely agree with the last point Jim said. This was a sign that we're doing something right. We've been rewarded," Miranda says.

"I am not as confident as these two," Matthew, the journalist, chimes in. "However, I also don't see any reason to panic. I don't see any reason to be worried right now. Even if you believe in global climate change, and I do, we are in a vastly greater position than we were. I think the world should sit down and discuss how to preserve more of this newly restored land, but I think we have a lot of time to do so now."

"Alright, well, it looks like though not 100%, these three are all in agreement. We shouldn't be worried about the world. Things will be fine and we should enjoy this gift that has been handed to us."

Rebecca keeps talking on the TV, but I stop listening. I hope this isn't how the majority of the world will respond. Though, I can't say I'm surprised if it is. I mean, I talked to Jess about this. About "magically" healing the world, and how ultimately that would just lead to people justifying reasons not to change. Or at least not be in any hurry to.

I wonder if she's watching this interview or paying attention to any of this. I mean, she must be. And I'm sure she's pissed. I just hope she's okay. I hope Bright is there for her. I should be. I'll try to be soon.

"Let's watch something fun, or play a game or something," I suggest.

"Sure, yeah, that sounds like a good idea. You two down?" Jason asks Mara and Kate.

"Yeah," Kate says. Mara just nods.

"Wanna play *Pandemic*?" Jason asks.

"I don't really want to think about saving the world," I whine. "Can we just play *Monopoly?*"

Jason laughs, "Spoken like a true capitalist."

I playfully push him, "Shut up."

But he's right. Not thinking about the problems isn't going to make them go away. I'm going to contact L.I.S.N. and I'm going to reach out to Jess and Bright, and I'm going to do my best not to stop thinking about my issues and the world's issues, but to be aware and to be trying.

BRIGHT

"What should I say?" I ask myself, standing outside of Jessica's bedroom door. I just got home from school. I decided to walk, and on my way home I promised myself that I would finally attempt to break down this barrier between me and Jessica.

It's been a few days since her big stunt and our getting grounded. I wanted to give her time and myself time. I needed to figure out what to do or say and how to do or say it. Unfortunately, I didn't figure any of that out, and I feel like it's time to stop waiting. So I knock on her door.

"Yeah?" she calls out.

"Can I come in?" I ask.

There's a moment of hesitation before she answers, "Yeah."

I open the door and she's lying on the ground, staring at the ceiling, listening to Michelle Branch's "All You Wanted."

"Are you okay?" Is the first thing I think to ask.

"Yeah. I mean … I don't know," She admits.

"Well, do you want to talk about … whatever's going on in your head? I mean—that sounded like an insult, I didn't mean it to. I just meant …"

"It's okay, I know what you meant. I know we haven't really talked in a while, but you're still my twin, one of the people I know the best in this world,"

Jessica says. I grin a little bit and wait for her to continue. "I don't know. I'm just a little … spun. I think that's the word I'm looking for? Or does that mean high or drugged out or whatever? I remember that movie *Spun*, that was like about cocaine right?"

"I think it was meth. I don't really completely know the difference."

"Well, you get what I mean. I just, I don't regret what I did. I'm happy to have helped, and to have got the world talking. But I do regret keeping you out, and I hate that Rachel's not talking to us. And I hate lying to mom and dad. I feel like I made the right move, but I didn't do it with the people I love and the support I need."

"Well, for one, I was keeping you out just as much as you were keeping me," I confess. "I've been ashamed. I don't know how you've dealt with this for so long. I killed somebody. The fact that we brought her back doesn't change that. I ended someone's life and I could barely stand to look at myself, yet alone face you or Rachel. "

"Bright …"

"I know it was an accident, and that I can't destroy myself over this, and for the most part I've been doing a lot of thinking and searching since it happened, and I've come to some peace, but it still hurts. Does it ever go away?"

"I don't know," Jessica shakes her head. "I don't think so. I think it stays with you forever. The pain comes and goes and I think you just have to realize that this is how this works. There's no forgetting completely, or 'getting over it,' at least not without doing serious damage. You have to deal with it and talk when you need to and allow yourself and others to help. And most of all you have to remember that you're a human being. You deserve love and forgiveness. There are no monsters, as much as we like to believe there are, and therefore you are not one."

I start to cry and I walk over to Jessica and lie down beside her, now also staring up at the ceiling. "I really like the way it feels to be crying, lying on your back," I say.

"What do you mean?" Jessica asks.

"I don't know, there's something … powerful about it. The tears streaming down into your ears, the way you're breathing and voice deepen when you're on your back, I guess it just feels more … intense. I don't know."

"I think I get what you mean."

"I love you, Jessica."

"I love you, Bright," Jessica responds.

We sit in silence, "All You Wanted" still playing in the background. "Is this on repeat?" I ask.

Jessica laughs, "Yeah, I was feeling angsty and I love this song." She then starts to sing as the chorus comes in.

"I get it," I say after a few more moments of silence.

"What?" Jessica asks.

"I get needing to help. Feeling like you have to do something. But you know you don't, right?"

"I know. But I want to. I want to help. I want to care. I know there are millions of ways I can do and show that, but we have extraordinary gifts. I'm not going to tell you how to use yours or if you should, but for me, I have to be doing this. I want to be the somebody who cares. I don't believe in fate or whatever, but I know that there's a path that leads to these powers making great positive change, and I just need to figure out what that is."

"Okay. Well, from here on out, I'll help you figure that out. We'll try and find a way to help the world. To show it we care, and show it why it should, too."

Jessica smiles, but doesn't say anything else. There's no need. There's both too many things to say and no effective way of conveying them. Words couldn't do it. Something special happens when we allow ourselves to understand each other. There's a … spark. Though, "spark" doesn't do it justice. It's like a light shines on a connection that's always been there, and sometimes the light stays on, and sometimes it's brief, but either way, what you see while it's on changes something in you and in the other person. As twins, Jessica and I have always been connected more so than others, but this felt like we finally saw each other as individuals.

I close my eyes and I let myself go. Tears stream, but there's a smile on my face. The music is swelling in my heart. I don't know what I'm doing, but there's a clarity. I'm going to help Jessica, I'm going to help myself, and hopefully somewhere along the line it'll all make sense.

RACHEL

Maybe I should have called first, but I feel like jumping directly into this is what's best. Or at least I hope. I'm standing at the Walkers' front door and I take a deep breath as I ring the doorbell. It's Bright who answers.

"Hey …" He greets.

"Hi," I respond. "Can I come in?"

"Yeah, of course." Bright opens the door wider for me to enter and I go in and stand in the entrance.

"Jessica!" Bright yells.

"What?" Jess calls. I can hear her walking towards the front steps. Bright doesn't answer though. "What?" she calls again as she's heading down the stairs. She stops abruptly when she sees me. "Rachel …" She continues to walk down the stairs, comes directly to me, and hugs me. "I'm so sorry," she says as she pulls away from me, tears in her eyes.

I hate seeing her cry. I start to tear up too. "It's okay. Well, I mean, it's not okay, but I understand. I get why you wouldn't tell me. I get how it'd be harder and harder to tell me as time went on. It's still a lot to process, but I can't lose you two. I need you both. You're my family."

Bright walks over and hugs me from the side. "You'll never lose us." Jess then hugs me from the other side. And I try to hug back as best I can. We stand hugging each other until Bright finally breaks the silence, "Your coat is so comfy."

"I know," I smile. "It's so puffy. I love it."

I bend down to take my shoes off, and then remove my coat and Jess takes it from me to hang up.

"So what have you two been up to? Besides running around healing rainforests?" I ask.

Bright laughs and points to Jess, "That's all on her."

Jess slaps Bright on the arm, "Jerk! C'mon, it was a good thing."

"Yeah, it did get us to finally tell Mom and Dad about our healing abilities," Bright admits. "It also got us grounded, so I'd say it's about even."

"You told your parents? Like, about everything? Me? Sarah? All of that?" I ask.

"No," Jess answers. "We came clean about the healing abilities, but we didn't tell them about the accidental deaths we caused."

"Figured we're still not ready for that. I mean, I'm having a hard enough time dealing with it myself, I have no idea what they'd do. I mean, if they think we're dangerous, or at least can't control our abilities, they might actually tell someone," Bright adds.

"Like turn you over to the government?" I ask. "You actually think they'd do that?"

"I don't know," Bright shrugs. "I don't think they'd intend to hurt us, but what do you do when your superpowered teenagers tell you they've killed two people?"

I don't say anything. I don't really have anything to respond with. But I understand even more why they kept this from me.

"So, I assume your parents aren't home then? If you're grounded and all I mean."

"They're not home yet, but yeah, you should probably not be here when they are. Though I don't know, they'd probably be happy to see you. I don't think my mom totally buys that you haven't been here because of spending so much time with Jason," Jess says.

"That's what you told her? Really? That I'd ditch you when I get a bae?"

"I just said you had a new relationship and you'd been busy with school too. I don't think it sounded that bad," Jess defends. "Also, please tell me you're not saying 'bae' now."

"And what if I am?" I ask. "I'm not though, that was purely ironic. Jason started saying it ironically, but now he just says it all the time and I'm doing my best not to let it spread to me."

"So you and Jason are doing pretty well then, huh?" Jess asks.

"Yeah. We even said 'I love you,'"

"SHUT UP!" Jess screams. "Really?"

I laugh, "Yes! I'm in love!"

"That's so awesome! I'm really happy for you two!" Bright congratulates.

"Thanks. It's pretty crazy. It's beautiful and terrifying having someone romantically feel the same way about you as you do them. For a while you're just scared you'll fuck it up, but then it's just comfortable. It's amazing."

"Well, you'll have to tell me about all of it, so I can live vicariously through you," Jess demands.

"Me too," Bright adds. "Hera knows I'm not going out with anybody anytime soon."

"Hera?" I ask. "You praying to Greek goddesses now?"

"Wonder Woman says it a lot. I've been watching a lot of *Justice League* lately," Bright explains.

"We both have," Jess adds. "Not a lot else to do."

I laugh and notice we're still standing in the entryway, "Let's go sit down," I suggest.

"We can go up to my room," Jess offers. "But we should grab your shoes and coat and bring them up with us. That way when Mom and Dad get home, we can just teleport you home and stay out of trouble."

"I love that you two are grounded. I mean, they know you can teleport right?"

"Well, I think they're just relying on us being trustworthy. They know there's not much they can do if we really want to leave, but they also know we love them and don't want to cause any more drama," Bright answers.

"Yeah, I know. I was just kidding." I grab my shoes and Jess grabs my coat and we go up to her room. "So, what's next? I mean, I assume you're done pulling stunts like this if you're not trying to upset your parents further."

"I don't know," Jess says. "My first goal was to fix things with you and Bright. And both of you came to me first."

"Well, it's still a mission accomplished," Bright tells her.

"Yeah, but my point is, I didn't even know how to initiate that, I have no idea what I should do next."

"Well, what do you want?" I ask. "Like, what do you imagine feeling like you've done enough looking like?"

"I just want people to understand," Jess responds. "I want them to understand and to empathize. I want them to care about each other and this place. I just want an all around mutual respect."

"And you want to accomplish that?" I ask. "I don't think it's possible."

"I do," Jess retorts. "I don't know exactly what it looks like, but I know we have the capacity to live among each other and other living things without needing to own it all. Without needing to control it. Without fearing it. I mean, how long did we live on Earth in harmony with it? We know how."

"We know how, but what would it take to live like that again, to be able to?" Bright asks.

"All it takes is understanding," Jess declares.

"Yeah, well that's a lot of understanding," I rebut.

"Yeah …" Jess sighs.

"Well, another thing I wanted to talk to you about is this organization called L.I.S.N. that Jason's mom told me about. Seems pretty cool."

"Listen?" Bright asks.

"Yeah, L-I-S-N. Stands for Low-Income Sustainable Neighborhoods. Just sort of trying to educate communities on why they should care about their environment and the injustices happening around them that they might not know about," I explain.

"That does sound pretty cool," Jess concedes. "Have you talked to them yet or anything?"

"No, I just have the director's information. I wanted to see if you'd like to go with me?" I turn my head toward Bright, "Both of you, if you want."

"Yeah, I mean, I think it'd be good to at least check out. Honestly, it sounds great, but I don't know if I want to commit to it," Jess admits.

"Why not?" I ask. "It's helping people. Informing them. And it's in the field you want to be helping and informing people of."

"I know! I just … I don't like to get involved like this. I just feel like joining an organization means time and commitment to that organization, right? I don't know if I have that or want that. I'd probably like to help out with events or certain aspects, but I want to be doing my own thing."

"It's not like this will be your life. You can be as dedicated as you want to be. I feel like there's a lot you could take away from this," I argue, starting to get irritated.

"I think there probably is too. I'm just thinking a hundred steps ahead, like I always do. Deciding what's going to happen and then letting myself believe that's the only way for it to play out. I definitely want to go with you," Jess clarifies, pacifying me.

"Sorry I was so pushy. I just, I want to help, but I understand what you're saying," We all sit, not saying anything for a few seconds. "So, what about you Bright?" I ask.

"I'm not really interested, but I'll go," Bright shrugs.

I laugh. "Okay. I mean, you don't have to."

"No, I want to. I'm trying to get out of my comfort zone. We'll see what happens."

Jess smiles, "Look at us! All together again! I love you guys!"

"I love you too," I reply smiling.

"Me too," Bright adds. "It's good to have you both back in my life."

"Let's never fight again," I declare. "Whenever we get upset, let's just yell 'I LOVE YOU!' really angrily. Try not to let whatever happens beat the love."

"Nothing can beat the love," Jess says conclusively. "Love is everything."

"Well, scientifically speaking, I don't know if that's true," Bright retorts.

"Scientifically speaking, what do you know about it?" Jess counters.

"Not much," Bright laughs.

"Anyway," I cut in, "I'll email this guy and set up a date to meet after school some time."

"If our parents let us," Jess notes.

"I'm sure if you explain it they will," I encourage.

"I admire your optimism," Bright wisecracks.

"Well you two are coming with, whether you have to sneak out or not," I assert.

It's really nice to be sitting here with these two again. Just hanging out and being family. I've missed them a lot. But I am concerned. Jess is serious about making people understand, and I'm worried about her if she can't accomplish that. I just wish she would work on smaller goals, not try to literally take on the world.

"Rachel!" Jess yells.

"What?" I ask startled.

"I asked, how did you know it was me who did the restoration stuff?" Jess repeats.

"Oh, sorry. I just guessed, but I mean, who else would have done it? And I figured if you had healing powers, I'm sure you've thought about trying to heal things other than people."

"Yeah, I guess it's not too big an assumption to think that I was involved," Jess concedes.

"Yeah, not really …" I smirk.

"You okay?" Bright asks after a bit of silence.

"Me?" I ask.

"Yeah, you look … sad or something," Bright observes.

"I guess I'm just thinking about a lot of things," I express.

"Like what?" Bright asks.

"Well, I don't know. I just, I guess I'm just now thinking about you two having to lie to me and your parents and keep your distance from others, and that sucks, you know?"

"Yeah. I think so." Bright says with a hint of sarcasm.

"Sorry, I just mean, I don't think I can do that same thing forever," I assert.

"What do you mean?" Jess asks.

"I just mean that, do I have to lie to my dad forever, and to Jason? I love you, and I'm not trying to say I don't want to be involved or anything, I just ... can't lie all the time."

"I don't know what to tell you, Rachel. I mean, your dad I can see, but Jason? How will we know ... ?" Bright trails off, looking to Jessica for assistance.

"Know what?" I ask.

"How will we know that if you break up, he'll keep our secret? Or that he'll keep it at all whether you break up or not?" Jess continues.

I want to get upset. I can tell the way they're talking they're assuming the relationship won't last. Not taking it seriously because it's high school and my first relationship. But I refrain, because I'm imagining how it'd look if this was a teen drama. Them trying to be honest with me, and me freaking out, not wanting to hear anything bad about my relationship. And I remember how much I hate those moments. "You just have to trust people at some point," I insist. "I mean, I wouldn't tell anyone I thought would hurt you. But also, you want understanding and respect? That requires vulnerability. From you just as well as everyone else."

"That's easy to say, but who knows what people will do? What they'll want to do with us," Bright argues.

"You've never hurt anyone. They ..."

"Except you," Jess interrupts me. "And Sarah."

"We've killed people," Bright bursts out. "That's not something people will take lightly, especially from black, superpowered teens."

I stop and think. They're right. I'm living in a fantasy world if I think people will just accept them without any objections. "There's got to be some way though," I implore. "I mean, you can just evade them. Or also, like, nobody knows you killed anyone. Nobody has to know. I'll never tell, and I'm the only other person who knows."

"So more lying then?" Jess asks.

"Maybe on this one thing, but you don't deserve to be locked up," I attest.

"Maybe Jess doesn't. Hers was a complete accident," Bright counters.

"And yours wasn't?" Jess asks.

"No. It was an accident, but not one due to my powers. If anyone else hit someone with a car and covered it up, they'd deserve to be locked up right?" Bright asks. "Jess didn't know she had superstrength. Nobody can fault her for killing you. For hurting you, yes, but ... I was just not being responsible. Not paying attention to the road. That's all on me."

"Bright ..." I start, but I don't know how to finish. Everything I can think to say just sounds cliché and not enough. "Look, I know you both. I know who you are. You're not killers. Neither of you would ever want to hurt anyone. We don't need to tell people about the killing. I mean, there's not even anyway to prove you killed us. It'd just be unnecessary."

"Well, I don't know about that. But it doesn't matter. We're not telling anybody," Bright orders.

"So you just decide?" I demand.

"Look, he's right. I mean, we can still think on Jason and your dad, but the world? Neither of us is ready for that. I don't even know how we'd do that," Jess jumps in.

"But you'll think about it? I wouldn't ask this of you if it wasn't important to me," I assure.

"We'll think about it," Bright agrees. "But for now, let's just figure out this L.I.S.N stuff and go from there."

I nod. I didn't even plan on asking any of that. Just all sort of came out. I don't know what will happen if they ultimately say no. That I can't tell Jason or my dad. I'd never tell their secret without their permission, but the thought of continuously lying to people I care about forever is hell. "Well yeah, like I said, I'll email this guy and I'll let you know what he says," I tell them.

I decide to leave now before their parents get home. I don't really know what else to say right now and I don't think they do either. We all just have to think for a while, or at least just be on our own. I put my shoes and coat back on at the door, and we all hug.

"I love you," Jess says before I go.

I smile back, "I love you too."

JESSICA

·⌒·

It's a Wednesday after school and we're driving to the L.I.S.N. office. Bright tries to avoid driving if he can most of the time now, so I'm at the wheel.

"I'm so tired," Bright announces.

"Nobody told you to stay up watching shit all night," I retort.

"I wasn't tired then," Bright defends.

"Whatever. So Rachel, is this like a whole class thing, or what're we going to be doing when we get there?" I ask.

"No, it's just us and the director. His name is Ryan Kranz. He said it'll be just a brief meeting. He'll tell us more about the organization and answer any questions we have," Rachel answers.

"Good. I don't really like walking into a whole group right away like that," I say.

"Yeah, he said he figured this would be less intimidating," Rachel concurs.

I nod. In the silence, I realize a song that I hate has just started on the radio, so I change the station. I don't recognize the song that's on, but I like it. The guitar riff brings the word "unstable" to mind. It perfectly captures the feeling of uncertainty and anxiousness I'm feeling right now. "Do either of you know who this is?" I ask after a minute or so of listening.

Bright shakes his head.

"I could Shazam it," Rachel offers. She pulls out her phone and she responds, "'Go' by Meg Myers. I like this too. I'll have to check her out."

"For sure," I agree. "Is this it?" I ask, pulling into the L.I.S.N. parking lot.

"What?" Rachel asks, having been looking at her phone. She looks up and catches on, "Oh, yeah, looks like it. Smaller than I expected."

"Yeah," Bright nods.

I park the car and we all get out.

"God, fuck the cold!" Bright cries stepping out of the car.

"You do realize we've been living in the great white north our whole lives right? You should be used to it," Rachel points out.

"I thought The Great White North was Canada," Bright challenges.

"Well, right under it then. Whatever," Rachel concedes.

Bright shoves Rachel playfully and we all start walking toward the building. It's a gloomy day out, all overcast.

"This is a little ominous. Walking toward this dimly lit office building, no sun shining. I mean, the guy could be a murderer," Bright alleges.

"You two could easily out murder him, so I think we're fine," Rachel counters.

"Can we not talk about killing people?" I say seriously. "This is supposed to be a new chapter for us."

"Yeah, sorry," Rachel grimaces.

I try to open the front door, but it's locked. I try the other one with no luck, so I knock. A few seconds later, a man appears and waves on his way to let us in. We all wave back.

"Hi!" he greets, opening the door. We all enter and he continues, "I'm Ryan."

We all introduce ourselves and shake his hand. Ryan then has the three of us follow him into a conference room. There's a whiteboard and a sole laptop on the conference desk with office chairs around it. We exchange a bit of small talk. He tells us he's 24 and a graduate from the U of M in environmental science.

After getting to know a little bit about us, he goes over the basics of the organization and then opens it up for questions.

"So, like, what exactly would we be doing?" I ask. "As beginners, I mean."

"Well, first we'd have you take some courses here on the information we'll be telling people. Once you feel like you're confident in that, we'll have you shadow a veteran member as they go around the neighborhoods so you can get a feel for what it's like and ease into it. It can be a bit awkward going door to door. You might feel like you're intruding on people. Also, it's safer going with a partner. You'll always be accompanied by at least one other person whenever you're canvassing. But yeah, basically after that, you'll be doing your best to immerse yourself into these neighborhoods. Going to block club meets, youth farms, farmers' markets, helping with community gardens, anything to really learn the people you're trying to help."

"That sounds great!" Rachel exclaims.

"Awesome! We always love recruiting new people. It's a fun process, teaching, and learning from them. A lot of time the people we recruit are from neighborhoods like we're trying to help, so they have a lot of insight on how to effectively communicate without sounding holier than thou, or too preachy, you know?"

"Yeah, that's something I'm really interested in," I reply. "Community bonding. Effectively listening and helping to bring understanding."

"Well, yeah, that's especially a lot of what we're doing in these months leading to and during winter. There's not as much outside activity to do, so we work on recruiting and strengthening our connections with the neighborhoods we're trying to help. Listening is probably the most important thing. We can spout our agenda at them all day, but it doesn't matter if they don't care. What we aim to do is actually listen to what their concerns are. Most of the time their issues are connected to our issues. I mean, that's just most of life. Generally, all our issues are connected, right?" Ryan pauses for a second. We nod and he continues, "A lot of these families and communities don't have easy access to healthy food options, the crime rates are high, there's a strong distrust of police, and they're skeptical at best about the government. People are working two to three jobs, taking public transportation—which is generally more time consuming than driving yourself—they're taking care of their children, their elders, and hopefully themselves. It's not that they don't care that their environment is polluted and that their health is at risk, it's just that there are so many more pressing matters to them. They don't want to hear about picking up trash, or starting community gardens, or contacting local officials to press for better environmental policies in their neighborhood. They want to have enough money for rent. They want to keep their jobs. They want their families to be safe. That's all they have time for. And if they have free time, they're tired. They don't want to do more work. So we have to listen. We have to hear them. And only then can we try and work together and show them that what we're proposing can help with some of these things. That it can lessen some of those burdens."

"It sounds like you're really passionate about this," I note.

"Yeah, it's rewarding work. I love what I do. And I mean, oftentimes we can't reach a whole neighborhood, but we can at least reach one individual or one household," Ryan responds.

"Do you ever get burnt out?" Bright asks. "I imagine you have to dedicate a lot of time to this. Do you ever get tired of it?"

"Well, sure," Ryan responds. "I mean, we all burn out at times. But I'm really happy doing what I do, and I couldn't just stop worrying about people and our environment. I do take vacations, though, and I take time for myself and friends and family, but they also know this means a lot to me and are understanding of my long work hours."

There's a small silence, and then Rachel asks, "So if we do sign up, when would we start?"

"Good question. We do our recruitment classes on the weekend so it doesn't interfere with school or work for most people. I think there's some classes this weekend." Ryan checks something on his laptop and then nods. "Yeah, this weekend. You guys wanna sign up?"

"Yeah!" Rachel nods, excited.

I look to Bright, and he's looking to me for guidance as well. "Yeah, I think

I'd like to try it." I say to Ryan.

"Me too," Bright follows.

"Awesome!" Ryan says and pulls some papers out of an envelope. "So we'll just need you to read these over and sign them, as well as your parents, and just bring them when you come back this weekend. The class starts at nine." We each take a signup sheet and begin looking it over. "If there's anything you need answered later, just give the office a call. Do you have any other questions for me now?"

We all look around at each other, and then shake our heads.

"Alright. Well, it was nice meeting you all, and I look forward to working more with you," Ryan says.

We all get up and he shakes our hands again, then he walks us out.

"Well, I think this is going to be awesome," Rachel states on our way back to the van.

"Yeah, I guess I still have doubts, but I am really interested to see how this goes," I admit.

I get in the driver's seat and Rachel sits next to me in the front while Bright gets in the back.

"So, what's up?" I ask. "What are we doing?"

"Well, I was actually going to head home. Told Jason I'd call him about how it went, and I've got some homework to do." Rachel replies. "And also, aren't you grounded?"

"Oh yeah," I recall as I start the van. "I keep forgetting. We've never really been grounded before. I'm not used to this. We still don't even have an end date."

"Well, I mean, it hasn't been that long," Rachel points out.

"Whose side are you on here?" I ask.

Rachel smiles, "I'm just saying, people are still sort of freaking out over this. Like, it's still everywhere."

"Yeah, I don't know if this is ever really going to blow over," Bright declares.

"Well, that was the idea," I reply. "But yeah, definitely could have been better thought out."

A lot of things I do could probably be better thought out, but this one definitely takes the cake. I mean, I've just confused everyone. Even the people I wanted to help. The world's scientists have no idea what happened. It completely throws off everything they know. Bruce Banner's line from *The Avengers* pops into my head, where he equates the team to a chaotic chemical time bomb. That's exactly how I feel. I thought I was helping, but I didn't do anything but throw everything into chaos. And I'm tired of confusion. I'm tired of feeling unsure. I'm tired of hurt and pain. I'm tired of tears. I realize that I haven't really listened. I haven't been hearing the people around me or the people of the world. I've been seeing the pain. And so it's been driving me insane, doing nothing. You can't see pain and want to do nothing. Not when you have the power to do things most could only dream of doing. But if I want understanding, and healing, and true connection, then I have to get uncomfortable. And I have to be patient. And I have to realize that though constant inaction is harmful, doing something—especially in the name of the entire human race—without real thought or understanding is probably just as damaging if not worse.

So though I'm not sure this is what I want to do, at least this is something thought out. Something I know is beneficial. It still feels like there's more to be doing, but I can't do it all at once.

BRIGHT

"How'd the meeting go?" Dad asks when we get home.

"I dunno, it was alright," I reply. "I mean, the Ryan guy seems pretty cool."

"Doesn't seem like you're too enthusiastic about it," Dad notes.

I shrug, "I think she is more than I am."

Dad turns his attention over to Jessica, "Yeah, how did you feel about it?"

"I'm really hoping it's what I'm looking for," Jessica responds.

"And if it's not?" Dad asks.

"I don't know, what does that mean?" Jessica counters.

Dad looks to Mom, who's standing next to him, "We just want to make sure you're not going to do anything like you've already done," He explains.

"We want to trust that you'll continue to be responsible, even if this doesn't work out," Mom adds.

"Then do. Trust me," Jessica states.

"We do. We trust you, but we also get that you're feeling like you're not being taken seriously. Feeling like your voice doesn't count because you're young and inexperienced. Or I mean, that's how society makes teenagers feel. So of course they want to rebel, and they want to feel like they're making a difference. And we get that you having the extraordinary gifts that you do makes that urge so much stronger," Mom says. She pauses to think about how she wants to continue. "We all make rash decisions throughout life, especially as a teen, and you—as we've seen—have the misfortune of being capable of making history-changing ones. We just want you to promise that you'll think things out. You'll talk to us about what's going on. That's all."

Jessica walks up to Mom and hugs her, "I promise I'll talk to you more about what's going on with me."

Mom hugs Jessica back, resting her chin on Jessica's head.

"So, like … does this mean we can be done with the grounding?" I ask.

Dad smiles, "No."

I slouch in defeat, "Okay, well I'm gonna get started on my health report."

"Yeah, I should get a jump on my homework too," Jess agrees, pulling away from Mom.

Jessica and I both head upstairs and into our respective rooms. I leave my door open and drop my backpack on the floor next to my desk, then sit down in my computer chair. A few seconds after I pull my health folder out of my bag, Jessica knocks on my door.

"Can we talk?" Jessica asks.

"Yeah sure, what's up?" I ask.

Jessica closes my door and takes a few steps in, but stays standing. "I have a feeling that Mom and Dad are right."

"What do you mean?" I ask.

"I still feel like there's something more I have to be doing. I'm going to do my best to take it slow. To realize that I can't do it all at once. I know I can't save everyone and everything. But there's so much happening. I'm not only thinking about the environment. That's just what I decided to work on right now, and it's hard to even scale that down. But if I see one more video of a black man or woman being gunned down by police, or a bombing in Europe, or a bloody child in Syria—things I'm for sure going to see, things I know I can't fix with my powers—how am I supposed to deal with that? No protesting, no appealing to officials, no local organization is going to bring change quick enough. L.I.S.N. is slow. And it should be. It has to be. The work they're doing can't be rushed.

But it's hard to accept that, Bright. I can't be sure that I'll be able to think that a slow method is the right option the next time something awful happens. And really, something awful is always happening."

"Jessica, you said it earlier that you think too far ahead. You decide what will happen and allow that to be the only outcome. You don't have to think about how you'll react to what comes next. You can't know. But I'll be there. Rachel will be there. Mom and Dad will be there. Talk to us. Even if you think it's annoying us. Even if you think it's the same shit you've been saying and we're tired of hearing it. You have to keep us in. And the same goes for us with you."

"Saying the same thing over and over makes me feel crazy," Jessica responds. "At some point I'd have to either accept that we're not going to agree or accept that I'm wrong. Either way, why would I continue to talk about it with you?"

"I'm saying that's not the only option. It's not like we're going to shut down everything you say. We may even agree with you. But your goal is to have understanding, so that means you have to continuously be showing people what you feel. You have to be talking. You have to be expressing yourself. And if you can't even do that with us, if you shut us out, then you'll shut the world out. And when people shut the world out, that's when they think they know everything. That's when they think they and they alone can know what's best. That's exactly what you don't want. Talking with us even if we disagree doesn't mean you have to accept that you're wrong. It doesn't mean you should just not talk with us. It means that we have different ideas and viewpoints, and hopefully together we come up with something we all can support."

"I know," Jessica sighs, "But think about all that's still going to happen while we're talking and making slow change. We're still going to be destroying the planet. We're still going to be destroying each other. I don't know how, but I know we can make lasting change with what we have. Our abilities have to mean something." She takes a few steps back and leans against the door, slowly sliding down to a sitting position.

"I don't know if that's true. I don't think it has to mean anything." I look to Jessica and she looks like she's on the verge of tears. "What do you see needing to happen to bring about what you talked about earlier? Making people care about each other, and our planet, and understanding."

Jessica thinks for a moment, "I don't know. I mean, I guess they'd have to be free to be able to. They'd have to not be distracted by bills, or having enough food, or a place to stay. They'd need to not be forced to think of other places as enemies, or outsiders. They'd need to know what's going on in the world. For real. They'd need to know what's going on with their own government. They'd just need to know."

"So how do we make them know?" I ask.

RACHEL

〽️

"So you want to try and out all acts of corruption, not only in the US, but in the world?" I ask Jess and Bright. We're all in my room after school. Jess and Bright teleported us here. Dad's at work and their parents won't be home for a little while either. "And how do you expect to be able to do this? I mean, you have a lot of powers, but I don't think they'll really make a difference in this case."

"I know. If only we had technopathy or something," Jess replies.

"Like Micah from *Heroes*?" I ask.

"Yeah. Then we could just hack our way into every government database and fuck shit up!" Jess exclaims.

"Yeah, I think you'd do exactly that—fuck shit up. Just because you'd have all the information—which even if you did have technopathy, you wouldn't know how to find or what to be looking for, nor is most of it even catalogued I'm sure—you'd have to prove it and have people believe it. I feel like it'd just throw things into chaos," I counter.

"My thing was that I feel like most people don't even trust the government completely. Most people assume shady shit is happening," Bright cuts in. "So, they just don't think there's anything they can do about it. And even if there is, they get to our dilemma of wondering what's even right to do."

"But it doesn't matter," Jess states. "We just need to give them the knowledge. We need to show them what's happening. And once the information is out there, whatever happens is up to them. Or us ... all of us."

We all sit in silence for a while before I ask, "Have you guys tried technopathy?"

"Yeah, of course," Jess replies.

"Since we don't know where our powers came from, or what they even are, we've tried doing pretty much everything we can think of. As far as we know, the powers we have are the only ones we'll get," Bright adds.

"Well," I say, throwing my hands behind my head to rest my head on, "It seems to me that there's no way of doing what you want to do. I mean, plus you'd have to be able to speak a shit ton of different languages to attempt that. I think you just have to stay on the smaller goals, Jess. Just keep with me with L.I.S.N. We'll figure something out."

"Yeah, I don't know. I guess you're right." Jess gets up, having been sitting on my bed, "I think we should probably go, Mom and Dad will be back soon."

"Tell Jason we say 'hey' and that we wish we could make it to the game," Bright tells Rachel.

"Yeah, I will. I wish you could be there too. His family isn't going to be there tonight, and I don't really know anybody else who'll be there that well," I express.

"Well, you can make some new friends, maybe," Jess says in a forced cheerful way.

"Eh, I'm good. Also ..." I trail off, afraid to approach the subject.

"What?" Bright asks.

"Well, I just ... I don't mean to nag you, but have you thought anymore about telling Jason and my dad about your powers?" I ask.

"Not really," Bright says, "Why?"

I get a bit annoyed at the question, "Because I don't want to lie anymore. And I can't make new friends, Bright. I can't let people into my life and keep such a huge secret from them."

"People keep their friends' secrets, Rachel. You wouldn't be the first," Jess argues.

"This is not just any regular secret. I mean, you're talking about outing all corruption in the world. Even if you're not going with that plan, that's huge. I'm helping you. I want to help you. I want to be a part of whatever happens, but I can't be having this on my mind and not be able to tell the other people I love about it." I take a few deep breaths, "I can already see that it's coming between me and Jason. With everything that's happened lately, I opened up to him a lot, talking to him about my mom and my relationship with my dad, my friendship with you guys, but he can tell I'm not telling him everything. I forgive you about my dying, but it's not something I'll ever forget. It's not something that's easy to get over, and not being able to talk to him about it is … it sucks. It really fucking sucks."

Jess and Bright look to each other, and then out the window and to the ground respectively. I can see Jess is starting to cry. "What if they hate us? What if they don't trust us?" she asks.

"What? Why would they hate you?" I respond.

"Because I killed you! Because we're potentially extremely dangerous, and I already killed you once. Why wouldn't they hate me?" Jess asks.

"Because you've been my friends for my whole life, and I trust you. My dad loves you like a daughter, he'd never hate you," I say.

"But Jason doesn't know us as well as your dad does," Bright points out. "And if you're planning on telling them everything, your dad is going to want to talk to our parents about it. I don't care what you say, no parent is going to accept that their daughter was killed and brought back to life and be cool with it."

"Well, I'm sure he'll be upset, but … I mean, maybe you should tell your parents," I suggest.

"Rachel, there's no way this is going to end well. There's no way everything will be okay," Jess retorts. "Either we'll have to tell our parents first or tell everyone together. If we tell our parents first, there's no way we'll even see you for months, maybe even years. They already grounded us both indefinitely for the forest thing. I honestly do think they'd consider telling professionals about us if they found out about you and Sarah."

I'm getting a bit flustered, so I try and take my time before responding, "Look, I'm telling you that I can't lie anymore. I know this is hard for you, but eventually I have to be allowed to let others in, and to let them in completely."

"This isn't just hard," Bright cries, tears forming in his eyes, "This is life altering. This could seriously change things for us, who knows what will happen?"

This time, I end up looking out the window. I don't know what to say. I get what they're telling me, but I'm not giving up on this. I can't continue to sacrifice my personal relationships. And I know they feel the same. I know they want to be more social and not be hiding forever. "Look, I get that everything any of us do is always judged. Through our gender, our race, our clothes, our schools, our families, we're already fighting hard not to be seen as an 'other.' Not to be judged before we even act. And I get that your powers make that much more dire for you than it is for me. I know that there's a lot of risk with what I'm asking you to do. But I think this is a first step to you not having to hide yourselves from the world. I know it's not what you want for your whole lives."

"I just don't know if I can do it, Rachel," Jess declares. "I guess all I can really say is that we'll think about it. Really, we'll go home and we'll talk it out, but I can't … there's no way I can promise we'll do this."

"I get it," I respond.

"We really should go," Bright insists.

I nod.

Bright and Jess gather their things. We all stand awkwardly in silence before Jess says that they'll talk to me tomorrow.

"Okay," I respond. The next second they're gone.

I let out a deep sigh and fall face-first on my bed. About a minute later, Rebel comes in and jumps right up next to my head. I roll to my side and scoop her into my arms. "At least I can tell you everything," I tell her.

I laugh at myself because I realize that if Jess and Bright don't go along with this idea, that I'll probably end up a crazy cat lady. They'll be the only other friends I can get close to and be honest with. I pull Rebel closer and I kiss her on the head.

I kind of wish I hadn't had that conversation with them before going to Jason's game tonight. It'll just add to me lying to him about what I'm feeling. But it needed to happen, and as long as they really are thinking about it this time, I've got to give them their time with it. Hopefully it's not too much time.

BRIGHT

"I'm afraid," I tell Jessica, as we get back to our house. "I'm pretty sure that I'm going to get the worst of this. If Rachel's dad or our parents or Jason respond negatively, I'm pretty sure it'll be because of me."

"Bright, it's not all on you. Don't do that to yourself."

"It is, though. It is. They might be afraid and upset after you tell them what happened to Rachel, but like I said, ultimately there was no way you could know that was going to happen. You didn't know about your powers. You can't be held accountable for that. With me hitting Sarah, that has nothing to do with powers, that was all on me. And then we covered it up. We healed her, and we covered it up. We did that on purpose. With Rachel, we didn't even heal her on purpose. It just sort of happened. It was all sudden and we knew nothing about what was happening. Yes we chose to lie then, but we were kids."

"We're kids now!" Jessica interrupts.

"Yeah, but we know this is wrong. This isn't excusable."

"Well, again, we all chose to do this. Or at least you and I did. You didn't act alone. I could have pushed you to respond like any normal person, tell you to call the police, get her to a hospital as quickly as possible, but I decided along with you and that we were going to heal her."

"I think you remember it differently than I do. You did push for a hospital. You pushed for more responsibility. You were the one who said someone should stay and make sure she got home safely. You were the one who stayed."

"But I still decided we should heal her. I was the one who said that to you. I didn't even think about going about it without powers."

I don't respond for a few seconds. Some of what she says sinks in, but then I remember the sound of Sarah's head hitting the hood, and the blood. I remember her body, limp and lifeless on the ground. "It doesn't matter. The point is, because I hit Sarah, and we brought her back, that shows more danger. Your accidentally killing Rachel can easily be forgiven, easily be seen as a child's error, even with the powers. But me killing Sarah and then us covering it up with our powers now … that's criminal. That's not something that anyone, no matter how much they love us, will take lightly."

I try to avoid Jessica's eyes, but in the end I can't. And when I see them, there's heartbreak and empathy in them. "Bright …" she starts. "I think Rachel is right, I think this needs to happen. I know this was just theoretical, but … I think you're fucked up." She must see the hurt in my eyes, because she quickly rephrases. "I don't mean you're a bad person or crazy. I mean, we're all fucked up. Rachel has to be allowed to talk about what happened, and so do we."

"I can't face that," I say.

"I don't know if I can either, but we have to. We have to do it, and we'll do it together." Jessica walks over to me and hugs me. "We need help, Bright."

Everything in me lets go. I cry into Jessica's shoulder. I sob. She cries too, but more reserved. She's holding on for both of us in this moment. For all the power we have, for all you'd expect of us, we're still just human. We're all continuously shattered, and rebuilt, and learning. We're all children. At all times. I know this now. Rachel and Jessica are right, we need help. I need help. And the only way for that to happen is to be vulnerable, to be honest. We have to tell them everything.

JESSICA

Rachel, Bright, and I are walking home from school. We're having all our parents and Jason meet us at Rachel's place. We felt it would be better for Mr. Crowley and Jason to be in a place of comfort for what we're about to tell them.

We don't really have a plan. We thought if we talked about it too much, we'd find some way to talk ourselves out of it. So we're walking in silence. We could teleport, but this way we do get time to prep ourselves a bit, and also we'd rather they were all there before us. We told them it was important and it couldn't wait, so they should all be there by the time we get there.

I can tell that Bright and Rachel are more nervous than I am. Bright wasn't wrong yesterday. I think there is more potential for him to get the brunt of the harsh reaction. And I think Rachel stands to lose the most. She and her dad lose the ground they've gained recently with their relationship, and she could lose Jason all together. She could even lose us as well. I know we'll at least have an extended grounding, and if Mr. Crowley responds negatively, he could refuse to let us hang out anymore.

I mean, the more I think about it, the more reasons I can think of not to do this. This is going to suck … .

We arrive at Rachel's house, and we all look to each other and hug.

"Thank you for doing this," Rachel says, "I know this risks a lot for you."

"You stand to lose a lot too, and I think we all stand to lose more in the long run if we don't do this," I respond.

"I love you both," Bright expresses. He's the most frightened I've ever seen him. He's shaking, and he looks physically ill.

"We love you too, Bright," Rachel comforts, rubbing a hand along his shoulder.

"We're going to be okay," I assure.

We all make our way to the door. Rachel opens it and we step in.

"We're in here!" Mr. Crowley calls from the kitchen.

We remove our shoes and coats and we all take hands for a moment, standing in silence. This is the closest I've ever been to praying, but I don't even think anything. I just free my mind and try to extend my love and energy to Bright and Rachel. I can feel something build inside of me. Or us, rather. Somehow I know we're on the same page. That we all understand. I feel what they feel, and they feel what I feel. It's similar to what I'd assume being "Drift Compatible" feels like, like they do in Pacific Rim. However, I don't share every aspect of them. I don't know their minds, but there's an understanding that I can't explain.

We let go of each other's hands and we head into the kitchen. Nobody is sitting except for Jason.

"So what's going on? Are you guys okay?" Mom asks. They all look worried. Though Jason looks more uncomfortable.

"We're okay, but we have some things to tell you that …" I start, not sure how to finish.

"We just ask that you let us get everything out. You listen and hear us, and let us get to the end, and then you can be … whatever you need to be," Rachel adds.

"What are you talking about, Rach?" Mr. Crowley asks.

Bright and I share a look, and then he starts to levitate, lifting slowly from the floor, and I teleport to the other side of the room. Jason jumps from the stool he's sitting on and Mr. Crowley almost falls backward as I appear right beside him.

"What the hell?" Mr. Crowley tries to formulate other words, but nothing quite comes out complete. Jason doesn't say anything. He just stares in shock at Bright, still hovering in the air.

"We have superpowers," Bright confesses.

"What are you doing?" Dad asks in anger. "You don't ... what ..." I know he's trying to ask us why we'd do this. Why we're risking this. I just hope he and Mom understand in the end.

"We have powers," I say, "And our parents know. Rachel knows also. We couldn't keep it from her. She's our best friend. And it was impossible for our parents not to find out. We developed these powers about four years ago, and our parents thought it was best to keep it hidden from everyone. We thought about telling you before, Mr. Crowley, but we were afraid of what you'd think. We were afraid you'd keep Rachel away from us. That's something I still fear, especially with what we're about to tell you."

I take a moment to gather my thoughts to see how I want to continue. Bright lowers himself back to the ground and then teleports over to me. He takes my hand in his for support. "So you've seen that we have teleportation and flight, but we also have superstrength, superspeed, and the power to heal. That last power we kept hidden from even Rachel and our parents until very recently."

"Why?" Mr. Crowley cuts in. "Why of all the ... powers, or abilities, would you feel you need to keep that one secret?"

"Because, we didn't want to talk about how we found out we could heal," Bright answers. He grips my hand tighter. He knows I'm the one who has to continue this.

"I found out ..." I start, but before I continue, Rachel joins me and Bright, and we're now all holding hands once again, Bright to my right, Rachel on my left, closest to her dad. "The way we found out we had powers was that ... one day while Mom and Dad were out, Rachel and I were playing Xena like we often did. And she accidentally hit me in the face with the broomstick we were using as a pretend staff. I got upset and ... I hit her back. Only I hit her way harder than should have been possible for any human ... and I ended up snapping her neck." Tears start welling in my eyes. The fear is setting in. This is real now. There's no turning back.

"What?" Mr. Crowley asks. "What do you mean you snapped her neck? Are you saying she died … ?" He's getting upset, and rightfully so.

"I died, Dad." Rachel confirms. "And I know this is upsetting. Not only for you, but for Mrs. and Mr. Walker, and for Jason. This is a lot to take in, but we need to get through it all, and I just ask that you let them continue." Mr. Crowley starts to protest, but Rachel cuts him off. "Dad, I'm fine now. I'm fine, and that's what matters. We want this to all be out in the open so that we all can heal. I asked them to tell you this. I asked them to come forward and be honest with everyone. They were afraid because they feared that you would fear them. All of you. And … just don't let them be right. Please …" Rachel looks all around the room. Everyone stays quiet for now.

"Jessica accidentally killed Rachel that day," Bright starts back up. "She screamed and she cried and I came down running. I eventually gathered what had happened and I panicked. I had always been told to call 911 in emergencies, to call my parents, but I didn't know what to do. I didn't want Jessica to be in trouble. I thought she'd be taken away. I wanted to protect her like I was always told to do, and I couldn't handle it. I couldn't figure it out. And so we sat and we cried, and I guess we were focused on wanting Rachel to be alive again. And we somehow brought her back. We started to notice color coming back to her, and then she was breathing again, and then she woke up."

"We didn't know what was happening," I continue. "It was all so overwhelming. And we didn't know how to explain any of it, or how we'd make anyone believe it, or how to do either of those things without being in trouble. So we kept it a secret. And over the next few days and weeks, the powers kept manifesting, and eventually we mastered them."

Nobody says anything for some time. Nobody knows how to process what's been said. "So what made you change your mind?" Jason eventually asks. It's the first thing he's said this whole time. "What made you tell Rachel?"

Bright is the one who has to answer this one. It's his burden to release. "We told Rachel, because she witnessed us bring someone else back to life.

About two months ago, I hit and killed a woman jogging. We were all in the van, and I was driving, and … I wasn't paying attention and … I hit her." Bright starts to cry, and I grip his hand firmly. "Jess and I brought her back to life, and we went on like nothing ever happened. But Rachel now knew about our healing abilities, and we knew we couldn't lie to her about them. We had to tell her the truth about what had happened."

I think that everyone in the room has tears in their eyes, expect for Jason. "What do you mean you went on like nothing ever happened? What happened to that woman?" Dad asks.

"Bright took Rachel home, and I waited with her until she was fully conscious. I told her I had found her passed out, and I helped her home. I've actually kept in touch a bit since then. She's a really nice woman," I answer. I notice the surprise in Rachel and Bright's eyes as I say this.

"I don't know what to say," Mr. Crowley expresses after a few more moments of silence. "So how did you find out about their healing then?" He turns to ask our parents.

"I'm also the one behind the massive restoration of the world's forests," I tell him. "I've been wanting to help world with our powers for a long time, and after the thing with Sarah—the woman we brought back to life—I really needed to do something. So I used our healing powers to restore forests, and Bright ended up telling our parents and, yeah, that's how they found out."

"None of this makes any sense. None of this makes any fucking sense," Mr. Crowley yells. He then turns toward Mom and Dad. "I just don't understand how you all could keep this from me. I mean, besides just as a common courtesy from one parent to another, Rachel and I had lost Katherine. Did you not think about how this could come between us? Making my daughter lie to me for an indefinite amount of time?"

"David, I'm sorry, but we had to think about our children's well being. We had no idea how you would act, and until just now, we had no reason to believe they were of any danger. We were always so careful, and so were they. Before now, we saw no reason to alarm you." There's a hint of plea in Mom's voice. I look to Bright, and I can tell he's feeling what I'm feeling. Mom said *before now* she had no reason to believe we were dangerous.

"So you think we're dangerous now?" I ask.

"What?" Mom responds, clearly not on the same thought process as I am.

"You see us differently now, don't you? Now that you know about what's happened. Now that you know we have the potential to kill," I insist.

"Honey …" Mom starts, but it's clear she doesn't know exactly what to say next. Or maybe she's afraid to say it. "You always had the potential to kill. Just like everybody else. But you're right, I do see you differently. Because you lied. Because you covered it up. That's what makes it so dangerous. Both of your incidents were accidents, and they're not excusable, but they were accidents. Lying and covering it up is not an accident. That is not taking responsibility. That's murder."

"Mom …" I want to tell her that's not fair. I want to say to her everything I said to Bright. I want her to understand that we were just doing what we thought we had to. But all of a sudden, it all just feels empty. It all feels like an excuse. I can see it in Mr. Crowley's eyes, and Jason's, along with Mom's and Dad's. We're no longer "good" in their eyes. We're monsters. We're murderers. We're dangerous.

Bright is crying harder than I have ever seen him cry. His worst fears are coming true. I didn't let myself think about it too much, but I'm quickly realizing these are my worst fears too. I had no plan for this. For everyone to be against us. I feel alone. Like a tether has been cut. Bright and I are Sandra Bullock and George Clooney out in space, hoping to hold onto one another. Wanting to believe—against everything that's before us—that it'll all be okay. That we'll find home again.

Home is gone.

RACHEL

I don't know what's happening. I didn't expect this. Their parents aren't being supportive. Dad isn't being supportive. Jason has barely said anything. Maybe I fucked up. I shouldn't have asked them to do this. Lying was better than this. What's going to happen now?

"I think you need to leave," Dad demands.

"What?" I ask.

"They need to leave, Rachel! This isn't okay! What do you expect me to say, that I'm over it? They killed you! I don't care if they brought you back! They killed you! And they killed again after that! They're dangerous. And clearly their parents can't control them!" I've never seen Dad yell like this. I've never given him reason to. He isn't wrong about what he said to Mrs. and Mr. Walker—my having to lie to him did hurt our relationship. I've been mostly thinking about how it would hurt it in the future, but keeping Bright and Jess's secret is a big part of what made me tell dad less about my life. And the less I told him the small things, the harder it got to tell him bigger things.

But that's not all on them. It was an amalgam of things that made that happen. And what were they supposed to do? There's no handbook for how to raise your superpowered kids. All of this is getting out of hand. All I wanted was for us all to be honest, to all be on the same page. Now I feel like there's a bigger division than ever.

"We're NOT monsters!" Bright yells. Jess tries to calm him, but he doesn't listen. "This is exactly why we didn't say anything. I don't care what you say, even if we had told you right away, you'd have still looked at us like you're looking at us now! We didn't decide to have powers. We didn't plan any of this. And we didn't want to lie, but what option did we have?"

"You always have the option to do what's right," Mr. Walker replies.

"Bullshit! The cards are stacked against us. Because we have powers, we're seen as unpredictable. Because we're teenagers we're seen as even more unpredictable. And because we're black, well, that just makes it a trifecta!" Bright counters.

"I don't think the race card is going to work with us," Mr. Walker retorts.

"I'm not talking about just you, Dad! Telling the truth would have meant telling a lot more than just you and Mom. You're the ones who've been telling us that the world wouldn't understand us, that they'd think we're a danger, that they'd take us away. We just talked about how you did the exact same thing when you decided not to tell Mr. Crowley! All we wanted to do was do the right thing, but in the way that we thought allowed us to still have a life. Rachel is alive. Sarah is alive. It's not like we're off killing people all the time and covering it up just for fun. We made the choices we thought we had to make." Bright's tears have ceased. I think he's cried all he can cry. Anger is taking over now. The adrenaline is pumping, and he's chosen fight over flight.

"The whole reason we're telling you is to end the lies," Jess adds. "To be open with you. All of you. Rachel wanted us to come clean so that she wouldn't have to lie to either of you anymore." She looks to Dad and then to Jason. She then turns back to her parents. "And we wanted to come clean, so that we could heal. We need to talk about this. We need to talk to someone ... professionally. And Rachel too, probably. We're dealing with heavy shit, and we're way over our heads. We need help and we can't afford to keep this all in anymore! I'm not going to hide myself forever. I won't."

"Nobody's going to believe this," Mrs. Walker claims.

"It's not hard to make them believe," Jess responds, lifting me up by the collar of my shirt with just one of her fingers.

"Hey!" Dad yells, "Put her down! That's enough. Get out!"

"She wasn't hurting me Dad!" I defend.

"I don't care! I don't care!" Dad throws his hands up in protest, "Look, I have no intention of sharing any of this, but as far as I'm concerned, this conversation is over. I don't need to hear anymore."

"This isn't about you Dad!" I yell. I'm so angry. He's being so mean, and unfair, and can he not see Bright and Jess are terrified? They're just kids. We're just kids! "Fuck! I'm sorry we lied! I'm sorry we kept this from you. And yes, we all kept it from you. I had a part in it too. Stop yelling at them! I get that you're angry, and scared, and hurt, but they're my family. They're your family. You've treated Bright and Jess like your own children our whole lives. Shutting them out when they're reaching to you for support isn't going to help. And it also means shutting me out. We just finally got back on track. This is why I wanted this to happen, so that we could stay on track. Stay together. Don't do this Dad."

Dad tries to fight it, but he can't anymore, and he breaks down. I run to him and hold him. We both fall to our knees. Me more so because I couldn't hold his weight. It hurts when we hit the ground. We stay there for a long time, crying in each other's arms. Nobody says anything. I look up a few times and I see Mr. and Mrs. Walker still standing away from Bright and Jess, and it makes me angry. Why aren't they going to their kids? Why aren't they holding them right now? Maybe they're afraid, maybe they think Bright and Jess don't want to be near them? At least, I hope that over the alternative—that they don't want to be near Bright and Jess.

After another long silence, Dad speaks up. "I'm sorry ..." he says. "Jessica and Bright, it took a lot for you to tell us the truth, and I now understand why you'd try so hard to keep it from us. I don't know how to move forward, but I want to help us all heal as best as possible."

"Thank you," Jess responds.

"Thank you, David." Mr. Walker nods. "I think Jessica is right. I think we need to talk to a therapist about all of this. I don't know what else to do."

"And what do I do?" Jason asks. I almost forgot about him. "So do I just lie to my family now? Act like I don't know any of this? Why am I even here?"

"I wanted you here." I explain. "Because I love you. I wanted to involve you because if I didn't … how could we make a relationship work?"

Jason doesn't say anything. I can tell he wants to, but it's not for everyone else. That's a conversation just for us, so I don't push it any further.

"I think maybe it is time for us to go," Mrs. Walker offers. "David, if you're okay with keeping this between us for now, then I say we all take a break. This has been … a lot, and I think we all need to process this and we can come together again later."

Dad nods. We stand up. My knees ache, and I'm sure his do too. We stretch them out a bit, and then I go and give Jess and Bright a hug. "Thank you," I whisper to them. They don't respond with words, they just hug me tighter. I tell them I love them, and they tell me the same. Then they join their parents, and they make their leave.

Now it's just me, Dad, and Jason. Dad recognizes that we need to talk, so he excuses himself and tells me we'll talk after. "Do you wanna go outside to talk?" I ask.

"Eh, maybe we can go to your room? It's kind of cold out," Jason replies.

I nod, and we head up to my room. Rebel tries to get in the door, but I close it before she can enter. We sit for a minute or so before either of us says anything. Jason is the first one to speak.

"I don't think I can do this."

"What?" I ask, but I know what he means. I felt it earlier. I knew this was coming.

"I can't lie to my family."

"I'm not asking you to," I move closer to him. We're both sitting on my bed.

"Yes you are. My parents aren't going to understand this. We'll have to go through all of this again with them, and we'd have to tell my sisters, and then what? Do they keep it secret?" Jason asks.

"Well, who do they have to tell?" I ask.

"Nobody really, but what about the forest restoration stuff? The whole world is talking about that. We'll have to lie every time that's brought up. And who knows what they'll do next!"

"Jess and Bright? I don't know, but whatever they do, it'll be what they feel is right. They're not going to hurt anyone."

"You don't know that, and neither do they. Jessica just decided to alter the Earth, just change it because she saw fit. Who says that was right? Who says she didn't do more harm than good?" Jason asks.

"We don't know, but right now it doesn't seem to have done anything too damaging."

"I don't trust them, Rachel. They hurt you. They killed you. I know it was an accident, but they can't be trusted to be in control of their powers. Do they even know where their powers came from?"

"No," I respond. I mean to say more, but he interrupts before I can continue.

"See? They don't know what they're doing!"

"They don't have to!" He's starting to make me angry. He's not even giving them a chance. "And they are individuals," I say.

"I never said they weren't." Jason defends.

"But you're grouping their actions together," I clarify. "They didn't kill me, Jessica killed me. But they did bring me back. They didn't kill Sarah, Bright killed Sarah. But they did bring her back. And it was Jessica alone who did the forest shit. Stop making them out to be villains. Stop lumping them together."

"Okay, sorry, but their individual actions still make me feel like they don't know what they're doing, and I don't trust them. I just don't."

"Can't you try to?" I beg. "They know they don't know what they're doing. That's what this was all about. They need to be able to talk to their parents and go to them for guidance when they need it, and I need to be able to talk to my dad and to you."

Jason just looks at me for a long time, I can see him fighting with himself inside. But finally he comes to a decision. "I'm sorry, Rachel. I can't do this. I know either way I still have to lie to my parents, but this way, at least it's mostly just one lie."

"What way?" I ask. I'm trying to hold back tears.

"I think we have to break up," he says.

I go numb. I'm feeling too many things to really feel anything. Part of the reason I did this was for him and … it doesn't matter. "So what are you saying? You're not going to tell anyone anything?" I ask.

"Nobody is going to believe me unless Jess and Bright show them. It'd be more hassle than it's worth."

Why is he being so careless? Why is he acting like this is easy? He's just being rational, and it feels so cold. "I love you, Jason. Can we please find a way to make this work?"

"I don't really see a way to. I can't deal with all of this, and … I don't want to. It's just too much for me."

I somehow hold onto my tears. Everything in me wants to cry, but I don't. I won't. Maybe I'm too numb to. Part of me doesn't want to just to spite him. He's hurting me, and I don't want to let him see just how bad. "So we're breaking up," I say.

"Yeah."

"Okay. Can you leave please?" I don't look at him. I can't. I can't tell if I'd cry, or yell, or attack him, or all of the above. So I keep my eyes on the ground.

He gets up and walks over to the door. He opens it, but pauses on his way out. "I love you too, Rachel. And I'm sorry. I never wanted to hurt you, and … I'm just sorry," he tells me, and then he walks out.

I stop fighting back the tears, but only a few fall out. I look up at the door and I stare at it for a long time. Eventually my eyes dry out and I lie down and close them. I don't want to go to sleep, but I don't want to be awake either. I don't want to be anywhere. I just want to leave existence completely. Not forever, but for now. That's not really possible though, so sleep will do.

BRIGHT

None of us are really sure where to go from here. Days pass and the weekend comes, and then it passes too. We don't go to the L.I.S.N. meeting. Not even Rachel. With her and Jason breaking up, and all that's happened, she's been rather angsty. I don't know what I've been. Mostly just in a perpetual state of "blah."

Mom and Dad don't look at us the same. I'm not sure they ever will. It's like for the first time they think of us as different. Like there's something wrong with us. But at least it's not all bad. It's all out in the open now. Everything. Jessica and I don't have anything to hide from any of the people we love.

Mom and Dad contacted a family therapist and we're going to start seeing her this week. Her name is Gina Howard. Mom did some research on her and thinks that she'll be understanding of everything we have to bring to her. I don't know though. Out of the four people we told our secrets to, only one was really understanding. Mr. Crowley was the only one to really accept it all and accept us. But Jason and our parents, the best they're doing right now is looking the other way. Tolerating us. So I don't have much confidence in people understanding.

It's Sunday night and I'm sitting alone in my room. I've been reading *X-Men* because for some reason, I thought it'd make me feel better. I thought seeing them go through all their shit and how shitty the mutants are treated would make me feel better by comparison. But of course, I understand all too well. The one nice thing for them is they have a home. They have the Xavier Institute. They can go and be themselves and not have to hide anything. They can have the benefit of knowing there are more of them. They have a large net of support. Jessica and I just have each other. And Rachel, of course. But it's only us with these powers. We're stuck, and we don't even know if we can die. We may be stuck forever.

I always thought it was better not having anybody else with powers. This way there's no way there can be super villains and it's not some big deal. But the trouble is if we're the only ones, then there's nobody to stand with us. Not really. If we were to go public and let the world know about our powers, the main reaction would be fear.

I don't even know if I believe me. I mean, superheroes are fucking huge now, people might accept us. It's really possible. There would definitely be people who say that we have a right to live in peace. Though I don't know how many of those people would hold that belief if they found out about us having killed people.

Ultimately, I just don't know. Who ever knows? As far as I can tell, everyone's just winging it. Nobody has any idea what they're doing. We're all just doing the best we can. All I know is it'd be a lot easier without powers. Powers don't make life easier—at least not having all the powers we do. It's just too easy to be seen as a hero or a villain. I don't want to be either.

I wish we had a pet. Any kind of pet. A dog, a cat, a frog—I'd really like a frog. I just need some living thing to teddy bear right now. Something to project my emotions onto and mostly just talk to myself out loud without feeling crazy. There would be no responses, which is exactly what I need. I don't want a discussion, I just want to vent.

Now I just have "Fall to Pieces" by Avril Lavigne stuck in my head. The chorus of this song is one of my favorite things in life. It's just so relatable and so powerful. Sometimes you don't want to fall to pieces or talk about anything, you just want someone to be there with you. You just want to cry or feel whatever you need to feel in the presence of another person. Someone who cares. Avril Lavigne is a fucking genius. I don't care what anyone says. She's genuine and I love the emotion in her songs. A lot of people write her off, but they're trippin' on that one. I just want to meet her and get to know her. I feel like she'd be really awesome to just shoot the shit with. Maybe one day ...

I get up and I make my way to my door, intending to go downstairs for a glass of water. But as I get to the door I stop, I just don't know what to say to my parents right now. I know they're down there. That's why Jessica and I have been in our rooms all day. Well, I mean, we're still grounded, but we just also don't want to deal with anything right now. Hiding out is so much easier for now. I hope that Gina Howard can fix us. Being honest and vulnerable is supposed to make things better, right? I'd like to start seeing that.

I head back to my comics, sit down, and continue reading. X-Men is bae right now. Who needs water anyway when you can't die?

JESSICA

·ᔋ·

So here we are at the therapist's office. Family bonding! Wooo!

I really hope that this is going to be worth it. Well, I hope that it doesn't end with Bright and me being locked up, really. If Gina Howard thinks that we're a risk to public safety or something, we may be fucked. Though, I guess they really couldn't keep us locked up really. Anyway, hopefully it doesn't come to extremes.

We're all in the waiting room, none of us speaking to each other. All probably terrified. All probably wanting to leave before it even starts. Everything here is gray, like really gray. Like I'm questioning why someone would make this room so depressing. I nudge Bright with my elbow to fill him in on it, but Gina comes to welcome us into her office at the same time. I tell him I'll fill him in on it later, and we all make our way into her office. I'm happy to see that it's much less depressing. The walls are evergreen and the paneling is all wood. It's like sitting in a forest. It's rather serene.

"So, Marion and Edward, you said that there's a lot of delicate and unique issues that you're dealing with right now. Ones that you don't think you can work through on your own," Gina begins after we're all seated and she's closed the door behind us. I can't tell if she meant that as a question or a statement. Mom and Dad nod "yes" anyway.

"Okay, well, you've read over all the preliminary information right?" We all nod. "Okay, so you're aware of the ways in which I can share what we talk about today, and that's still alright with all of you?" We all nod. "Good, so Marion, why don't you fill us in on what's happening with the family. Try to stick to facts. Don't add your opinions on the events, just catch me up. And I'd like the rest of you to please listen until she finishes. I find this is best, as to avoid any arguments or bickering right off the bat." We all nod. Then Gina nods to indicate that Mom should start speaking.

"The first thing that you need to know can't be told, it can only be shown," Mom tells her.

"Alright then," Gina nods, looking apprehensive.

Mom nods to Bright and me, we look at each other, and then we pretty much do exactly what we did to show Jason and Mr. Crowley. Except this time I levitate and Bright teleports. Gina screams, and then gathers herself quickly.

"My children have powers," Mom explains.

A few seconds later there's a knock on the door. "Gina, is everything okay in there?" Gina doesn't respond at first, and the person asks again, more worried.

"Everything's fine, Arthur. I just almost knocked my computer off my desk. Sorry."

Arthur chuckles, "Okay," he says and then walks away.

"So you have powers?" Gina attests.

"Yes," Bright confirms.

"Right ..." She takes a few deep breaths. "What all can you do?" she asks. I tell her all of our powers, showing off the superstrength, just talking about the others. "Okay, so fill me in on what's going on then."

Mom takes a deep breath, and Bright and I return to our seats. Then Mom starts telling Gina everything. She covers it all, she even does well not to inject her opinions into any of it. When she finishes, Gina is in shock. She doesn't look terrified though, just like she's been on an exhausting trip.

"This probably sounds really stupid coming from someone you hired to help you through your problems, but I have absolutely no idea what to say," Gina tells us.

"Do you think we're bad people?" I ask. I surprise myself, and looking around the room, it looks like I surprised my family as well. It's what I want to know. It's what's been bothering Bright. All I want to do is help the world, but what does that even mean anymore? It's not that I think I don't have the power, but how can you tell if you're the villain or the hero, and is it even possible to be one without also being the other?

These are things that I probably should be asking out loud. I mean, this is the place to do it. To get all of my frustration and emotions out. This is the time. I don't speak up, but Mom does.

"You think you're a bad person?" Mom asks me, then also works to include Bright, "You think you're bad people?"

"Don't you?" Bright asks. "Isn't that part of why we're here? You—neither of you—have looked at us the same since finding out about what happened with Sarah and Rachel. I've experienced a lot of judgment, for a lot of different reasons, but it's never bothered me all that much until it happened from you and Dad. The looks we get from you. It's like, in your minds, we've become everything society thinks black adolescents are. Dangerous, ignorant, violent, careless. Every time you look at me, I hear 'They're right.'"

Bright and Mom stare at each other, hurt deep in both of their eyes. I can tell mom wants to embrace him and to tell him that he's wrong, but she can't. Not completely. "I don't think they're right," Mom insists, "They aren't right about you, Jessica, or anyone else. The reason I've looked at you differently is because now, for the first time, I don't see you as kids. And on that scale, I do see you in society's eyes. They don't view you as a kid, they see black youth and they see calculated, premeditated, adult. They judge you as an adult no matter what. They call you dumb or savage—though not directly—yet they hold you to impossible standards as if you're some kind of dangerous master-mind. And now I can't not see you as an adult. Yet I don't quite see you as my equal. You're my child, and I see you as someone I need to protect. So at the same time I think I need to make decisions for you, like you can't possibly be able to make your own. But I know you can. I don't know. I guess what I'm trying to say is the innocence is gone. I don't think you're bad, but you're becoming an adult. And we see adults as capable of anything. We don't really view children that way. Not that that's right either, but … it's true."

We all remain silent for a while. I feel a sense of relief, but it's not quite comforting. "Silhouettes" by *Of Monsters and Men* comes to mind. That song has been on my mind a lot lately. It begins with lines about finally being at peace, but it not feeling right. That really resonates with me right now. As teenagers, all we want is to be taken seriously. Hell, even as kids. Even adults! Everyone wants to be taken seriously. But as teenagers we're so close to being adults. We're told we're being prepped, we're told we're expected to act like adults, but then when we try to get the respect of an adult, we're told we're "entitled" or "smart asses." Sure, some of us may think we know more than we do, but adults are no different. Hubris is found throughout all ages and all cultures.

So we teenagers want to be treated like adults, we want a say in what happens around us, and what we do, but just as adults underestimate what we go through, we underestimate them too. Being an adult isn't that fun as far as I can see. Once you're told you're an adult, you no longer get any benefit of the doubt. You're no longer allowed to be unknowing. If you fuck up, you should have known better—you're an adult for god's sake! Teenagers fuck up, and it's expected, and that's both really comforting and really fucking frustrating. Everyone expecting you to screw up sucks, because then when you do succeed, it's not seen as success, not really. It's people going, "Holy shit, this fuck up actually did something cool." It's seen as an exception, and then they expect you never to fuck up again. People should always expect the best from you—or not expect it, but know it's possible. And they should also know fucking up is possible. Human beings—at every point in their life—are capable of amazing things. Amazing in every sense of the word. We just have to be willing to always see that.

Again, this is something I should probably be saying out loud. But I wouldn't even really know how to start, and I'd get jumbled up, and frustrated with myself, and in the end, it wouldn't come out nearly how I want it to.

Gina Howard doesn't have much to add. She tells us that this is a good place to start, and we should take a break and come back in a week. She tells us that she also has a lot to process, but assures us that as of now, she sees no reason as to why she should share any of what we've told her. We thank her for her help, though she really didn't do anything, and we exit her office.

Being back out in the gray room feels almost right after so much emotion. It feels neutral. As we exit the building, we find that the gray has followed us. The skies are overcast and it looks like snow, maybe. Snow is the only thing I like about the winter. Well, not the only thing, but I hate the cold. I don't even like saying that I hate the cold, the cold is just being itself. It's not intentionally trying to do me harm. It's not doing anything. How can I say I hate it? I don't really. There's so much that the cold makes better, or just makes possible at all. I just don't do well in the cold.

RACHEL

It's been about a week since the breakup. I mean, all in all, we weren't a couple for that long. I shouldn't be this broken up about him right? I've got more important things to worry about. Jess and Bright came clean about everything, I should be focusing on them. I should be helping them.

Though, maybe not. I always help them. I'm always thinking of them. I deserve to feel what I'm feeling. And what am I feeling? Confusion all around. I don't know how to feel. I wish I could just be mad at Jason for giving up on us. I wish I could yell at him, slap him, rage, tear shit up, just fucking go off the rails. I wish I could just be closed-minded. Just once.

But no, I get it. I get how it's too much. I get how we're still in high school and the kind of thing we dropped on him is a life secret, something that's life altering, and he just has to sit on it. I get that he was even understanding about it. There's nothing to be mad about. He's not in the wrong for feeling the way he does. He didn't mistreat me, and I didn't mistreat him. I think that's the shittiest part of all of it. There was no problem with us, not really. We didn't break up because we stopped loving each other, or because one of us fucked up. We broke up because we knew we couldn't continue. Because if we did continue, we knew resentment would come with us. We knew we weren't equipped to deal with this, or at least, there was no way we could given our circumstances.

I didn't think I'd ever really fall in love, but I always thought that if I did, it'd be forever. You like to think that you're different. That the problems you've heard other couples having won't be problems for you and your partner. Or partners. But knowing that's not true is terrifying. Knowing you could not even fall out of love but still fall out of a relationship is fucking awful. How am I supposed to want to try again knowing that? I dunno … .

Dad says that eventually you realize that no matter what, any relationship you get into can end for many different reasons, and not just romantic ones. He says that one day I'll get excited again about love and I'll want to risk getting hurt. I don't know if I believe him though. I don't think his excitement for romance ever returned after Mom. Though that's completely different, I guess—years of marriage and years of being a couple before that can't be compared to months of dating.

Right now I don't really care much if he's right. I'm enjoying wallowing in angst. I've been listening to a lot of angsty hits, but Meg Myers has had me gone lately. I love her. She's amazing. And her music is just what I need right now. The right amount of self-deprecating, self-pity, and self-empowerment. Her song "Heart Heart Head" is one of my favorites. I've listened to that one the most—much to my dad's displeasure, I'm sure. The screaming she does in the end is just pure angst. It's fucking brilliant.

I decided to make another attempt at keeping a journal. It never really works out, but I need it, I think. I know the Walkers are trying therapy. They suggested going to the one they're going to, seeing as how she knows every-thing already, but I dunno. I just don't feel like it's for me. I know the impor-tance of talking through my emotions and allowing myself to feel, but I think I do that enough with my dad, and Jess and Bright. And the rest I feel confi-dent in working out on my own. Though, I don't know, maybe I'm being foolish and I really do need to see a professional. I'm sure there's years' worth of shit to go through.

Who knows? I guess if I ever feel like something happens that I can't handle, I'll give therapy a go.

I don't really know where Jess and Bright are at with moving forward with trying to change the world. I'm kind of mad at myself for not going to the L.I.S.N. meeting. I just couldn't really think about doing anything this past weekend.

I remember after Mom died I just wanted to keep going. I didn't really wanna talk about it. I wanted to accept it, but I wanted to be there for everyone else more than I wanted anyone to be there for me. This is the exact opposite, and I feel so stupid because it made sense for that. A parent dying, especially when you're a child—people are supposed to be there for you. That's understandable. But I just didn't want to seem like I was looking for sympathy. I didn't want to be an "attention whore." I didn't want to be treated specially.

Now I just want my dad to buy me ice cream, and I want Jess and Bright to be here trying to shit talk Jason, and I want the attention. Only I know right now that I don't even deserve all the attention. I mean, I know I need to talk, but I can't expect people to be concerned with me and only me right now. But all I can think about is Jason and how torn I am about it all.

Ahhh!

The real shitty thing is I haven't even seen Jess or Bright outside of school because they're still grounded. I just want to be with them, doing nothing, watching movies maybe, eating shitty food. I'm in great need of a hang sesh.

The chorus to "Heart Heart Head" comes in and I turn the music up louder even than I think is necessary and I sing along. Rebel makes a quick escape as I go to shut the door before Dad complains. Until a hang sesh is doable, Meg Myers has my back.

JESSICA

"What do we do now?" I ask Bright as I sit down on the floor of his bedroom. The door is shut, and Mom and Dad are at work. I don't even know what I'm really asking. Sometimes I just ask things or say things with no real plan on a follow up. Something just pops into my mind and I need to expel it. This was one of those times.

"What do you mean?" Bright asks.

"I mean, how do we move forward?"

"Aren't we moving forward now?"

"I don't know …" I stop, needing to think about what I'm even trying to say. "It feels like we just opened up a box . Or like, we broke out of our shell, but it turned out we were just in a bigger egg."

"What the fuck are you talking about?" Bright asks. He sets down the bag of gummy worms he's been chewing on.

"I mean, yes we told Mom and Dad and Mr. Crowley everything, but we're still hiding. We're still forced to suppress ourselves in public and hold back. We still can't make friends. We're still kind of like prisoners. How can we really do anything we want to do? How can I make the changes I want to make if we're always lying and hiding?" I can tell by the look on his face that Bright's been waiting for this moment to come. Only it doesn't look like he's annoyed like I expected. It's more understanding.

"I know," he states simply. "I've been thinking about it a lot. I've been thinking about what it would mean to come out. Completely. Just put it all out there, with everyone. And honestly, it's scary, but not as much as I thought. For me, I think the hardest part is over. But if we do this, we're going to have to tell Sarah Murdock what happened. And we're never going to be free. We won't be in a shell anymore, but we won't have privacy. I mean, we can bring people back from the dead, Jessica. Do you know how many people are going to be knocking on our door every day? And sure, people might accept our story and not be afraid of us, but there is no way they're going to leave us alone. They're going to ask to test us, to get our powers. This is historical, Jessica. We're historical. And then of course, there's still the chance they do fear us, or they don't ask, then it's us against them."

"'Us against them?' Is it really that black and white?" I ask.

"No, that's what I'm saying. There's a lot to think about and a lot of decisions to make after that."

"Like if we don't come out, how long until they find out anyway? Or what do we do, trapped in this shell? How long until we can't take it anymore and let the world know in ways less thought out, or less careful?"

"Yeah. And what do our loved ones do?" Bright asks. "This isn't going to be the only time Rachel is going to fall in love. What happens the next time? And what if she wants to make more friends? She's going to need to do that. And it would be a load off of Mom and Dad too."

"But then what will they do when we have all the attention of the whole world. What will they do when they also can't be left alone? If we bring ourselves out of hiding, are we binding them? And by binding them, will we be forcing them to either choose to stay with us, or leave us to free themselves? If we tell the world our secret, would that separate us from it even more?"

We sit in silence. I think we both are thinking the same thing. That there's no way to be able to predict everything that will happen on either side of what we choose.

"How about this?" Bright asks.

"What?"

"Why don't we shelf this until we graduate high school?"

"Why?" I ask.

"Well, for one it gives us more time to think on it," Bright starts.

"But if we're still thinking on it, we're not shelving it," I interrupt.

"I meant that we shelf making a decision until we graduate. We get more time to think on it and we avoid fucking up our education along with Rachel's. I mean, we both want to finish high school. We'll need to. And I know things will still come up between now and then, but I feel like dealing with those things as they arise is better than making this huge decision now."

I think on it for a bit. He's got a point. Of course I can come up with a lot of "what ifs," but the more I think about it, the more this seems like the right thing to do. We finish high school, we try to expand, grow ourselves more, see what happens in these last years. And this way really is the fairest to Rachel.

"Okay," I say.

"Yeah?"

I nod. And as I do, this swell of relief waves over me. A smile breaks across my face. "We might actually be alright." I tell him.

Bright laughs, quoting the chorus line from "Alright."

I laugh, "Put that shit on right now!"

Bright jumps up and puts on Kendrick Lamar's album *To Pimp a Butterfly*. For the first time in a long time, I feel right. Like, I'm making the right choice. I'm doing not only what's best for me, but for those around me. I feel like Uncle Ben would be proud of me. We're making the most responsible choice we both can see right now.

Bright and I rap along to the opening lines. And as the beat kicks in we get hype and dance as Kendrick assures us that even though we're fucked up and all need healing, we will make it through.

And I believe it. I have no idea what's going to happen. I have no idea how our lives are going to turn out. Shit's fucked up, but it always is. And we will be alright.

RACHEL

᭝

Mrs. and Mr. Walker allow me to come sleep over at their house. They said that with everything going on, even though Bright and Jess are grounded, they understand that we need time with each other.

So Jess, Bright, and I are all sitting in Jess's room listening to this playlist I made called Pick Me Up and Keep Me Up. It's got some bangers on it. "Make a Mess" by Matt and Kim—well basically their whole discography, "Today Was a Fairytale" by Taylor Swift, "Good Day" by Nappy Roots, "A Thousand Miles" by Vanessa Carlton, "Everywhere" by Michele Branch—which if you ask me, is a song about love itself, and not about being in love with someone specifical-ly—"Die Tonight" by Charli XCX, "Why Not" by Hilary Duff, "And We Run" by Within Temptation featuring Xzibit, "If It Makes You Happy" by Sheryl Crow, and a bunch more awesome songs. Over a thousand. This is going to be a great day.

Right now, "I Don't Wanna Go to Work" by Lissie is playing. We've got lots of gummy candy and lots of chips and crackers. Ice cream and Popsicles downstairs in the freezer. We're probably going to order pizza later. This is just what I needed—It's just what we needed.

"Did you end up texting Jason?" Bright asks.

"No," I reply. "I just … I don't think there's really anything to say, at least not right now."

"Yeah …" Bright looks for something more to say, but nothing comes.

"Well, today is about us just relaxing right? No break up talk, no figuring out life. Let's just fucking have fun," Jess expresses.

"Well really, today was about just getting quality time together to talk and just hang out, but I'm cool with making it an angst-free day," I agree.

"Let's make it an angst-free rest of high school," Bright insists. "If we're shelving any big decisions until then, I think we can make that happen."

"You're dreaming," Jess says.

"I mean, Ryan and Seth couldn't even last a night of angst free, so we'll be lucky to get that," I attest.

Jess laughs. "Duuuude, let's watch some *O.C.* right now. Let's watch that episode!"

"No!" Bright says. "If we're truly going angst free, then by definition, teen dramas are off limits."

"I think anything worth watching would be off limits then," Jess counters. "And this playlist would definitely not make the cut."

"Well, the playlist stays," I demand. "I spent like two hours picking all of these songs."

"Okay, fine, let's just keep listening. Keep talking," Bright tries to move things along.

"Yeah, and we could color!" Jess gets up to get some coloring books out.

"Color?" I laugh. "I feel like it's been forever since I've seen you pull out the coloring books."

"I know! I just really wanna color though!" Jess exclaims. "Okay, so I got … some Frozen ones, Marvel characters, Scooby-Doo, and that's it." She laughs and throws the books down between us all.

Bright flips through the Marvel book and tears out a picture of She-Hulk and The Thing to color, I take one of the whole Scooby gang, and Jess picks one of Storm from the X-Men.

"Keep Your Head" by The Ting Tings starts playing as we start coloring.

"I really liked this album," Bright says, "but I totally didn't keep up with them. Do you have any of their newer stuff?"

"No, I should look them up later," I reply.

"I wish my name was Ororo," Jess sighs.

"What?" I ask.

"Storm." She points to her coloring picture, "Her real name is Ororo. I think that's such an awesome name!"

"You sound so white," Bright tells her.

"What?" Jess asks incredulously.

"'This name is so cool, because it's a culture I don't know and I like it. I'm gonna call myself Ororo!'" Bright laughs, "You're so white."

"Shut up!" Jess laughs back. "It's a fucking cool-ass name, that's a fact!"

We all laugh and continue coloring for about an hour. Some great songs come on during that time. "Everyone's a Winner" by Hot Chocolate, "Pretty Girl Rock" by Keri Hilson, and now "Damaged" by TLC is playing.

"Woah, *Damaged*?" Bright asks.

"Yeah?" I question.

"How is this a 'Pick Me Up and Keep Me Up' song?" Bright asks.

"Do you hear this?" Jess exclaims. "This is a jam!"

"Yeah," I add, "and like really it's about falling for someone and opening up to them and letting them know that you've been hurt and mistreated and you hope that they can accept that and work with you. I mean, it's a bit of a downer, but it's clearly hopeful, and like, what's more 'up' than trusting someone enough to be vulnerable with them?"

Bright gives in and shrugs, "What do you wanna do now?" he asks.

"Show off our coloring skills, duh!" Jess laughs.

"Yes, yes, I like that idea." Bright agrees.

We all hold up our pictures and after careful consideration we all decide that Bright has the best picture, but mostly because She-Hulk and The Thing are awesome.

"Do you ever wish that superheroes were real?" I ask.

Jess and Bright just stare at me.

"Shut up!" I say embarrassed. "But really, I just really wish I could talk to them, you know? Like The Thing? I wish I could just chill with him."

"Well, he'd probably want you to call him Ben Grimm rather than The Thing," Bright retorts.

I chuckle, "Yeah, you're right."

"Everything's OK" by Lenka is playing and we all just sit, sing, and bob our heads along for a moment.

"I get what you mean," Jess says. "It'd be really awesome if we could just have people who knew what we were feeling and could really relate."

"I was just thinking this the other day!" Bright yells.

Jess and I laugh, "No need to get so excited," I tell him.

Bright laughs, but continues, "I just ... I know that it'd be awful, probably, in reality, but being able to go to Xavier Institute would be fucking awesome."

"It would just feel nice to belong," Jess admits.

"No, no, no, c'mon guys! This is an angst-free night!" I protest.

"You're the one who started this," Bright counters.

"I said it'd be cool to hang with Ben Grimm, I didn't say, "Let's all mope!'"

"Well you may as well have," Bright insists.

I roll my eyes and yawn.

"What, are ya gettin' sleepy?" Jess asks.

"I'm always ready for another bout." I answer smiling.

"That movie is so damn quotable," Jess says.

"It really is," I concur.

"So you wanna order pizza yet?" Bright asks.

I think on it, but Jess answers, "Yes!" right away.

"Yeah, I guess I'm getting pretty hungry," I admit.

The pizza takes less than 45 minutes to arrive. We get a huge, magnum-size pepperoni, pineapple, green peppers, and olives. None of us have the stomach to finish this whole thing, but we push ourselves. In the end we're all laid out on the floor, stuffed and wanting to never move again.

"Gucci Gucci" by Kreayshawn is playing and we all rap along. Only it's less like rapping and more like incoherent mumbling with bursts of laughter throughout.

"Why do we always get a magnum when we know we can't eat the whole thing?" Bright asks.

"Because our stomachs are bigger than our eyes," I reply.

"You mean our eyes are bigger than our stomachs," Jess corrects.

I laugh, "No, like, because you're stomach is in charge. Your eyes can see it's too big, but your stomach is like 'I'm hungry! I'm large and in charge!' And so the stomach wins and you order something too big and then your eyes mumble, 'We fucking told you.' And your stomach yells 'Shut up!' and then cries itself to sleep."

"Yeah, that sounds about right," Bright laughs.

Jess moans and rolls onto her stomach, "I think I have to poop."

"Thanks for the info," Bright grimaces.

"Yeah, and let's keep that end pointed toward the ground." I say pointing to her butt.

"I don't want to move," Jess whines, elongating the "move."

"Jess, you have the power to teleport. Just go to the bathroom," I demand.

"Fine," She play pouts and then vanishes the next second.

Bright and I sit in silence for a while before I ask, "Do you ever think about how weird it is that, like only humans and trained animals worry about where to go to the bathroom?"

"Not really," Bright shrugs.

"I just think it's weird. Not necessarily like bad or anything, but just weird," I state. "Like, if a lion has to take a shit, it doesn't care. It's not really a concern, it just poops. A bird flying overhead isn't thinking about what's below, it just poops. It's only a concern for us. Like it will be an actual troubling issue. We'll dwell on it. If we're standing in line at the bank and all of a sudden you really have to poop, that's a huge issue. You're stressing out. It really matters. If you poop your pants, that's going to change your whole day, maybe even your life to an extent."

Bright doesn't really respond. We just lie in silence and I think about my life's journey. It's so weird. Born in Korea, adopted by a Chinese man and a white woman, and come to America. My best friends end up having superpowers. I get killed by them, brought back to life. And like, now I'm just lying on the floor, stuffed full of pizza, still heartbroken from the breakup, and thinking about how weird it is that humans worry about where they poop.

"Life is just so crazy," I say as Jess reenters the room.

"Yup," Jess responds matter-o-factly as she joins us on the floor.

"How was your poop?" I ask.

Jess laughs, "Everything I hoped it would be."

"Well good, you deserve the best," I reply smiling.

"Aww, thanks," she says. "You do, too. And you too, Bright." She nudges him with her foot.

"I probably deserve to die here right now for letting myself eat this much," Bright groans.

"If It Makes You Happy" by Sheryl Crow comes on and I recite the title as a response to Bright.

"I don't know if it makes me happy or not," he responds.

"Everyday is a Winding Road," I state.

"What are you even saying?" Bright asks laughing.

"I don't know, I'm just trying to think of titles to Sheryl Crow songs that I can just spit out as responses to what you say," I admit.

"You're so weird," Bright says, shaking his head.

"Yup. And that's why you both love me, because you're weird motherfuckers too," I reply.

"That's us. Weird, pointless motherfuckers," Jess agrees.

"Pointless?" I ask.

"Yeah, like in the sense of just living. Right now we've got no point, no direction we're specifically heading. We're doing us. We're pointless," Jess expresses.

"I like that," I nod. "Pointless mothafuckas!"

"If we were in a movie, it would be called that, and this would be the part where we inevitably say the title of the film," Bright points out.

"That's always a hit or miss for me," Jess says. "I either *love* it or just find it really jarring."

"Yeah, it's cliché, and cliché isn't bad. Things are cliché because they're true for the most part. So familiar, we're tired of them, but if it works and is done right, and it can strike something that connects with someone, then it's gold," Bright agrees.

"I feel like we've talked about this before," I claim.

"Probably," Bright admits.

"A glitch in the matrix," Jess adds.

"We're so lame," I shake my head smiling.

Jess lets out a big relieving sigh and stretches back out across the floor. "You know, I love you guys," She tells.

"We love you too?" I respond.

Jess laughs, "I just, I don't know, I feel so stress free."

"That's the idea, isn't it?" Bright says.

"Yeah, but it's easier said than done," Jess pauses for a moment. "There's just so much that's happened lately. And I feel like I should be wanting to do more, to keep pushing, but I don't."

"That's not necessarily a bad thing," I counter.

"I know, I'm not saying it is," Jess responds. "I just, I'm saying I'm okay with just allowing myself time to figure it out. Allowing myself to be in the moment and be happy. I still feel kind of weird about it. I still have the thought that I need to be doing something more, but I can't weigh myself down with that."

Bright and I smile at her, but don't have anything to add. It's all really been said before.

"And I just felt like telling you two that I love you," Jess starts up again. "I'd definitely be somewhere without you, but it'd be nowhere near as awesome as where I am now."

"Well, that's an odd way of saying that," Bright tells her. "But, we love you too."

"We love you!" I add.

"I don't want to do anything anymore," Jess vents after another moment of silence. "Let's just stay here on the floor forever."

"Sounds good to me," I accept mid-yawn. I stretch and move myself into a more comfortable position. "Could you guys actually stay here forever and not move?"

"I mean, I think, maybe, but it wouldn't be pleasant by any means," Bright responds.

"Who needs pleasant when you've got forever?" I shrug.

"Sounds like words to live by," Jess laughs.

"Words to live by," Bright says in a weird accent. We all laugh, and I don't think any of us know why. It's just one of those things that's incredibly funny for no reason. Something's said in the perfect way, at the perfect time, and the people it's said to are in the perfect mood, and it just strikes something deep inside. Ignites memories of something else, or just makes you forget about everything else for a while.

We laugh for a long time. I laugh so hard I cry. And the fact that it was at something so stupid and so meaningless makes me, and us all, laugh even harder. My stomach hurts, and it's hard to breathe, and I can't help but keep laughing. Over time, our laughter starts to slow and we think it's over, but then Jess gets another huge burst and we all start up again.

And in this moment of intense, uncontrollable laughter, where I can't breathe and my abs feel like they're going to explode, and tears are streaming down my face, time stands still. And though I'm lying on the floor, I feel like I'm floating through space. I feel like I'm Karolina Dean, I feel like I always want to feel. I feel like my whole self. I feel complete.

This laughter will pass, and so will this night, and time will continue, but one of the most comforting things that I've ever heard is that there aren't any endings. And I suppose that could also be terribly frightening, but I take solace in it. I love these beautiful people I'm with, I love my life, and I love myself. And that love is forever. That love doesn't end.

CPSIA information can be obtained
at www.ICGtesting.com
Printed in the USA
FSHW020719240519
58393FS